WHEN WE WERE TWINS

History has many cunning passages and contrived corridors, wrote
T.S. Eliot, and Danuta Hinc takes us down several such dark alleys as
she explores the human realities behind the so-called "War on Terror."
Along the way she reveals just how intricate and surprising the weave of
history has become, or perhaps has always been. The threads here twine
from Egypt to Poland to Afghanistan to Palestine/Israel, and many
places in between. The questions her novel explores--about love and
war, about family, peace, and the price of freedom—couldn't be more
urgent. Hinc's imagination here revs at full throttle, and we would be
wise to go along for the ride.

—**Askold Melnyczuk**, author of *The Man Who Would Not Bow*

Infused with urgency and propelled by a sense of the world in catastrophe
mode, Danuta Hinc's *When We Were Twins* exposes the tangled fates of
people caught up in events they cannot control. The prose finds its pulse
right from the start and the reader feel its animating force throughout.

—**Sven Birkerts**, author of *Changing the Subject: Art
and Attention in the Internet Age*

In this deceptively simple novel brimming with visions and allegories,
Hinc has created a mystical work of historical imagination. Ultimately,
When We Were Twins confronts us with a demand that politics, religion,
and the rise and fall of nations be understood as a single, tragic human
story.

—**Maria Bustillos**

Danuta Hinc has produced a lushly written, intricate drama between a
radicalized Muslim and a Polish fellow traveler who encounter each other
in Afghanistan as well as New York City. It's a startling and unexpected
novel about friendship and terrorism, love and hate, forgiveness and its
opposite.

—**Michael Scott Moore**, author of *The Desert and the Sea: 977
Days Captive on the Somali Pirate Coast*

A young Egyptian man becomes increasingly radicalized in his devotion to Islam and struggles to resist the call to violence in Hinc's novel. Taher is born in Ismailia, Egypt, in the midst of great violence during the Six-Day War in 1967 with Israel; he comes into the world on the heels of a fraternal twin sister, Aisha. He is a well-behaved, studious boy, impressing his family by memorizing the Quran by the time he is 6 years old. His bond with his sister, even as they drift apart as years pass, is mystically profound...

Taher is first exposed to a mixture of Islamic radicalism and political dissent by his cousin Ahmed who, along with hundreds of others, is sent to prison after the assassination of Egypt's president Anwar Sadat. Taher eventually travels to Afghanistan and joins the mujahedeen to fight against the Soviet invasion—though by moving to Germany to attend college, he seems to express a desire to live a normal life as well, a peacefully bourgeois existence similar to his sister's. However, he begins to lean into extremist ideas about political resistance, an organic development intelligently charted by the author. Taher is a memorable protagonist—deeply thoughtful and morally sensitive, he disdains killing despite his political commitments. ... Hinc's portrayal of him as a saintly, blameless child who grows into an adult capable of hijacking an airplane is delicately rendered—it is never quite clear what ultimately motivates his transformation ... As a psychological snapshot of radicalization, this is a subtle work, one that astutely highlights the many ways in which Egyptians could feel betrayed, not only by Western powers more interested in their resources than their freedom, but also by their own leaders.

—*Kirkus Reviews*

With empathy and compassion, Danuta Hinc's fine novel erases the line between "us" and "them," shedding light on the variety of human circumstances and delivering the uncomfortable truth that extremism is often in the eye of the beholder. When We Were Twins is a lean, beautifully written, important book.

—**Clifford Thompson**, author of *What It Is: Race, Family, and One Thinking Black Man's Blues and Big Man and the Little Men: A Graphic Novel*

When We Were Twins is both a troubling and beautifully written story. It is a brilliant and complex tale of the human experience at the intersection of identity and ideology. Effortlessly compassionate, the novel restores our sense of humanity even in the face of senseless and irrational violence. Hinc's writing is instantly enthralling with its vivid imagery and powerfully convincing characters. She captures her readers in a world that is both distant and familiar.

—**Dennis L. Winston**, Editor-in-chief of *Words Beats & Life: The Global Journal of Hip-Hop Culture*

"Hinc has written a lucid, utterly gripping speculation expanding our understanding of who hijackers [are] and what motivates them. She provides an important new perspective to event[s] that transformed our lives."

—**Rabbi Martin Siegel**, author of *Amen: The Diary of Rabbi Martin Siegel*

'In *When We Were Twins*, we are witness to the horrors of war, and if we can be saved, it will only be by walking through the savage beauty of work like Hinc's. Her unsparing prose will lick your soul dry.

—**Catherine Parnell**, author of *The Kingdom of His Will*

Childhood moments draw us into the character of Tahir, a cherished boy who turns from aspiring doctor to terrorist. With brilliant prose, author Danuta Hinc unspools his path backwards, holding the readers in suspense. We witness what brought him and his allies to radicalization and the most unthinkable moments—all while compelling us to hope for a different future for such a sympathetic character. Great care was taken with research to illuminate points of view we rarely see so close-up.

—**Laura Lipson**, documentary filmmaker, *Standing on My Sisters' Shoulders*

Hinc's enticing narrative draws us into a world we might prefer to ignore, even despise. We identify with and appreciate the humanity of the protagonist—until we discover what he has become. Through *When We Were Twins*, we discover a whole new perspective on some of the people and cultures we find hardest to understand and embrace. The story is fascinating, blending fantasy with stark reality, and memory with reflection. The message is compelling, and we are made better for the experience.

—**Charles F. "Chic" Dambach**, president emeritus, National Peace Corps Association

When We Were Twins is a beautiful, devastating, and heart-wrenching treatise on faith in family, in friends, in politics and God. Danuta Hinc's superb writing and powerful imagery at once can explode like a Molotov cocktail or cradle you like a child in need of care.

—**J.R. Angelella,** author of the novel *ZOMBIE*

From the riveting first scene of a man with a box cutter, a flight attendant on a commercial flight to the U.S., and Islamic prayer, we know how the story will likely end. But do any of us know how it began? This gut-wrenching fictional story begins with a little boy in Ismailia and ends on a plane in despair. What drives some to darkness? What allows some to twist the double helix of life/death so that it becomes utterly unfamiliar? Unfathomable? Beastly details unfold via lyrical, strangely beautiful prose to tell a story we often don't want to face.

—**Pamela Gerhardt**, author of *Lucky That Way*

The brilliant novel, *When We Were Twins* by Danuta Hinc, portrays Taher as a sensitive young boy who grows into a compassionate and sensitive young man, who demonstrates his loyalty to his Muslim brothers by participating in the war against the Soviets in Afghanistan, and lastly, in a hijacking. The author doesn't excuse his extreme behavior and choices. Rather, she helps us understand the forces and choices that led him to commit such a horrific deed. No one wins in war. We all lose. What's most extraordinary about this tale is Danuta Hinc's courage to tell it from the hijacker's point of view. Through beautifully written landscapes, poetic imagery, and dreams, the author has written a compelling novel that underlines some universal truths: we are all friends and we are all foes. It all depends on what we believe and the choices we make.

—**Diana Stevan**, author of *Paper Roses on Stony Mountain*

WHEN WE WERE TWINS

A NOVEL

DANUTA HINC

Plamen
Press
Where Words Ignite

Washington, DC

Plamen Press

9039 Sligo Creek Pkwy, Suite 1114, Silver Spring, Maryland 20901
www.plamenpress.com

Author copyright © 2023 by Danuta Hinc
Published by Plamen Press 2023

Printed in the United States of America

10 9 8 7 6 5 4 3 2 1

PUBLISHER'S CATALOGING-IN-PUBLICATION DATA

Hinc, Danuta
When We Were Twins / Danuta Hinc;
Silver Spring, MD: Plamen Press, 2023

LCCN: 2023938143

Identifiers: ISBN 978-1-951508-31-9 (paperback)
ISBN 978-1-951508-32-6 (PDF) | ISBN 978-1-951508-33-3 (Epub)
ISBN 978-1-951508-34-0 (hardcover)
LCSH: Polish/American Literature

Polish Literature--21st century. | Eastern European Literature.

BISAC: FICTION / European / General. |
FICTION/Historical/ General

Edited by Rachel Miranda

Cover design: Walter Carlton © 2023
Portrait photography: Amy Smucker © 2023

for Tim and Alex

Contents

Evocations

The moment he looks in the mirror—long shadows cast down in sharp strokes—he knows it has started, and he can't go back. He feels exhausted. The overhead light makes his face look yellow, sagging. His lips, narrowed by dried skin, form a straight line. *It's okay,* he whispers, seeing the reflection of his lips move. He closes his eyes, looks up at the ceiling, and takes a deep breath. *Allahu Akbar,* he says, remembering the garden in Ismailia—lilies floating in the flower pools, faces in the crowd turned towards him in awe— *Taher is pure,* his grandmother had said to Aisha, his twin sister. *So is Aisha,* Taher had replied, but Aisha didn't smile.

He tries to talk to himself the same way he talked to Aisha when they were children, *It's okay.* But all he feels is a rapid heat infiltrating him and the space around him. He knows that stepping out of the lavatory puts him on a new path—irreversible—with consequences he can't predict. He wants to know if this is the beginning or the end of his new life, but there is no way to know, unless he follows the instructions given to him over a year ago. He has to go through with the plan. He thinks of Ahmed, his cousin—the images are overpowering—and the plan makes sense to him again.

He raises his hand with the box cutter and looks at the reflection of it in the mirror, and then he looks at the box cutter itself. His palm opens. *Small,* he whispers. Images of the garden rush back in—black and white pebbles on the paths between heavy pink blooms and the low sun of the late afternoon. He closes his eyes again and feels the small space contracting around him. *It's okay, Aisha.* He opens his eyes and sees his reflection in the mirror getting smaller, fading away. *Stay calm,* he whispers, opening the door and stepping into the cabin.

The moment Taher raises his knife up high, above the heads of

1

the passengers, and grabs the flight attendant from behind, he is as scared as she, maybe more. His body shakes as if in a high fever. He thinks only about the knife slipping in his sweaty palm. The plastic handle seems to shrink, dissolving in his fingers.

The flight attendant tries to escape. She pulls to one side awkwardly, like someone who has changed her mind and needs to go back, someone who forgot something.

"Don't," Taher says, and pulls her closer.

Both look at the passengers in bewilderment, though for different reasons. She is extending her arm; he is waiting for them to notice. The passengers are busy looking out the windows, observing the earth escaping between the clouds, listening to music with headphones, or falling asleep. No one is looking at them.

*

Taher presses himself against the flight attendant, not knowing what to do next. He tries to remember the instructions—he had practiced them for months—but nothing comes to his mind except the words, *Allahu Akbar,* and Aisha's face. He decides to tell her everything once this is over. The truth, he will tell her the truth.

"It's a hijacking!" he finally shouts, but his voice breaks, leaving him in distress. The woman in his arms is trembling, shrinking. He wants her to stop. He knows it would help him if she stopped.

Only a couple of people from the first row lift their gazes in confusion and disbelief.

"This is a hijacking!" he tries again after a short cough, and lifts his knife up for everyone to see.

Passengers start rising from their seats.

"Stay in your seats!" he shouts, pressing against the flight attendant.

*

Her skin is soft and warm. He feels it through her blouse, her back against him. Her warmth seeps slowly into his own flesh, exchanging with his, amplifying, until it reaches a place deep inside his chest. Sudden tenderness overtakes the moment, rushing through him amid his indecision and shaking.

Her hair is pinned up high, and it smells of sweet bitterness, a scent he knows from his home in Ismailia. The scent is sweet like jasmine and bitter like burnt ginger. He turns his head to see where two of his comrades are heading, and his face sinks into the massive tangle on her head.

He takes a deep breath and feels a sudden rush of tears under his skin. For a moment he can't remember if he is holding a hostage or someone he loves.

The flight attendant has his twin sister's eyes—almond-shaped and framed with heavy eyelashes. He had noticed that when he entered the plane. Her eyes hold the same spark of strength and courage as Aisha's, the same defiance. She has his mother's tiny frame, long fingers, and shiny hair. He thinks she has someone else's smile, straightforward, inviting, a little bit too broad, but he doesn't know for sure. And now, holding her close, he feels himself immersed in scents and moods of the distant past that remain in the present with no explanation. There is no distinction between remembering and the woman he is holding.

Twins

Just a couple of minutes after midnight, Laila awakens with a sharp pain in her abdomen, followed by a hot wetness spreading quickly on the sheets under her ripened body.

"Omar," she whispers, gently touching her husband's shoulder. "Omar."

"Uhm . . . " he groans, arriving from a deep sleep.

"It's time," she says, raising on her elbows.

"What time is it?" Omar speaks slowly, keeping his eyes closed.

"Midnight," she answers, lowering her feet to the floor.

"We still have plenty of time." Omar turns over.

"Oh, no. Not for the *Al Fagr* prayer," she says, getting up. "I mean for the baby."

"The baby!" Omar screams, jumping up on straight legs. "My son!" He runs around the bed toward his wife, kneels in front of her, and kisses her knees. "Everything will be all right, just breathe deeply," he says, embracing her thighs.

"Omar, you silly, stop it!" Laila laughs. "Of course, everything will be all right. Now, get up, and let's go." She runs her fingers through her husband's hair.

Grandmother Rumaisa, excited and happy, has packed the necessary things for the hospital, praying under her breath constantly. "God Almighty, grant us a baby boy, healthy and strong, healthy and smart." This long-awaited grandson, son of her eldest son, is to ensure the continuity of the family's lineage. The boy is to be a blessing for the family and a reward for the unconditional patience offered for five years to Omar's first wife, barren Fatima.

The hospital welcomes them amidst crowds of wounded soldiers. Some are carried hurriedly on stretchers; some wait in a long hallway to be seen by a doctor. Their uniforms are ripped or disheveled, soaked with blood and soil.

The air is filled with cries. Some ask for help. Some pray, *"Allahu Akbar—"* Some curse the enemy. Some dream their last dreams. The air, still thick with smoke and fire, slows every movement.

A young soldier with a baby face stretched into a spasm clenches something in his hands and cries, "Ommi! Ommi!" Mommy! Mommy! He repeats the one word. His broken glasses are covered in blood.

At the sight of the soldier, Laila bends forward with a sharp pain. Omar embraces her shoulders and helps her to endure the contraction. Laila, holding her stomach, tries to breathe according to Rumaisa's instructions. "Pant! Pant!" Rumaisa is leaning forward, holding her own belly.

"When is it going to end?" Rumaisa asks after Laila straightens her spine. "Those evil Israelis!" She raises her hands to the sky. "Go back where you belong!" she screams at the top of her lungs. "To hell!" one of the passing soldiers whispers, forcing a smile. *"El makateea!"* Monsters! Rumaisa nods toward him.

"To the left. To the left." A young doctor directs the traffic of patients. The nurses are helping with the stretchers coming from the trucks. "Here. Here." Voices mix in commands. "Slowly. Gently." Everybody is busy. In despair, Omar, Laila, and Rumaisa observe the chaos.

"They won't have a place for me today," Laila whispers, still holding her belly.

"We have to check," Omar says firmly, stepping toward the front door.

The hallway is crowded with wounded soldiers pouring from different directions, with no order. Some are carried. Others make their own way, often leaning on makeshift crutches. People help one another bandage the wounds. Someone offers water to the ones sitting on the floor against the wall. Another covers the faces of the dead lined against the opposite wall. Nobody pays any attention to Omar and the women. And they, bewildered by what they are witnessing, don't know how to ask for help.

5

It takes several minutes before a nurse with a heavy tray of medical implements notices pregnant Laila. "There!" she screams through the busy crowd. "Over there." She waves her hand toward the door at the end of the hallway. And as they turn to go, the air is cut once more with a high-pitched cry.

"*Elhakoni!*" Help! A man carrying three small children rushes through the door.

There is no time to discuss anything. Laila grabs Omar's hand. "Stay," she pleads. Her big black eyes are terrified. Rumaisa understands everything without words. She looks up and shakes her head exactly the same way she had when Laila had entered their house for the first time. Omar stops for a moment and then, putting his hand on Laila's belly, says, "I'll be right back."

After a few seconds, he is holding a little girl. She is unconscious. Her blue dress is stained with blood. Her bare shoulder is tied to her torso, and her forearm is limp at her side.

"Everything will be all right," the father of the children says to himself, breaking with coughs. His forehead is covered in sweat and debris. "The man will help us," he says to the boy in his arms. The boy cries, "I want my Ommi! I want my Ommi!" The man looks at Omar and whispers, "Killed. She is dead." And then louder to the boy, "Later. Later."

The voice of the boy mixes with those of the soldiers, doctors, and nurses. For a long moment, the man stares helplessly, not knowing what to do.

"I have wounded . . . I have wounded children . . . "

Nobody pays attention, until a young nurse with round wire rimmed glasses waves over the heads of others and motions the man to follow her. Omar glances toward his wife and mother, and then disappears around the corner.

Wounded soldiers are still coming through the front door. The nurse at the door tries to direct the traffic. "Stretchers to the right!" she commands in a high-pitched voice, waving her arms high in the air. "You, third door to the left." She directs those who can walk without help. "Here. Place the dead along the wall to the right." She doesn't stop even for a moment. The river of people, steered by the nurse's arms, floats along the high banks of the hallway, pushed by its own rules of disarray.

Laila and Rumaisa, waiting for Omar, lower themselves onto chairs in the corner of a small, distant corridor.

"Just don't cry!" Rumaisa tries to keep her spirits up with precise commands. "I have a little cap," she starts, opening her bag. "And a blankie for my grandson." She smiles to herself.

"What if it's a girl?" Laila interrupts her, looking straight ahead.

"So what? If it's a girl, it's a girl!" Rumaisa doesn't stop rearranging the contents of her bag. "But I know! I know it's a boy!" she says firmly, and to validate her words, cuts the air quickly with her hand.

Laila takes a deep breath and says nothing.

"You can sigh all you want!" Rumaisa knows how to talk to her daughter-in-law. "Just mark my words. One day you will understand everything I say to you, and you will be grateful," she says. "I had five sons and four daughters, and I always knew what I was carrying!"

Laila jumps off her chair. "I know exactly what I'm carrying!" Her eyes grow bigger. "I am carrying twins!" She holds her belly as if to prove her own words.

Rumaisa looks up. "You don't know anything!" Her voice rises with the same old sarcasm. "The doctor knows!"

Laila moves back. "She said herself she wasn't sure!" Laila's voice is higher than normal.

"The doctor said it, only because you forced her! Forced her with your constant complaints!"

Rumaisa lowers her bag to the floor and gets up from her chair. Now, they are standing face to face—with their eyes burning, both breathing faster.

"No, it was you who forced your suggestions on the doctor," Laila says, repeating the same accusation for months now.

"You are going too far, Laila, too far!" Rumaisa waves her index finger at her. "And stop being nervous! You're carrying a baby! Stop making yourself nervous! It will make your labor difficult! Do you want to have a difficult labor? Why do you have to be this way?"

Laila covers her face and starts crying.

"Now, now . . . just sit." Rumaisa moves a chair behind Laila. "Here." She helps her to sit down. "Calm down, and think about the baby. That's all . . . that's all."

The nurse, carrying a tray covered with a linen cloth, approaches with a smile and informs them that the midwife is currently helping with the wounded. "Don't worry, she will come in time." Laila takes a deep breath and says nothing.

The midwife comes earlier than expected. After doing a quick check-up, she announces that since Laila's water has broken, she needs to stay in the hospital. She also gives instructions to the nurse and leaves in a hurry.

Hours of waiting allow the entire family to gather at the door of the delivery room. And even though their reasons for being there are personal, all they can talk about is the war.

"I heard fourteen children were killed," someone says.

"Yes, a building collapsed, killing all of them," someone else says. "The Suez Canal is still blocked."

"It might stay like this forever . . . or at least as long as the war goes on."

"When is it going to end?"

"When will they go back?"

Their voices mingle with the distant voices of the wounded, underlining the uncertainty of their lives. No one is safe. No one is assured of another day. Everyone hopes for better days after the war.

Omar paces the corridor. His relatives ask him about the wounded children he helped earlier, but he doesn't have any answers. "I don't know. Their father stayed with them." He keeps coming back to the door and listening, but after a second starts pacing again.

Angry, Rumaisa can't believe she has been asked to leave the delivery room, and is wondering if this is the hospital's policy or maybe just a secret wish of her ungrateful daughter-in-law. "The war! Silly excuse!" She battles her own thoughts. "So many healthy religious girls in Egypt. And he had to marry a Turkish woman! Why?" She looks at the ceiling, the same way as always, searching for answers from above.

It is a long night for everyone—for Laila, weakened with labor pains; for the family members, waiting with anticipation; and for those affected by the war. Doctors and nurses work long hours, and often their efforts bring nothing in the end.

In the early evening, the sky becomes clear with a strange light. The warm, moist air, carrying the smell of battle, penetrates the skin, leaving an unforgettable nauseating trace. Low, unfamiliar sounds are coming from the east, just as it is announced that a ship is sinking in the Suez Canal.

When, finally, the high-pitched cry of a newborn fills the air, the family jumps to the door. Omar freezes. A familiar sweet dream he has treasured for years resurfaces in his mind. He sees—in this dream—a little boy holding his hand and looking up straight into the sunlight coming from the morning window, mingled with the sounds of the garden. "Abba, what is it?" the boy would ask, clenching his little fingers. "Grandfather's flamingos at the pools," Omar would answer quietly, as if trying to bring this little boy slowly from a dream to the light of day. "Flamingos?" the little boy would ask, lowering himself to the floor and stepping toward the window into the soft pool of light on the bedroom floor. "Yes, my son," he would answer and follow the boy. They would stay there together, watching the morning garden unfold slowly, listening to the birds, and watching the surface of the calm water of the flower pools.

"The husband! Please, only the husband!" The nurse peeks through the door. "Everything went well," she adds, scanning the faces, still and focused. "It's a girl, a healthy girl," she says and asks Omar to step in.

"A girl?" Rumaisa runs to the door. "A girl?" Her eyes become round and white. "A girl?" She raises her hands to the ceiling. "Eight-and-a-half months after the wedding! Eight-and-a-half months! That's why! That's why!" She covers her face in disbelief, rage rising in her body like a desert storm.

"A healthy girl ..." Someone is trying to console her. "Next time it will be a boy!"

"Next time?" Rumaisa looks at the gathered with absent eyes. "She is too skinny to have another one!" She stomps her foot and lowers herself into a chair. "My firstborn! My Omar!" she wails into her palms.

Cries and groans of the wounded come from the other end of the hallway. Nurses, carrying trays and bins with bandages and clothes soaked in blood, appear and disappear in the halls.

Omar's family anxiously awaits the details, but no one questions the midwife's decision that they must stay away from the delivery room. "The war ... bacteria ... better to wait outside." After a long while, Omar finally comes out. He looks for someone in the crowd, and Rumaisa runs to him.

"What happened?" she asks nervously.

"Laila says there's another baby ... " Omar starts, lowering his gaze.

"Because it's a girl?" Rumaisa doesn't understand.

"No, she says there are twins. Do you know anything—?" He doesn't finish his sentence before his mother explodes.

"Why Turkish?" Rumaisa raises her arms. "Why?"

"Stop it!" Omar says. "Stop it right now!"

A loud, strange cry like a wounded animal cuts the thick air. Everybody freezes, looking at the delivery room door.

"I have another baby!" Laila screams. Her voice is unfamiliar, coming from a place of desperation and heartache. "Help me!"

"No, you don't." The nurse puts her hand on Laila's forehead. "It's normal to think that way. It's just contractions. It happens all the time." She moves her hand down on Laila's stomach. "The girl is beautiful and healthy. Be happy, rest."

"I have another baby inside me," Laila says quietly and starts sobbing. Omar goes back in, closing the door behind him. The family members pace the floor, exchanging suspicions and comments.

"What if she's right?"

"Is she ever right?"

"She mentioned something before."

"What was she saying before?"

"The doctor."

"When?"

They all stop talking for a moment when the midwife leaves the room, hurriedly directing her steps toward the wounded section. Nobody tries to stop her. They know the war has changed everything. There is no time for answers, no time for explanations, no time for understanding. Life is about surviving another week, another day, another hour.

"She was saying something about two heartbeats."

"They've been confused from the beginning."

Everybody is trying to remember the doctor's comments, the midwife's remarks, and Laila's observations, but nobody is sure of anything. They remember that she didn't agree with her doctor. They remember she didn't agree with Rumaisa, but then again, she rarely did. But they can't remember exactly the reasons for the disagreements and misunderstandings.

"Stop it, all of you!" Rumaisa yells, catching everyone by surprise. "It's a girl! Healthy girl! We should be grateful! Allah is great!" She speaks fast, as if trying to convince herself. And when, finally, everyone at the door starts getting used to the idea of a firstborn girl, the door swings open.

"She's in labor again!" The nurse rushes through the crowd.

Soon, both the nurse and the midwife are running back. The midwife changes her apron, and the nurse holds her mouth in distress. Now all the events come rushing like an avalanche. First, Omar is asked to leave the room. He comes out holding his head in both hands.

"Everything will be fine," someone says.

"I'm not sure she has enough strength to push," he sobs quietly. "She's very weak." He looks at everybody absently. "There is no doctor to do a Caesarean," he explains slowly. "Every single doctor is with the wounded." He covers his face with his hands.

"She is strong! Skinny, but strong! All Turkish are strong! She will be . . . " Rumaisa doesn't finish, quieted by Omar's sharp glance.

Omar paces the hallway in silence. He looks at his watch. Ten minutes. Eternity. At the other end of the hallway, he hears the prayers of the wounded. Some are carried away on stretchers, most with faces covered in white sheets. These are lined up on the floor against the wall, awaiting burial in the morning.

When the nurse appears in the door, those gathered freeze in anxious silence. Nobody moves except Omar, who slowly steps forward.

"A boy!" she says, raising both hands. "A healthy boy!"

"A boy?" Rumaisa jumps off her chair again. "A boy! That's a miracle! I knew it! I knew it! *Allahu Akbar!*"

"What about my wife?"

"Very weak. She lost a lot of blood. She needs a transfusion, and I wanted to ask . . . " She hasn't finished her sentence when a tall and slender woman comes forward. It is Fatima, Omar's first wife.

Fatima, not taking her eyes off the nurse, approaches her slowly. She glides silently across the floor, pushed by the longing of her barren body. She rolls her sleeve up. "Take my blood for her." Other members of the family, taken aback by the sadness in her eyes, step aside.

Omar flinches, knowing that they won't be able to accept her help.

The nurse, surprised and moved, tries to find an answer in the eyes of the people around her, before she finally says, "Laila has a very rare blood type." She hesitantly looks at Fatima. Now everyone except Rumaisa rolls up their sleeves.

"Take mine!"

"Take mine!"

The voices rise and fall. Fatima stops, resigned.

"She has a rare blood type," the nurse says again. "O Rh negative." After this announcement, some roll their sleeves back down; others ask if their blood could be checked. Fatima gives a long cry, covering her face with both hands. Her last chance of becoming closer to the children is gone. Someone hugs her tightly. "Don't cry."

Rumaisa finally gets up from her chair, moves through the crowd, and rolls up her sleeve.

"I have the blood type you need," she announces solemnly, bringing her chin up. "I know that. Laila knows it, too. Take as much as you need!" She stretches her arm forward.

The nurse nods with a smile and asks Rumaisa to follow her. Rumaisa, passing the family members, silent with amazement, carries her bare arm like a trophy. Omar presses his right hand to his chest. "Thank you, God," he whispers, closing his eyes.

They embrace Omar with congratulations. And considering the unexpected nature of the boy's arrival, they express the belief of God's special blessings offered to the family.

"*Allahu Akbar!*" The rejoicing voices fill the hospital's hallway.

"God is merciful! God blessed us all!" The words of praise and hope and gratitude are shared like bread—in the middle of war, between the newborns' first cries and the last breaths of the wounded soldiers.

No one remembers the wounded for a moment. No one wants to remember the war. All want to feel the joy for the new and long-awaited life. Family members embrace one another. "So many blessings!" The ecstatic words lift everyone's spirits. Everybody feels rewarded. Even Fatima smiles. "I could raise the girl," she whispers to herself. "I would give her a name, Aisha. Aisha would be her name." She clasps her hands to her heart. "Aisha," she whispers several times.

"A boy!" someone says loudly. "It's a miracle! He will be someone special!" They rejoice until the door of the delivery room swings open again.

"The husband! The husband!" The nurse's face is covered in sweat. "The husband and one more man!" she adds, jumping back in.

"Hamzah!" Omar grabs his younger brother by the hand and pulls him quickly.

Someone stops the door from closing, and everyone rushes in. They want to see what's happened. The white tiled floor under Laila's bed is covered in blood, smeared with footprints in all directions. The midwife is lying on top of Laila, holding onto the railings of the bed and screaming orders to Omar. "Fast!" She is trying to catch her breath. "Fast!" Despite the midwife's efforts, Laila's body is bucking up and down with convulsions. "Don't let her fall off the bed!" the midwife screams again, unable to fight the seizure. "Help me, hold her down!" Her commands are fast and precise. "More blankets! On top! On top! Not the stomach!"

Laila's body, stretched in an arc, offers strong resistance. Only after the two men press her to the bed are both the midwife and the nurse able to cover her with blankets. They maneuver under the arms of the men to cover her as tightly as possible. "Hold her down." The midwife wipes her forehead with the back of her hand.

After Laila is secured under a pile of blankets, the nurse notices the crowd at the door. "The door! Close the door!"

The midwife waves her arm, but no one moves. "Close the door, now!" Her voice is worn.

Laila's face, translucent as parchment paper, is motionless. Only her thin purple lips are twitching as if trying to say something. Her half-closed eyelids reveal narrow slices of white moons, and her forehead is covered with a wet shine sliding down her hair all the way to the pillow, where it forms a dark circle. The convulsions slowly cease under the weight of the men's bodies, in the silence of the motionless crowd at the door.

When both men get up, wiping the sweat from their faces, Omar looks into his wife's eyes and gives a loud cry.

"Don't cry." The midwife places her fingers on Laila's neck. "She is alive. *Allahu Akbar.* All in his hands. She is alive," she says, wiping Laila's forehead.

Omar buries his face in the blankets covering his wife, embracing them as if trying to reach her. He doesn't stop crying until Rumaisa puts her hand on his back. "Come," she says gently. "Let her rest." She helps him up. "She will be fine. I promise you." She pulls him away toward the table in the corner.

"They look so much alike," he says, looking at his children.

"Yes, that's rare," the midwife comments with a smile.

"Why rare?" Omar doesn't understand. "They *are* twins, after all."

"Yes, but they're not identical. Fraternal never look alike," she explains with medical conviction.

"It's so unbelievable." He looks at his sleeping children.

"It's a miracle," the midwife adds, placing his children carefully in his arms.

He studies their faces.

"Like two drops of water," he says finally.

"Like two drops of water," the midwife confirms with a smile.

"This is the boy," the nurse says, pointing to the infant in Omar's right arm. "I gave him this hat," she says, wiping her nose and face with her sleeve.

Omar approaches Laila's bed.

"This is Taher." He lowers the infant to Laila's sleeping face. "And here, close to my heart, is our daughter," he says, lowering the other infant. "You can name her later. When you gain your strength back," he adds softly.

Now, all are crying—the midwife, the nurse, Omar, Hamzah, and all the family who circle Laila's bed.

"Poor, skinny you." Rumaisa strokes Laila's face. "Gain your strength back quickly."

"She will be fine. *Allahu Akbar*," adds someone from the crowd.

"*Allahu Akbar*," adds Omar, kissing his wife's forehead.

Home

It is a colonial villa, like many of those built for foreign engineers working on the Suez Canal in the 1860s—in sepia colors with a multilevel roof covered in dark red shingles. Old palm and fruit trees that give off a subtle fragrance invite those seeking quiet moments in the shade. Many walk the numerous paths around the house and marvel at the beautiful gardens. Some rest on benches and swings. Some love the expansive flower pools, blooms, and leaves—as big as dinner plates—that sway softly on the silver surface of the calm waters.

The villa is separated from the wide boulevard by a high, white fence covered in ivy. For Taher and Aisha, the house and the gardens are an island that protects them from the outside world.

Their favorite places to play are the terraces, lined with brown shutters and shaded with wide roof overhangs. The shutters' purpose and meaning changes with every new discovery the children make. Sometimes they serve as curtains for their puppet theater, exactly the same as the one Taher knows from a book in his father's library. Sometimes they are a dark and silent forest. On other days, they become the wings of an airplane.

The big garden behind the house is a place of adventure and happiness, but also a place of solitude and comfort. Spacious and mysterious, the garden invites the children for safe expeditions.

In the center of the garden, two long flower pools, filled with bright goblets of lotus flowers and lilies, reflect the sky. The many paths of white and black stones lead to the flower pools among soft carpets of tiny blooms of *El Foil*. The paths, shaded with various fruit trees, are drowning in scents of sweet figs, mangos, guavas, refreshing lemons, and dwarf apples. Between the two pools, where all the paths meet, there is a small pavilion shrouded in grapevines. This is where six-year-old Taher stands facing Mecca, reciting the Holy Words of the Qur'an for family and guests, their faces turned towards him in adoration.

"What a blessing," they comment among themselves. "A reason to be proud." They congratulate his parents. "Miraculous!" They nod in assent with Grandmother Rumaisa, remembering the birth of the twins and discussing the war.

For the children, the garden has its own hidden mysteries that are revealed in the deepest corners, behind the azaleas thick with heavy and sweet blooms. One day, the mysteries reveal themselves as the fear and helplessness of a spider's prey, seeping slowly through the tight cocoon when Taher tries to free a butterfly. *"Teery!"* Go! he cries as loud as he can, throwing the sticky and motionless body in the air, still hoping, not yet grasping the radical power of death.

Another day, the mysteries come in the form of discovering the forbidden, when Aisha crawls under the bush and helps Grandmother Rumaisa's favorite cat deliver her naked and defenseless kittens.

"Katkaut." Pussy cat. Aisha reaches for them without hesitation. *"Meshmesh."* Come here. She crawls on her stomach. "Don't be afraid. *Meshmesh*," she says, stroking the soft fur stained with blood. "My little babies!" She embraces the huddled, squealing, blind creatures with pride and gratitude for having witnessed the beginning of new life.

The day Aisha confesses her envy to Taher, they are alone in the garden. Tired from running, they decide to rest at the edge of the flower pool.

The air, thick with sweetness, hovers in the sweltering sun, slowing their breaths, filling their bodies with blissful weight. Receding behind the tall palm trees, the sun throws long lines across the flower pools. The day, closing slowly to the *Al Maghre* prayer, evokes silent anticipation.

Taher closes his eyes and tilts his head slightly back and to the side, and his imagination takes over.

He arises like a bird or a cloud, lightly and silently, with no effort. He stretches out his arms and glides toward the highest roofs, where he stops for a while to look at the minaret shimmering on the background of the clearest sky, and the silver surface of the lake surrounded by white beaches at the edge of the city. After his eyes finally feel satisfied with all he wanted to see in the distance, he steers himself above the roof to find the long swords of palm leaves that strayed into the drainpipe. Controlling every single movement of the descent, he lowers himself and reaches for the leaves. He picks them up gently between his fingers and studies their rough surface, always with the same astonishment. "They're drying up already," he whispers, and busies himself with finding more and more different colors, from greens to dark browns, depending on how much time they spent in the blazing sun. He inhales deeply the high air filled with the smell of the sea.

The sun is lowering itself to close the day with the silent gentle breath of a soft breeze, when suddenly Taher is jolted by cold blades. Only after he opens his eyes does he understand it is water.

Aisha laughs, hitting the surface of the water in the flower pool, splashing her brother and screaming, "Wake up, Taher! Wake up!"

"You are so stupid!" he screams, jumping off the edge.

"Me?" She laughs louder and hits the surface of the water with all her might.

The wide fans spring toward Taher faster and faster, darkening the edge of the pool and the polished river rocks covering the path under their feet.

"Stop it!" Taher yells, moving back and wiping his face. "You're stupid!"

"And you sleep all the time!" She mocks his voice.

"I don't!" Taher defends himself. "I don't sleep! I think!"

"About what?" She doesn't give up. "Making up silly stories again?"

"You're jealous!" He knows how to hurt her.

A long silence falls over the garden. Aisha wipes her hands on her dress and starts to pick at her nails. For a while, she looks at the goblets of the lotus flowers and the flat leaves speckled with fast-drying drops of water, and then she moves her gaze to the pebbles on the paths, to the tips of the trees. Kicking her right foot in the air, she stays silent.

"It's different for you, Aisha." Taher sits down next to her. "It's different, because you're a girl," he says softly.

"They all see only you!" She looks him straight in the eye. "They cheer only you! *Taher is a true miracle! He memorized the Qur'an! Taher! Taher! Taher!*"

"And you're the faster runner, remember? And also—" Taher doesn't finish. She jumps off the edge, as if on fire.

"Do you always have to be such a saint?" she screams, stamping her foot.

"I'm not a saint—"

"You are!" she interrupts him again, stamping her foot one more time.

"And you are too!" He spreads his arms helplessly.

"No, I am not! I am not, and I don't want to be! I don't want to be good! I don't want to! And I don't want to be myself!" She holds back her tears, shivering.

"What are you talking about?" Taher takes a step toward her. "You're crazy!"

"*You're* crazy! You! You're stupid! Like everyone else!" she screams, running toward the thick azalea bushes in the farthest corner of the garden.

*

On the first level of the house, there are two fountains designed to cool the hot summer air and bring relief, longed for by all who live there. The bigger one, sitting in the middle of the foyer on a large square, emits the low sound of deep water. The smaller one, situated in the back of the house facing the garden, is rarely visited by anyone except Taher.

Taher spends long hours there, listening to the gentle patter of water and observing the garden. He sits on the steps that lead with a gentle pitch to the bottom, where water shimmers like silver coins.

Behind the window, the world is sharpened by sunlight, but here, everything gives way to soothing sounds and rhythms.

The half-circle bottom of the fountain and the wall with the spout are covered with tiny multicolored tiles that form a symmetrical design, flickering as much as the water.

On the day when Aisha splashes him with water at the garden pools, Taher finds something extraordinary at the back fountain. Because of a mechanical failure in the pump, the usual silver ribbon of running water is replaced by single drops coming off the spout in regular intervals.

The single drops falling on the motionless surface arouse soft waves that form perfect circles. The waves make their way toward the outer edges of the bottom, running one after another—one circle, a second, and a third. Perfectly symmetrical and widening, they rush toward the edge to vanish there and be reborn in the single drop of water trickling down the spout. Waves disappear and new drops are born, one after another—one drop and the beginning of a wave vanishing at the edge.

Taher sits at the top of the stairs and watches in amazement. The drops seem to be identical. *Is this the same drop of water coming back every time, or is this a different one?* He asks himself. *The same one starting the waves and coming back in the spout or a different one, since the first one was dissolved in the water?* He fixes his gaze on the surface. *Can a drop be dissolved in an ocean of drops? Can it be lost? Or does it stay the same drop and come back as itself? Can it be identical and self-contained at the same time?*

"Each one is different, and they are all the same." He remembers what his father had said at the lake not long ago. They were on a boat, just the two of them, in the middle of Lake Timsah. The surface of the water was silver and black, idyllically smooth, motionless.

"Now, throw the biggest one you have," his father commanded.

Taher reached into a tin can and retrieved a big rock with a smile.

"Here!" Taher swung his arm.

The rock, vanishing into the water, started a series of waves. One after another, they rushed through the lake, pushing each other, multiplying in strength and scope. Growing bigger and bigger, they made their way toward the shore and the boat.

"Now, throw the small one," his father commanded when the surface became still again.

This time smaller waves rushed from the center, but they were as symmetrical as the first ones, pushing each other in the same systematic way, with the same consequence, irreversibly set in motion with the fall of the rock.

"You see?" His father pointed to the spot where the rock disappeared. "A big rock makes waves, and a small pebble makes waves. They make waves the same way. The same round waves that make their way from the center to the shore. One after another, the same way."

"And all the waves are rushing the same way," Taher continued his father's story. "The same way from the center, where the rock hits the surface, to the shore, to our boat, and all the way around."

"That's true," his father confirmed with a smile. "After the fall of the rock, you can clearly see how similar they really are, so similar that it's hard to distinguish them. Almost identical."

"The waves or the drops?" Taher liked asking questions.

"What do you think?"

"Well, really . . ." Taher stopped for a moment, thinking. "Really both, I think." He looked at his father, awaiting his response.

"You're right. They are almost identical."

"And they always rush like that after a hit." Taher squinted his eyes, looking at the surface.

"Yes, the hit gives them their beginning. Invariably."

Sitting at the top of the steps, Taher notices that the drop of water in the broken fountain plays the role of the rock. The drop, like a rock falling on the smooth surface, creates waves—first one, then a second, and so on. The next drop and the next circle. Indistinguishable. Which drop? Which circle? Different? The same? Still the same? Different and identical. Like two drops of water.

"Why are you sitting here?" Aisha is towering over Taher.

"I'm not sitting. I'm squatting. Go away." Taher doesn't look at her.

"Oh, no!" Aisha says, covering her mouth. "Oh, no!" she says again, lowering her arms slowly. Her eyes grow bigger.

"What?" Taher jumps up.

"Taher broke the fountain!" she screams. Her voice bounces off the walls.

"I didn't! It was this way when I came," he says, pointing toward the spout.

"No, you always break things!" Aisha looks him straight in the eye, pointing her finger at his chest. "Ommi! Ommi! Taher broke the fountain!"

After a moment, they hear quick steps in the hallway.

"What happened?" Laila catches her breath.

"Taher broke the fountain! Taher broke the fountain! Taher broke—"

"I didn't!" Taher struggles to hold back tears. "Stop it!"

"Yes, you did!" Aisha steps closer to her mother.

"Aisha, stop it this instant!" Laila moves away from her.

"But he did." Aisha freezes. "Just look." She points toward the spout.

"He didn't break anything!" Laila waves her finger at Aisha. "Stop accusing your brother! That's enough!"

"I told her I didn't do it. It was like this when I came." Taher wipes away his tears.

"I know," Laila says softly. "Don't worry about what your sister said." She embraces Taher gently. "The small pump broke this morning. Father already knows."

"How was I supposed to know?" Aisha says. "He was sitting over there . . . " Now she is holding back tears.

"I wasn't sitting. I was squatting. I told you that, too!" Taher drawls. "You never listen!"

"I always listen, but sometimes I don't believe!"

"Children, children." Laila embraces Aisha and leads them both to the top of the fountain's steps. "Let's sit down here."

They sit down and look at the water.

"I have only you two. Only you two," she starts slowly, gathering her thoughts.

The drops of water are trickling down, creating waves, causing the water to shimmer. Perfectly round, they rush toward the edges of the fountain. The multicolored mosaic of the bottom moves with the rhythmic waves. Taher squints and looks out the glass door. The plumes of the palm trees in the garden are gilded with the light of the withdrawing sun.

Laila doesn't say anything for a long while. She pulls her children closer and stares at the water.

"Ommi, are you cold?" Taher asks, breaking the silence.

"No," she whispers.

"I know." Aisha embraces her mother tightly. "You don't want our father to marry again. You don't want him to have a third wife."

"Oh, no, no," she says quickly, swallowing her tears.

"Don't worry, Ommi," Taher adds. "She might be nice."

"It's not the same," Aisha says. "Don't you understand?"

"I understand!" Taher leans forward to meet her gaze. "Grandmother Rumaisa says that maybe this way I can have a brother."

"You only think about yourself!" Aisha scolds him.

"Stop it, please," Laila interrupts. "We shouldn't even be talking about it."

"We didn't say anything to anybody." Aisha looks at Taher.

"It has nothing to do with the two of you." Laila wipes away tears. "Besides . . . Father didn't decide anything yet," she adds calmly.

"Grandmother says that we want to have more children." Taher strokes his mother's hand.

"I know. I know," she says, embracing them even more tightly.

The world shrinks to the size of her body, to her warmth and the smell of jasmine and burnt ginger that accompanies her always. She strokes their hands, kisses their faces. They remain silent and watch the individual drops of water hitting the surface in the same spot, with the same speed, with the same result, one by one.

"We are one family and will always remain this way," she says firmly, as if trying to convince herself more than her children.

Those words will stay with them for many years after they are spoken and will become even more significant when Laila decides to leave the house.

"The differences are not important. Only the similarities," she says softly. "Just look at yourselves and try to see what you have in common, not what is different."

Taher and Aisha look at each other and grin.

"Taher, you must try to find yourself in Aisha," she says softly. "Aisha, you must try to find yourself in Taher," she says, turning toward her daughter. "Do you understand?"

"Maybe . . . " Taher isn't convinced.

"No, I don't." Aisha shrugs.

"Taher, you are in Aisha, and Aisha is in you. Aisha, Taher is in you, and you are in Taher." Laila smiles. The children look at her, confused but intrigued. She knows how to gain their attention. She kisses their faces again. "It's simple. You just need to try."

"With love?" Aisha snorts.

"With openness." Laila is trying to simplify the complexity of her thoughts.

"Hmm." The children nod unanimously.

"You have the same hearts. The same blood is in your veins." Laila opens their hands, following with her finger the tiny blue branches. "Here. And here." She traces her finger slowly along the little niches of their palms. "And here. And everywhere."

The children cling to their mother and, holding hands, embrace her tightly. Close to the warmth and scent of her body—jasmine and burnt ginger. Close to the everlasting water and to the setting sun. Close to each other in a way that seems strange and inviting, awkward and appealing.

*

The complications during the delivery of the twins have left Laila barren, and this has become a source of many misunderstandings and tensions between her and Omar. In the end, Laila decides to leave the family and ask for a divorce. She won't agree to live in the shadow of the third wife.

"I want to have more children," Omar pleads with her for years. "Don't you understand? They will be your children too." He tries to convince her to accept something that is unthinkable to her.

"Only Taher and Aisha are mine. Nothing will ever change that." She believes strongly in her words.

Rumaisa enters into their marital problems with the momentum of a lady of the household, invoking the unyielding laws of heritage. "It's our tradition! What do you expect?" she reprimands her daughter-in-law. "You are standing in the way of our family's expansion and growth! You are egoistic!" Rumaisa never chooses her words carefully.

Laila reaches for her own beliefs with equal conviction. "The world around you is changing!"

But nothing can convince Rumaisa. "It's decadence, not change. Maybe in Turkey you call it change. Here it is called a straight road to the edge of a cliff! God still exists. And someone needs to be the mainstay in the world!" She wags her index finger at Laila. "And who—I ask—who delivers a baby eight-and-a-half months after her wedding?"

Rumaisa doesn't stop short of any argument to prove her own opinions and isn't quick to accept the uncomfortable explanations of the midwife that twins rarely come to full term.

"Well, then, I want a divorce."

"Please, think about it," Omar pleads. But finally, he accepts the inevitable.

"I can't stay." Laila knows he understands. "It wasn't supposed to be like this. You said different things back in Turkey."

"I remember." He is leaving her slowly, against his own desires. "But we didn't know then what we know now. I know you understand."

"Two children aren't enough for you?" Laila, knowing the answer, repeats the question with new hope.

Omar can't look her in the eyes.

"All my life I struggled with your mother," she says, crying. "I don't have the strength to struggle with anyone else."

"You don't know how it all will turn out."

"I do know," she says hurriedly. "I know because I finally understand poor Fatima and her place in the family."

"Fatima loves you like a sister." Omar tries the same argument as always.

"Omar, she hates me! She hates me because I gave you children! Because I took her place in giving you children! This is the truth!" she cries out.

"Don't be egoistic," he answers with the same tired response.

"Really?" Her eyes grow wider. "Don't forget to add that I am also *bad*. This is your mother's line as well!"

*

When the twins turn nine, she leaves the house and moves to Cairo. Omar buys her a comfortable condominium and makes sure all her needs are met. Laila sees her children once a week and, fulfilling all their wishes, spoils them with presents, movies, and ice cream.

None of this lasts long. After only a year, she becomes gravely ill and is taken to a hospital. Omar, who is abroad at the time, visits her after a month.

"It's my fault." He sits on her bed and cries, holding her hand.

"Nonsense," she says, stroking his hair gently. "Cancer is cancer. Nobody's fault." She looks at him with the same tenderness as when they first met in Turkey, but he can't recognize anything but her voice. Her petite body has become a shadow lost in blankets. Her head on the pillow reminds him of a baby bird. Her hands, just skin on bones, are cold and stiff, and the rings on her fingers slide up and down with the slightest movement of her wrists.

Omar closes his eyes and lowers himself onto the bed next to her. He tries to remember the smell of her body, but it isn't there anymore. "Say something," he implores, trying to resurrect the remains of their past.

"I'm sorry I couldn't love you the way you needed to be loved," she says after a long silence.

"No, it was me, not you," he answers, pressing himself closer to her. "I broke the promise."

"You had no choice," she says softly.

"There are always choices in life. Always. I just refused to see it," he sobs.

"Let Fatima raise our children." She gazes out the window. "Promise me it will be her."

"I promise."

"Omar . . . " The pupils in Laila's eyes become wide and soft. She looks at something that appears to be close and far away at the same time. "Omar," she says softly.

"Yes?" He lowers his face and tries to understand what she needs.

"Omar, I'm dying." She closes her eyes.

The world withdraws in a strange and distant silence that claims all the words and gestures.

Their final embrace, unrecognizable, comes with Laila's last breath.

Omar looks at her in disbelief, unable to accept what just happened. He holds her hands, ready to follow her over the precipice. "Wait," he says softly, but only the fading hum in the air answers his last request.

The thickened air above her body glistens for a while in translucent colors. It moves in a soft wave coming from her feet up her chest, finally freeing her. She stretches her arms wide and rises freely, like a bird or a cloud. She brushes her husband's face for the last time and pushes toward the horizon. Weightless, gilded with the warmth of the setting sun, she drifts away in the pounding rhythm of his heart. He closes his eyes and follows her for a long time, all the way to the end of her flight.

Sacred Room

At seven, Taher loves the family escapades into the desert and always awaits them anxiously. He daydreams about them, even when they are not planned for the near future. Sometimes, he thinks about them all day, looking into the calm waters of the flower pools in the garden, especially when he can't find anything to do.

He sits on the edge of the pool, thinking about his father with tenderness, remembering the family adventures and his father's stories. He knows that on each journey, another mystery will be revealed to him, another step in grasping the meaning of life. There, in the middle of a distant desert, in the company of other men, he belongs.

Taher yearns to understand his father's words. "Every man must recognize his destiny. Every man must know what to choose." The words leave the boy's heart pounding and his eyes wide open late into the night.

The desert is a place where one confesses the mistakes of his life and where absolution from sin happens with force and assurance. All worries and cares disappear, making a new, clean space in the heart. Taher can never decide whether that is possible because the sun burns out all that is painful, or because the vastness of the plain dissolves worries into nothingness, or maybe because the silence absorbs thoughts and ill feelings. All of his worries and cares disappear behind the horizon with the vibrations of hot air. He doesn't know but is grateful to God for the gift of redemption coming from the desert journeys, where he always feels the presence of a power greater than anything he knows, a miraculous power he wants to understand and be part of, a power that touches everything in his life. From losing races to his twin sister Aisha in the garden, to the blue butterfly caught in the web, to his mother's disappointments—all disappear in the sweet relief of forgetfulness offered by the most sacred of places, the desert.

*

Taher can't remember what time they left. He thinks it was early morning, and then he thinks it was the middle of the night, but he remembers his mother standing at the front door, waving. As she stepped forward, her dress billowed with thousands of soft waves. Then there was a quiet groan, but he couldn't tell if it was his mother or maybe the door hinges. He prefers to think it was the door, since her sadness would have made him quiet for many days. Nobody needed her tears. Not Taher, not his father, who always became confused, and certainly not his mother, who, with every single tear, grew more distant from the family.

That day, they travel longer than ever, and Taher knows that this journey is different. Not only because every man in his family is coming to join them, even those from abroad, but also because this is his seventh birthday. He is a little concerned about meeting them all because of the indescribable weakness he feels after the removal of his tonsils and the weeks of high fever he experienced afterwards.

His mother wanted him to stay home, and only after a plea from his father and his own forceful assurance, did she give permission for him to go. They all agreed to celebrate his birthday at home immediately upon their return.

The white ball of the sun hangs high above the earth, enfolding everything with swelling heat, when his father stops the jeep and says, "The rest of the way is on foot. It's not that far."

Taher feels a strong pull downward, something is trying to bring him to his knees, and his body becomes heavy again. He knows the fever is coming back by the way the ground is slipping out from under him when he lowers himself from the car. He looks straight ahead, trying to understand why the fluid mass of heat is entering his chest. Every single breath is labored. His father's voice is fading in the far distance. Taher sees himself leaving the car many times, repeating the task of opening the door and lowering his feet to the ground. After that, everything else repeats—putting up the tent, arranging the camp with blankets and sleeping bags, setting a place for food and water. He is tired already.

Before they came here, his father told him about the Sacred Room, and Taher knows that it is the most important place on the planet, since all decisions are made right there.

"Every man enters the Sacred Room many times in his life." His father had leaned toward him the same way he always did when revealing the secrets of life.

"Why?" Every cell of Taher's body waited for the explanation.

"Because this is the place where one makes decisions." His father's index finger rose to the sky.

"Decisions?" The boy's eyes grew wider.

"Choices," his father explained. "You choose what you want to do, or what you want to have, or who you want to be when you grow up." His father raised his eyebrows. "You choose black or white."

"Stones?" The boy came up to his knees. "The ones in the garden, near the flower pools?"

"Sometimes the stones, and sometimes . . . something different." His father's explanation was complicated, but convincing.

"Daddy, but I don't know what I want. I like the white stones, but I like the black ones, too." Taher wanted to learn everything.

"You will have to choose between the two of them." His father's voice carried a sad note.

"What if I don't?" Taher lowered his voice.

"Then someone else will choose for you."

"What if the other person knows best? Just like you?" Taher leaned forward.

"Someone else might know better and choose for you when you are a child, but when you become a man, you must choose for yourself. Do you understand?" his father asked.

"What if I will always be a child?" Taher said, shrugging his shoulders.

"We both know that's impossible, right?"

"Yes, we both know." Taher nodded.

His father's stories were etched into him like words carved into stone. They structured his world in Ismailia, where he was born and grew up. And even as he grew older and the interpretation of the stories changed, they remained his oracle until the end. The most controversial and the most discussed story was the one about the Thirst.

"Only the people of the desert can grasp the truth of life." His father looked into the starry sky, putting his hands behind his head and stretching himself out on the ground. "It's a necessary survival skill and an art required to build a meaningful life." His words were slow and quiet. "But most people, greedy and imprudent, live their lives unconsciously, and that's the time when water turns into lead."

"Into lead?"

"Yes." His father looked straight into Taher's eyes. "Water always turns into lead when there is too much of it, and when there is not enough of it."

"Impossible!" The boy eagerly pointed out the contradiction.

"Only the people of the desert know the exact amount of water that won't turn into lead," his father continued slowly. "They know exactly what amount of water is essential, and they know this is the amount, exactly the amount, they should take with them. People not familiar with the desert either take too much water, or not enough. Those who run out of water are imprudent. They always go farther than they should, and that's why they never come back. Those who take too much water, rapacious ones, overburden themselves and their animals, slowing down the journey dangerously, never arriving at their destination."

His father always looked at him before the last sentence. "Remember, this is very important! You must become a man of the desert before you take upon yourself the journey into the desert. You must become a man of the desert before you take upon yourself the journey into life. Prepare before you go!"

"Life is a tremendous journey through the desert." These words became a mysterious conundrum to Taher. "Life is a tremendous journey through the desert, and a man's thirst is his biggest challenge. Through his choices, it can become his biggest strength or his biggest weakness." Taher repeated these words and pondered their meaning.

*

The visit to the Sacred Room takes place at midnight. His father wakes him with a gentle shake. "It's time," he says softly. The boy gets up fast and immediately notices that the ground under his feet is hard and steady. His body is light and fresh, just the way it is in the garden, when he plays with Aisha. He remembers to be cautious and picks only one small goatskin of water.

They take a couple of steps, and there it is. A gigantic wall appears before them, out of the darkness. Surprised, Taher trips over his father's heels, but is rescued by a firm grip. The same grip pulls him into a long corridor. "Let's go!" His father's voice is anxious. The coolness and dampness of the stone walls help him forget the unbearable heat of the day. Excitement makes his breath soft and shallow. He tries to concentrate on following his guide, but the rhythm of his own heart pounding in his temples overwhelms all his efforts. He shakes as if with high fever again, but his mind is clear and alert.

When he sees the warm light at the end of the corridor, he knows this is the place—the Sacred Room. Unable to control the trembling of his body, he reaches for his father's hand and clutches it with all his might. His father tightens his grip, and they cross the threshold.

The room is in the shape of a cylinder. Its obsidian floor is opaque and glistening. The ceiling is a canopy of brilliant stars. The high walls are covered with engravings and divided into three sections, equally tall and parallel to the floor.

The lowest section is filled with ocean life. Deep, dark waters from the bottom of the ocean travel up the silver lines of light, where dozens of stingrays float under the shimmering surface. Their flat bodies, culminating in a long, sharp arrow, twinkle with a willow-green flash. Schools of dolphins, cutting the air with long arches, swim toward the crimson horizon. In the distance, blue whales spurt water into the sky, dispersing flocks of noisy seagulls, the very ones that just a second ago had been diving into the waters in search of silver prey.

Taher releases his father's hand and walks around the room in awe. He studies every detail with amazement, until he notices the sharks. They don't belong with the stingrays, or the dolphins, or the majestic whales; they don't belong to the light under the surface. They belong only to themselves. He notices it in the blink of an eye. The sharks circle the waters restlessly while he waits, unable to take his eyes off them. They are silent, with many rows of white, crooked teeth in their jaws and small, black eyes. They look focused and determined in every movement. Taher knows that they are on a hunt. After a while, the sharks streak through the dark waters, striking ferociously—fast and nimble turns, snapping jaws. The waters boil in an instant, frothing with blood and pieces of white flesh—then the heads of the prey fall to the bottom in a slow and fluid motion. Scavengers flash into the image, reaching for the remains. And then all of it disappears into the impenetrable darkness.

Taher looks at his father in relief, but only for a moment, because the sharks come back. His heart sinks when he sees them return. He knows what it means—all of it is surreal, and at the same time, it is the most vivid experience.

Without warning, the sharks reemerge from the darkness and point themselves toward the middle of the room. Taher can't take his eyes off them even for a split second. Bewildered, he watches them approaching his face, realizing that he has gone from a spectator to a participant in the bloody spectacle. Now he is the target of their hunger.

The sharks circle his body many times, narrowing the distance, until they completely separate him from his father. He is on his own for the first time. His heart strikes as he falls to his knees, saying the only words he remembers, *"Allahu Akbar . . . Allahu Akbar . . ."* His voice is soft, held back by the overwhelming experience. The sharks reveal their rows of teeth and come even closer. Now he can touch them with his hand. He smells their nauseating breath, and in that very moment when all hope disappears, he discovers the mystery of his biggest strength.

What happened?

He turns his eyes away from them, and the sharks freeze in midair. Everything around him becomes still. He understands immediately. The pictures are moving only when he looks at them. He breathes life into them, and they are alive only as long as his eyes are on them—that is the only life they can have. He feels a wave of strength come up from the floor, through his legs and into his chest. His feet become light; his face turns up to the starry ceiling. He lifts his arms with open hands.

"I am!" he screams at the top of his lungs. "I am!" he screams again, amazed by his own words.

In the top section of the walls, innumerable flocks of birds, awakened by Taher, race towards the sky. Lone eagles and hawks from the forests and mountains. Black clouds of ravens and crows on the snowy plains. And thousands and thousands of slender swallows and crimson cardinals. Taher raises his arms gracefully, conducting the symphony of wings. "Look! Look!" he calls to his father. "Look how high!" Rainbows of enormous macaws drift through the air like open umbrellas. *Swoosh, swoosh,* their wings cut the moist, hot air. Flocks of geese leave for the distant horizon, and lone gray herons float down the shimmering streams without touching the water. In the distance, slow flamingos lower their heads over shallow waters, cobalt plates of a darkening sky on the ground.

Enormous pictures on the walls, brought to life by Taher's gaze, fill up the Sacred Room, surrounding him and his father, until they both become part of this surreal world.

The boy looks to the middle section of the wall, bringing to life herds of wild horses that charge forward in clouds of dust. He leads them with his hands, calling them and making them run away, marveling at their manes flowing in the wind. He makes giraffes cast long eyelash shadows by squinting their eyes. He brings their heads up, reaching for the highest branches of the smooth tree trunks. He reaches for the black mounds of hippopotamus in the muddy waters, soft white bears buried in the snowdrifts, and watchful penguins balancing precious eggs on their feet. He reaches for gigantic deer antlers clashing with a low sound that is carried above the marshes and herds of oxen, powerful in stillness. Lemurs, jumping between the thick crowns of the dark trees, fill the air with a high-pitched scream, and white wolves wait for the night. Taher gives them life. His hands direct their steps. All is possible only with his presence— life unfolds, and he makes it happen.

The lions sit in high grasses. Taher sees their amber eyes above the waves of soft greens. Then he notices a movement near a small herd of gazelles. He steps forward, and suddenly he senses the sweet smell of blood. Not spilled, just hanging in the air like a cloud, announced by the raw instinct he is about to discover. He sees the gazelles lifting their heads, and then their reflections in the amber eyes. The nostrils of the lions and the boy's palms are wide open and ready. The boy knows that everything depends on him. He takes another step forward. "Someone must live, someone must die," he whispers. The gazelles lower their heads in the grasses, and the light runs down the swords of their antlers. The gazelles don't suspect anything, even though this is the order of things. Taher raises his hands up high above his head, and with this signal, the chase of the lions and gazelles begins as fast as a cut, as short as the beat of a startled heart. First, the colts, their necks limp like morning stems. Then two young mares are dragged with effort—they don't make a sound.

The boy sees teeth sinking into the warm flesh of the sacrificed. He falls to his knees, trembling. "*Allahu Akbar . . .* " he says, remembering his father's words—"This is the nature of things. Just the nature of things," spoken to him in the garden in Ismailia, among the azaleas, where black spiders preserved the bodies of blue butterflies in their sticky wraps. Taher closes his eyes, and everything in the Sacred Room grows still.

The memory of the night in the desert, the night before his seventh birthday, will remain vivid for him for many years—the piercing wind of the Arctic and the moist heat of the tropics; the impenetrable darkness of the oceans and the inexhaustible plains of the desert light; the unattainable lightness of the birds and the stillness of blue whales; the strength of the lions and the undeserved weakness of the gazelles. All join together in a vivid picture of life, made possible by Taher's gaze.

*

This faith in his own strength, which he gains that night, changes him. And although he never shares with anyone what happened—understanding that the most intimate experiences should be secret—all his relatives notice the transition.

"He is so quiet," they say.

"Pensive," they observe.

"Still a little bit weak," they speculate eagerly among themselves.

The night before his return home, an unexpected closeness between Taher and his cousin, Ahmed—eleven years his senior—is born under strange and amazing circumstances. The difference in age would typically seem to rule out such a connection, so everyone is surprised when Ahmed announces that Taher is like a brother to him.

At midnight, when everyone except Ahmed is sound asleep, and the campfire's glow is still shooting toward the starry sky, a giant lizard slides between the tents.

Ahmed, sitting next to the fire, is reading the Qur'an. This is the way he spends all his desert trips. By reading, meditating, and fasting, he strives to renew his covenant with God. He never refuses an invitation to family escapades, but usually he goes to the desert by himself—to search for peace and reconnection, to distance himself from everyday life in the tranquility of the vastness.

Taher is coming out of the tent, half asleep, when the giant lizard stops close to Ahmed, who is completely absorbed in his reading. The shape of the animal's gray body is vibrating in the golden glimmer of the campfire. It appears and fades in the darkness, leaving Taher puzzled for a moment. He can't decide if what he sees is real or just a dream still haunting his eyes, until the lizard steps forward and looks at him.

Taher recognizes the lizard immediately. The memories of a previous encounter with a similar lizard come rushing back. There was this little boy, stiffened in his mother's arms, and her scream, "Help! Help!" She rocked him, saying "Wake up! Wake up!" The little boy stayed lifeless.

Taher's father had tried to explain to him the nature of the lizard, and that its bite paralyzed the victim for only a few hours, but rarely kills. Taher hadn't believe him, because nothing was as convincing as the legend in which the giant lizard possessed the power of his ancestors, as old as 130 million years. According to the legend, during an attack, the lizard undergoes a metamorphosis and changes into a deadly snake, and this ability is common knowledge among the people of the desert. The lizard grows and lengthens with air sucked up as fast as a desert storm, allowing him to tower over his victims. He is able to produce sounds so piercing that some die just from hearing them. Others die from the sight of the dance the lizard performs during the attack, and some die from the strike. This makes the lizard the most feared and most respected animal of the desert.

Now that lizard is behind Ahmed, who is lost in the Qur'an. Taher sees the razor-thin pupils of the monster's glowing eyes, and his shadow projecting all the way back between the tents. "Ahmeeed!" Taher whispers through his teeth. Ahmed doesn't move. "Ahmeeed!" he tries again. Nothing. Only when he turns a page, Ahmed notices his little cousin, frozen in fear.

"Don't move!" Taher's lips whisper. "He is behind you."

Ahmed understands immediately.

"Where?" Ahmed's lips move slowly.

"Behind you."

"How far?" Ahmed's eyes are fixed on Taher's face, but his mind is somewhere else.

"Meters," the boy whisperd, and discreetly shows him seven fingers.

Taher is waiting for the next question, ready to help, but for a moment nothing happens. The desert is still. The sky is still. Ahmed is still, and the lizard is still. Even the glow of the campfire seems to transform into a bright, motionless column. After a moment longer than eternity, Ahmed slowly moves, gets down on his knees, and faces the monster. With one hand holding a blanket, he raises the other toward the lizard as if to say, "Stay!"

"Knife!" Ahmed hisses, but Taher doesn't move.

Taher wonders, *Where is it? The bag? Tent?* Finally, not able to decide, he whispers back, "Where?"

"In my backpack, next to the fire." Ahmed's words are slow and clear.

Taher lowers himself, disappears into the shadow cast by the pile of boxes containing water and supplies, and slowly crawls to the campfire. He finds the knife. *What's next?* he thinks. He can't decide if he should throw it to Ahmed. *What if I injure him?* Or if he should crawl toward his cousin. *What if it takes too long? What if I fail? What if I am not strong enough? What if my aim is not good enough? What if I faint again?* He can't decide.

"Come here slowly, now!" He hears the steady voice and follows.

Taher is crawling toward Ahmed, shaded by his cousin's body, invisible to the lizard. He is crawling toward a sleeping volcano, just seconds before the eruption, not knowing that he is approaching yet another challenge.

When he is a meter away from Ahmed, and all he needs to do is to reach, the creature rises up on its hind legs and opens its mouth full of white, sharp teeth. What happens next is both expected and feared.

The lizard initiates its primordial dance by moving its neck from side to side, then by puffing its chest, opening its mouth wider and wider, and making a low growl. Ahmed and Taher understand that this is the beginning of the ancient metamorphosis. The lizard closes its eyes and sucks up the air with enormous force. Widening its neck as if trying to burst into pieces, it starts to rise up higher and higher on its hind legs, coming up on its tail. "Grrr . . . grrr . . . " comes out of its swollen throat. "Grrr . . . grrr . . . " comes louder and louder. Finally, its eyes turn red with blood, its head and body become one, like a tall tower swiveling above them. "Grrrsss . . . grrrsss . . . " The growl changes into a hiss. "Rrrsss . . . sss . . . " Its body changes into flowing silver, and finally its tongue splits at the end.

Taher stands next to Ahmed, with the knife in his extended hand, thrilled and bewildered. "Knife!" He hears Ahmed's voice, but doesn't understand what it means. "Knife!" Everything turns into silence as if disappearing behind the horizon, leaving just the beat of Taher's heart, darkness, and the vastness of an empty space.

In one sudden motion, the lizard-snake leaps forward. Taher, pushed by Ahmed, jumps to the side and falls to the ground.

"Knife! Taher, give me the knife!" Ahmed presses something to the ground with his entire body, and Taher realizes it is the blanket. Ahmed is strangling the lizard in his blanket. The sound is coming back slowly. Ahmed's body is shivering as with a high fever.

"Knife!" Taher gets to his knees and slowly brings himself forward. Ahmed grabs Taher's hand, pulls it fast, and drives the knife, still holding the boy's hand, into the blanket. There is a faint resistance of the lizard's flesh and a strange warmth and stickiness. Taher's hand is soaked in blood—once, twice, and once more, driven into the motionless softness under the blanket. "Tttssaarr . . . " The lizard's life dissolves in the last sound, a soft shush.

Taher can't let go of the knife. His grip grows into his own existence, beyond the boy's control. After a while, he sees his father and other relatives coming out of the tents, approaching him with the small circles of their flashlights. All of them want to see and touch him.

"Taher saved my life." Ahmed is asked to tell the story over and over again, until the sunrise. "He warned me! He had the knife! He pushed it in like this!" Ahmed makes a stabbing motion. "Seven times!" His words—round and polished—make the brotherhood possible. Make it happen, and make it real. Years later, both of them will remember. Both of them will lean on this moment.

Ahmed

After four hours of waiting, Taher becomes uncertain. *Maybe it was a different day? Different time?* He goes through his pockets again and finally finds the faded piece of crumpled paper with a note in blue ink. "October 17, noon." The note is just as he remembered. *He won't be released.* Taher feels a sudden heaviness overpowering his entire body.

When the gate of the citadel roars open, Taher freezes in anticipation. Shading his eyes from the blazing sun, he fixes his gaze in the direction of the sound and stops breathing. He hears a brief, muffled conversation behind the wall, and then a thin old man appears at the gate. Resigned, Taher falls to his knees.

The medieval citadel reigns over Cairo on a high hill, casting long shadows that have traveled over the same roads in wide circles since the beginning of remembrance. It is a massive monument, unattainable and portentous. Nothing can be said of the place, except that it marked many with suffering, leaving a trace of ever-changing but never-forgotten stories. These stories shaped lives throughout the ages with sorrow and pride. No one knows exactly when those two melded into one and were simply called *everyday life*.

Taher looks away from the gate. At the foot of the hill, the city sways in the soft light of late afternoon. The noises of the busy streets hover in the distance. He feels suddenly hungry and remembers he hasn't eaten. The picture of his anxious morning comes back in a flash—broken glass and milk spilled on the floor, a new pair of pants, a missing button on his cuff, and the regular phone call from his grandmother Rumaisa, starting always with the same accusations. "Why don't you call me? I am still alive and well, waiting for you to remember to call once in a while!" He remembers cleaning up the bathroom in a hurry and unclogging the kitchen sink.

"I didn't recognize you." A voice breaks into his thoughts.

Taher looks up and sees the thin old man towering over him. The blazing sun coming from behind the man makes it impossible to see his face. Taher looks at him for a moment and then stands up.

"Ahmed?" he says in disbelief.

"And your voice has changed too," Ahmed says slowly, as if talking is difficult.

The next day, Taher doesn't go to school. He decides to stay home for a couple of days, not knowing that the short break he planned in order to care for Ahmed would turn into weeks of silence and grief.

"Are you hungry? Some tea? Do you need anything?" Unanswered questions fill the air with pain.

Ahmed isn't interested in anything. He spends his days in bed, staring at the ceiling. He doesn't ask any questions; he doesn't want any answers. He doesn't pray, doesn't change his clothes, doesn't wash himself. Twice a day, always at the same time, he gets up to go to the bathroom. He eats his meals in silence, chewing his food reluctantly. He ignores the newspapers smelling of fresh print, folded neatly by Taher, leaving the piles of *Al-Ahram, Al-Akhbar,* and *Al-Gomhorejja* untouched, day after day. Sometimes he curls up with his knees to his chin, covered with a blanket, and sobs quietly. In moments like this, Taher leaves him and wanders the streets for hours, trying to recognize in Ahmed the person he knew before this unbearable hopelessness.

Every night, Ahmed fights his enemies. Kneeling on his bed, he stares into the darkness of the room, breathing heavily, his face covered with sweat. He grabs his blanket or pillow and presses it with the weight of his body, as if killing the giant lizard over and over again. Then he freezes as if waiting for something. Trying to recognize sounds in the silence, trying to see shapes in the darkness.

Half asleep, bewildered, Taher watches his cousin, unable to decide if what he sees is real, or just a dream still haunting his eyes.

He holds his breath, waiting for the battle to end. He prays for Ahmed to get better. "God, let him come back in strength. *Allahu Akbar.*"

After weeks of waiting, the silence is finally broken, and Ahmed suddenly comes back with words, coherent and powerful, as if he has been practicing to speak them for eternity, polishing them into smooth surfaces.

"That was the first time I understood her," Ahmed says and slowly gazes out the window. "That was the first time I began to understand what she was saying." He clenches his hands tightly. "I remember how I wanted to kill her for the embarrassment she caused our family. How I hated her." He looks at Taher. *"Ha Hah Illa Anta Sobhanuka Innyi Konut Mena El Zalemin.* There is no God but Allah. You are the greatest. Forgive me my mistake." He finishes with the words of a prayer

"I don't understand what you're saying," Taher says quietly, trying not to interfere.

"You might not remember. You were only seven or eight," Ahmed answers after a while.

"But who are you talking about?" Taher is relieved to ask questions.

"I'm talking about my sister. About Jihan."

"What happened to her?" Taher still doesn't understand.

"It was 1975. We thought she was crazy. We thought she had a mental problem."

"Mental problem?" Taher is lost but anxious for answers.

"It was her senior year. She was becoming a doctor. Just like the rest of us." Ahmed looks out the window again, as if trying to find his past somewhere far on the horizon. "She decided to wear a *hijab.* Do you understand? No one could talk her out of it." Ahmed's words are slow. "In the beginning, we all thought it was just a phase, some religious phase. But it wasn't. Nobody could believe what was happening. Jihan was the prettiest of my three sisters, tall and slender. And she loved her Chanel suits and dresses more than anything else. She always updated her wardrobe with the latest trends in Paris fashion. I remember we used to laugh that she spent a fortune on perfumes alone. And then she decided to wear a *hijab.*

An educated woman, a doctor, she decided to cover herself like an ignorant village woman, like a backward peasant. The family was devastated. I was so angry. Maybe because I was the youngest, I don't know. But I can still remember how much I hated her." Ahmed closes his eyes and covers them with his hands.

"Nobody wanted to marry her. There were many suitors, but they all had one condition: for her not to cover herself like that. She refused. No one wanted her to be so religious. "Why is she covering her hair?" all of them were asking. "She doesn't have to be so religious," they pleaded with my parents. We were viewing this as backwardness. People were laughing at us. Friends were at first sympathetic, then started avoiding us. "What a pity!" they would say. "What a shame!" Those who hated us started spreading false accusations about our past and our ancestors. It certainly didn't help Father in his teaching career at the university. Suddenly, all his accomplishments were ignored; the only thing that was important and worth talking about was his backward daughter."

"Why didn't I know anything about this?" Taher asks.

"No one wanted to talk about it, I suppose. It was taboo. We were all ashamed; no one understood her," Ahmed says quietly, looking out the window again.

"No one understood?"

"Well, maybe Mother. They were very close. Jihan was the only one who memorized the Holy Qur'an. When she started wearing the *hijab*, she was studying the Qur'an all the time. It was what changed her. She seemed so distant, so different. But she didn't try to push it on us. She actually never talked about it. Maybe because she knew it wouldn't change anything. I remember she once said, 'You will understand me one day.' I told her then, I remember the exact conversation, 'People have problems understanding progress sometimes, but never backwardness.' And I was very proud of myself for saying this. I still remember her eyes." Ahmed closes his eyes, recalling the moment. "She smiled sadly and said, 'Yes, but do they really know what progress and what backwardness are? The heritage . . . ' she stopped in mid-sentence. I remember someone stopped her. I think it was Father. I don't remember exactly."

"And what happened next?" Taher can't believe what he is hearing. "What did she do?"

"She prayed all the time, especially at night. She read the Holy Qur'an at night. Mother would often find Jihan in the morning fast asleep with her forehead pressed to the ground."

"And?"

"The worst part was that she said she wanted to become a martyr. That was her dream."

"A martyr?" Taher opens his eyes widely. "She really lost her mind."

"That's what we thought back then." Ahmed looks at Taher. "You're too young to understand," he starts slowly. "How old are you, anyway?"

"Sixteen." Taher tries to sound serious.

"The last time I saw you . . . you were thirteen. You've changed so much. You're so tall, and your voice has changed." Ahmed looks at his hands. "You didn't recognize me at the prison gate."

"The sun was shining straight into my eyes," Taher interrupts him immediately. "I was waiting for you for four hours. Besides, I was starving."

"You don't have to explain," Ahmed says calmly. "I lost forty kilos, and I was never overweight." He laughs bitterly. "I know how I look and feel."

"Don't worry. I'll take care of you. We'll beef you up fast. You know I was using your apartment for all these years . . . it made it so easy for me to go to school here." Taher is speaking fast, as if covering Ahmed's tiny body with words would help to make him feel better.

"You don't have to." Ahmed lowers himself on a pillow. "Really, you don't have to. I need maybe one more week, and I'll be fine."

"Do you want me to move out?" Taher asks sadly. "It won't be a problem at all." His voice isn't convincing.

"Oh, no . . . you can stay as long as you want." Ahmed closes his eyes and soon falls asleep.

Taher watches him closely, marveling at the change. This is the first time his cousin sleeps on his back—his chest rising and falling slowly, his palms facing up, his face freed from the unbearable heaviness.

The next conversation between the two of them not only renews their friendship but also reveals their longing for closeness. They become the brothers of the desert again, remembering the lizard, remembering the family escapades.

"Taher," Ahmed says, "I will tell you everything. You have to remember what I say for yourself and for others. Forever," he says, lowering himself on the bed.

"Who are the others?"

"All who need to know." Ahmed raises his hand and sweeps the air. "As many as possible."

"Okay." Taher isn't convinced, but he is ready to listen.

"After the assassination of Sadat, they arrested about eight hundred of us," he says, leaning on his elbows.

"I know," Taher interrupts him eagerly.

Ahmed looks at him, surprised, but doesn't say anything.

"Everyone was talking about it," Taher adds.

"Some of us were released after a couple of months. I'm not sure, but this is what I heard in prison. I want to tell you that those three years in prison have changed my life forever, and there is no going back." He looks at Taher as if making sure he has his undivided attention. "For me, there is no other way. I will tell you why, and I know you will understand," he adds and looks at the ceiling. "I didn't have anything to do with the assassination, and I won't pretend it was otherwise. I won't pretend I was brave and fearless. I wasn't. I had nothing, absolutely nothing to do with it." He stops for a while, closing his eyes. "I didn't have anything to do with it, but the day I was arrested became one of the most important days of my life. And not because I finally understood my older sister." He gives a short laugh, confusing Taher. "Do you understand?"

"No, not yet," Taher answers honestly.

"I meant Jihan . . . "

"Oh, I get the part about Jihan, but you didn't say anything about yourself yet."

"I will tell you something about someone else . . . and it will be about all of us. About this young boy named Khaled, about me, and even about you." He closes his eyes again, falling into a long moment of silence.

Ahmed's face changes rapidly under the weight of memories. It becomes cold and dull. It becomes a translucent parchment of dark blood.

"They hanged him from the ceiling."

Ahmed's eyelids are closed tightly.

*

The prison's dark corridor reverberated with the sound of the slamming door. It hung in the air, alerting the prisoners. They knew something was going to happen. First came the familiar echo of the guards' steps, then a white shirt soaked in blood. It was Khaled.

All of the prisoners silently moved forward in their cells. Some of them clenched the metal bars; others fell to their knees and looked away, burying their faces in their hands or sleeves.

"Khaled, hang on!" someone finally spoke up.

"*Allahu Akbar!*" another voice followed.

Then there was silence. One of the guards pushed Khaled to his knees. The second one grabbed his hands and tied them behind his back. Khaled leaned forward and touched the ground with his forehead. The third guard kicked him in the ribs. Khaled groaned. "Piece of shit!" The guard's voice was low. Khaled moaned again.

For a while, all three guards struggled with a tangled chain hanging from the ceiling. After it came undone, they kicked Khaled from both sides, forcing him to stand up. Then they connected the chain to his hands that were tied behind his back.

*

"On the chain hanging from the ceiling—the chain was attached to a hook on a pulley—so they . . . they raised him." Ahmed's eyes are closed, but Taher knows that Ahmed is crying. "They wanted us to see him in this unbearable pain ..." Ahmed sits up on the bed and brings his hands behind his back. "This is how they did it," he says. "And then they pulled him up. Like this." Ahmed lifts his arms up behind him. "They don't go too far up on their own," he adds softly.

*

Khaled lifted his head and looked toward the metal bars dividing him from those who had become his friends. His narrow, swollen eyes were trying to find someone. *"Ja Rab! Ja Rab!"* God! God! he moaned.

The guards began pulling the chain and Khaled's arms jerked up. He leaned forward as far as he could and gave a loud roar when his hands reached the height of his shoulders. He was still leaning forward and, holding his head close to his chest, breathing heavily, spitting saliva and blood. *"Ja Rab!"* he repeated over and over. His white shirt, soaked in sweat and blood, stuck to his back. The guards looked at him, gloating when his feet left the floor.

"Murderers!" someone yelled from his cell. One of the guards spit on the floor in the direction of the voice.

Khaled's feet flailed desperately, looking for support. His body gave up slowly. He fought for every breath, leaning forward in the hope of withstanding his own weight. The prisoners beat the metal bars. "Let him down!" someone yelled. The guards laughed. *Allahu Akbar. Allahu Akbar.* Single voices started slowly inviting others. More and more joined, and after a while, the prison was filled with incantations. The words echoed through the corridors, off the walls and ceilings, multiplied with revived strength.

*

Ahmed's face becomes white, then gray. He stops talking. His eyes are focused on something beyond the room, far away, in his past, which is slowly becoming his present, which is slowly becoming his future.

"He fought for a few minutes," Ahmed continues his tale. "We saw him drenched in sweat. He was brave, very brave. We stopped our prayers in midsentence. We couldn't continue. We just looked at him, hoping for a miracle, but it never came." Ahmed closes his eyes again and waits a long while. "I still remember the silence. Silence and waiting for the inevitable. And then the sound of his bones." Ahmed starts sobbing.

*

Khaled's scream cut through the air. The sound of his bones being wrenched from his shoulders came like thunder that hits a tall pine, splits it open, and makes it fall to the ground. The guards looked at his limp body approvingly. "Take him down!" someone screamed. "What for? He can't feel anything now." The guards laughed at their own remarks.

Khaled's motionless body was hanging like a rug. Single drops of blood and urine formed a pool underneath, in the middle of the corridor, between rows of cells filled with men who, in this moment, became his family.

*

"I can still hear the sound of his bones. I can still see his limp body on the thick chain. He lost consciousness from the pain and was hanging there by his arms torn from his shoulders. They left him there all night. None of us slept. We prayed until the guards came back in the morning." Ahmed stops for a moment. "Helplessness is unbearable," he starts again slowly. "Us behind bars and him, hanging there. Khaled was sixteen, just like you." Ahmed looks at silent Taher, who is trying not to cry. "The guards returned in the morning with dogs. They took him down and threw him in our cell. They said to me, 'Here, doctor, your first patient!' And they laughed. No one moved because they had dogs." Ahmed reaches for a handkerchief and wipes his face. "It took me forever to put his shoulders back in place." Ahmed wipes his face one more time. "Later on, Khaled told me that he had nothing to do with the assassination. Just like me. And he was grateful to God for imprisonment. Just like me. He said prison ripped his shoulders and opened his eyes. 'There is only one way. We have to fight back.' That is what he said. 'God, never let me forget the pain I endured. Don't let me forget the bloody taste of my sweat. Let it stay with me forever. Let it become part of my body as long as I live—forever.' He was so young, just like you. And he was a poet."

*

Taher is silent. He glances around the room—a table at the window with several weeks of neatly folded newspapers, water in a glass for Ahmed and a view of the city, a teaspoon in a sugar bowl and a bottle of milk, the corner of a plastic tablecloth, a chair with Ahmed's shirt on it, the zipper of a sleeping bag, shaving cream, a small lamp on the night table, a notebook, a pencil, an empty yellow wall, a windowsill, and the wing of a bird in motion. The sky.

Taher tries not to look at Ahmed. He rubs his fingers, stretching them until they give a popping sound. Only the sound of his knuckles cracking fills the space between them.

"There is nothing you can do to erase memories like that," Ahmed says. "Nothing. You can't return to your previous life. It's impossible." He looks at Taher. "When you stop feeling pain, the moment you stop feeling pain, you become a piece of meat. You become just a piece of meat to them and to yourself. No dignity, no humanity." They look at each other for a long moment before Ahmed says, "Only a new life can make your life possible. It can give you a new face and a new identity. There is no going back. Change is the only salvation."

"What did they do to you?" Taher asks hesitantly.

"They locked me in a cell with wild dogs. They beat me with cables." Ahmed takes a deep breath and stops for a moment. "They did this to all of us. I wasn't the focus of their attention because I didn't know anything. They figured that I was a doctor, just out of college. They knew that many of us, medical students and engineers, sympathized with the Islamic movement, but weren't really involved in any activities. Almost all of the students sympathized, but that's all. But those who were involved in the assassination were tortured every day. They would put them in cells with those who were arrested based on their confessions." Ahmed closes his eyes again. "They wanted to break the movement from the inside."

"And what happened in the cells where they all met?"

"What cells?" Ahmed opens his eyes.

"Where they were together . . . those tortured and those captured because of the confessions of the tortured?"

"They said what every Muslim would say to another Muslim." Ahmed wipes his eyes. "They said, 'I am sorry you have to live with the weight of your confession.' They knew everyone has his limits. They had their limits too."

Ahmed tells Taher the story of his three years in the prison, day after day. He quotes conversations he witnessed and describes people he met—for a week, he speaks of nothing but his life in prison. His body is speaking as much as his words. He paces around the room for hours immersed in painful images, his eyes absent, his voice cracking. Sometimes he continues his stories till dawn, not noticing what is changing around him, as if nothing else exists but memories burned into his flesh.

Taher rarely says anything. He listens and observes this vaguely familiar stranger from the past. This isn't the Ahmed he knows from the trips to the desert. It isn't the Ahmed he knows from the excursions to museums in Cairo. It isn't the Ahmed he knows from studying the Holy Qur'an together. This is someone else, someone strange yet exciting. Someone Taher is getting to know.

*

They came back to their cells drenched in blood. Heads shaved. They prayed with their foreheads pressed to the floor for hours. Joined together in suffering and Holy Words. Taking care of each other, dressing one another's wounds with shreds of their clothing. Some lost consciousness, others died in the arms of their comrades. Still others promised to carry on in memory of the dead. Some promised revenge.

*

"We were one family in suffering and in the words of the Holy Book. We supported each other, even, or maybe most of all, when we were forced to turn on each other." Ahmed looks into Taher's eyes. "Do you understand? There is unspeakable strength in this," he says. "Unimaginable power in such a union. It surpasses understanding; it surpasses death."

*

Those with dislocated shoulders were leaned against the walls. They were unable to kneel and prostrate themselves. They whispered their prayers; some moved their lips silently, they didn't accept water. Those with swollen stomachs died fast. Those with their tongues as dry as wood died slowly; with their eyes swollen shut they languished for hours, sometimes days. Immersed in the monotonous melody of the same words, repeated over and over again. "*Allahu Akbar. Allahu Akbar.*" God is great. "*Ja Rab Awinyi.*" God, give me strength. "*La Hah Illa Anta Sobhanuka Innyi Konut Mena El Zalemin.*" God, you are the only God. You are the truth; forgive me for losing my way.

*

"We were afraid of the dogs." Ahmed closes his eyes, choking back his tears.

*

Hungry, wild dogs, frenzied by the smell of blood, were let into the cells. Their teeth sank easily into the flesh of the weak, tearing up their arms and legs. Some prisoners attempted to fight back. Weakened by torture, none were able to fight the beasts. The floors of the cells were drenched in blood and excrement. The dogs didn't stop for a moment, even after a long fight. They were unable to part with the dying.

*

"The trial began on the fourth of December, 1982," Ahmed starts again and then becomes silent for a long moment. "It was broadcast around the world. They put us in a long cage. There were about three hundred of us. In a cage like animals."

"I know," Taher interrupts him. "I was there. And your mother was there with me . . . "

"Some were shouting the names of their relatives. I didn't. I was afraid she was there, and I didn't want her to see my scars. I didn't want her to suffer. And I wasn't ready to admit to her that Jihan was right," Ahmed adds softly.

"She was convinced you weren't there." Taher tries to hold back his tears. "She thought you were dead."

*

The prisoners were dressed in clean white shirts. They chanted and prayed into the cameras of the international news organizations. Some yelled the names of their relatives in hopes of seeing them in the gathered crowd. And then, with a signal from a young man, it all stopped. He wore a white shirt with a gray shawl and black-framed glasses. He was calm and focused. Staring straight into the cameras, he spoke for all of them.

"Now, we want to speak to the whole world! Who are we? Who are we? Why did they bring us here, and what do we want to say?" His English was perfect, precise, and forceful. "About the first question, we are Muslims! We are Muslims who believe in our religion! We believe in our religion, both in ideology and practice, and hence we tried our best to establish an Islamic state and an Islamic society!"

"*Allahu Akbar!*" the prisoners answered with a roar.

"We are not sorry. We are not sorry for what we have done for our religion. We have sacrificed, and we stand ready to make more sacrifices!" His hand reached through the metal bars toward the cameras.

"*Allahu Akbar!*" the roar came again.

The young man extended his arms even farther, as if reaching beyond the cameras, directly to the people in front of television sets, on the other side of the earth, in the comfort of their homes.

"Where is freedom now?" His eyes were full of fire. "Where are the human rights? Where is justice now?"

"*Allahu Akbar. Allahu Akbar.*"

Some prisoners pressed forward to support the young man's speech. Others, disoriented, covered their faces in disbelief, trying to hide.

"They imprisoned our wives!" His eyes shone like quicksilver. "They imprisoned our mothers! Our fathers! Our sisters! Our sons!" His slow words fell like rocks.

He looked into the cameras, as if expecting a response. His breath was fast and shallow. He grabbed the metal bars tightly.

"In the worst Egyptian prisons, we suffer the worst imaginable atrocities!" He stopped to take a deep breath. "We are beaten, we are kicked, and we are electrocuted. We are tortured."

The prisoners started undressing, removing their shoes and raising their shirts. The cameras zoomed in. Arms reached out of the cage, sharing their scars with the world—long dark stripes, black smoky marks, and half-healed wounds.

"They set dogs on us!" The young man's voice grew stronger. "They hang us with our hands tied behind our backs!" He pointed his finger emphatically.

New prisoners approached the metal bars revealing their wounds. One after another, showing teeth and ligature marks.

"We are murdered! We are murdered in the prisons!" the young man shouted.

The prisoners covered their arms and retreated. They lined up along the bars in silence. No one moved when the first name was spoken, then the second, third, fourth. The young man recited the names slowly, one after another.

"These are the names of those murdered in the prison." He looked directly into the cameras.

After his last words, the prisoners started a prayer in memory of the murdered, kneeling and rising together. Eyes closed. Young and old, men and women—a steady melody of chanted words filled the space, loud and strong, rhythmic and united.

*

"What were we accused of?" Ahmed looks at Taher. "Because we want to preserve our way of life? Because we want independence from the West? Freedom for the suppressed Muslims? Because we are against our corrupt governments?"

"What happened after the trial?" Taher asks anxiously.

"Nothing." Ahmed shrugs. "No one supported us. No one noticed. They could kick us. They could set wild dogs on us. They could starve us. They could refuse us bathroom breaks for hours. They could refuse us medical attention." Ahmed looks out the window into the darkness. "Nothing changed. Nobody cared."

"I think I knew." Taher lowers his voice. "I think I always knew, maybe from my father? I don't remember."

"This is the man." Ahmed unfolds a piece of newspaper he had in his pocket. "He spoke on behalf of all of the prisoners. His number was one hundred thirteen. His name was Ayman al-Zawahiri."

"And he was beaten every day," Taher says, staring at the picture of the young man in glasses.

"Yes. Beaten and tortured," Ahmed confirms. "He helped us to understand the meaning of our imprisonment, the meaning of Muslim life. His charisma united us all." Ahmed takes the newspaper clipping from Taher and, looking at the picture, adds, "He will do great things. I know it." He hands the picture back to Taher.

While Taher is still looking at the picture, Ahmed reaches for the bag he brought from the prison and retrieves something covered in a piece of fabric.

"This is for you, Taher," he says, kissing it and handing it over to him. "I want you to know this is the most valuable thing I possess, and I want it to belong to you."

"What is it? Why are you giving it to me?" Taher reaches for the gift hesitantly. "Why don't you want to keep it?"

"I won't need it where I'm going." Ahmed looks out the window into the darkness again.

"Going? Where are you going? You can't go anywhere, you just got out of prison—you need to rest and gain your strength back." Taher's words come out fast.

"I'm going next month. I still have some time to recover," Ahmed answers. "Maybe even in the beginning of December. I don't know yet, but I'll be fine by then."

"But where? Where are you going?"

"To Afghanistan, of course. Where else?"

"I'm going with you," Taher says immediately.

Ahmed looks at him, surprised.

"I am going with you!" Taher repeats.

"I'm not sure that's a good idea," Ahmed says.

"You know it's a good idea." Taher's eyes grow wide. "Of course, you know," he adds.

"You have to finish school." Ahmed tries to find a good reason. "I'm going there because they need doctors."

"I can take a few months' break and help you." Taher opens his arms. "I'm sure I can be useful."

"No. You can't go to war. It doesn't make any sense."

"So, why did you tell me all of this? So I can sit here and learn geography while my brothers are dying in Afghanistan? Who do you think will help them? Have you read the newspapers lately? Do you know how many stories were published about the war? I can tell you. I can tell you." Taher's eyes grow bigger and bigger with every word. "Zero! Zero! Nobody cares. Nobody is even interested. Nobody cares about the millions of refugees. Nobody cares about Muslim children frozen to death in the camps or those dying of starvation. I don't know if the rest of the world even knows about the war." Taher gets up and starts pacing the room. "You don't want me to help my brothers in Afghanistan the same way nobody helped you when you were in prison? And this makes sense to you?" Taher stops, and looking at a quiet Ahmed, he sees that he has already won the argument.

"Well . . . " Ahmed starts quietly. "You are too young."

"Oh, really? And do you remember him?" Taher joins his wrists and lifts his arms overhead.

"You would have to have your mother's permission. She won't allow it."

"Ahmed, my mother is dead. Remember?"

Ahmed looks at him, totally surprised. "I can't believe I forgot," he says quietly. "I remember your father dying in the plane crash." He tries to refresh his memory. "I forgot about Laila . . . I forgot about your mother completely."

"I'm going with you," Taher says. "Do you remember the giant lizard? In the desert?"

"Lizard? What lizard? Oh, the one you killed mercilessly?" Ahmed smiles for the first time since coming back from the prison.

"We!" Taher smiles back. "*We* killed it!"

"Oh, no. You killed it. Now your memory is going." Ahmed laughs.

"Okay, whatever," Taher laughs along. "But . . . I am going with you."

"It doesn't make any sense," Ahmed says without conviction.

"Fine. It doesn't make any sense. And now you tell me what makes sense. Go ahead. Tell me. Tell me what makes more sense than kicking Russians out of Afghanistan." Taher knows all along that Ahmed will eventually give in.

"Nothing," Ahmed says quietly. "Nothing anymore."

"Do you remember what my father said after we killed the lizard?"

"Yes, but Taher, he didn't know he would die in the crash," Ahmed answers.

"So what? He trusted you," Taher says. 'Take care of Taher. He is your brother now,' Remember? He said 'brother.'" Taher nods, raising his arms up, still holding the little thing covered with a piece of fabric. "And don't tell me he would say that studying geography is more important than helping our brothers in Afghanistan."

"I won't say that," Ahmed says finally.

The gray dawn is making its way through the night. Cairo is waking up with the first sounds in the streets. A yellow circle of light from a night lamp shines on the few objects on the table.

"What is it?" Taher remembers the thing he is holding.

"It's a present for you," Ahmed answers. "A present for a younger brother." He smiles.

Taher unwraps the present. It is an old and worn copy of the Holy Qur'an.

"Do you still remember the entire book?" Ahmed asks.

"I do," Taher answers. "You never forget the words once you learn them."

"This is a copy from the prison," Ahmed explains. "We all prayed with it."

"Didn't they confiscate them?"

"They did. This is the only copy we had left."

"And the stains?" Taher runs his finger down an open page.

"Blood," Ahmed says quietly. "Blood of the martyrs."

They are both silent for a long while. Ahmed is overcome by memories once again; Taher is stunned by the weight of the meaning, both unable to speak. The clock on the table shows four-thirty in the morning. The new day is starting with the stained pages of the Holy Book in Taher's hands, a new day, a new beginning.

"It's time for *Al Fagr,*" Ahmed says, looking at the clock. "Time to pray."

"I have something for you, too," Taher says, closing the book and leaving the room.

He returns with a new prayer mat.

"We think like brothers!" Ahmed says, giving him a long embrace, as if finally greeting him for the first time after his release from prison.

They both kneel facing Mecca and pray in unison. Their voices and breaths become one; their bodies join in one wave of motion, with foreheads pressed to the ground and palms facing the sky.

*Allahu Akbar, Allahu Akbar, Allahu Akbar, Allahu Akbar, Ash'hadu
an la illaha ill'allah, Ash'hadu an la illaha ill'allah Ash'hadu anna
Mohammed ar-rasulAllah,
Ash'hadu anna Mohammed ar-rasul Allah,
Haya ala salah, Haya al salah,
Haya al falah, Haya ala falah,
Allahu Akbar, Allahu Akbar,
La illaha ill'allah.*

After the day's first prayer, Ahmed takes the Holy Qur'an and says,
"In prison, we used to finish with a reading of *Al-Fath,* The Victory
Sura," and then he opens the Holy Qur'an in a place marked by
another newspaper clipping.

> He it is Who sent down tranquility into the hearts
> of the believers that they might have more of faith
> added to their faith—and Allah's are the hosts of the
> heavens and the earth, and Allah is Knowing, Wise.

His words, slow and clear, greet the light of the distant horizon.

"And what is this?" Taher points to the clipping between the
pages. All he can see is a sleeping child's face.

"Take it out and see." Ahmed hands him the book.

Taher studies the picture. He sees a dead child.

"All I can see is the head and one arm," he says.

"It's a four-year-old Palestinian boy. Killed by Israelis." Ahmed
puts his folded mat on the bed.

"Why do you keep it in the Holy Qur'an?"

"To remember." Ahmed sits on the bed. "To remember where
to go."

"Where to go?"

"Yes, the direction for my life," Ahmed answers. Taher looks at
the picture for a moment and then places it back between the pages
of the book.

*

Two days later, Aisha calls. Taher takes the phone to the bathroom and closes the door.

"Grandma called me again," she says, her voice agitated. "I can't do this, Taher! You are missing school, and Grandma is calling me to tell you to call her. She says you are not picking up the phone."

Taher sits on the floor and leans back, closing his eyes. It takes him a long moment before he replies.

"I am not a child anymore, Aisha. I can fight in a war. She needs to leave me alone," he says.

"Grandma says our parents would have been so so so disappointed. She feels responsible. Don't you get it?" Her voice changes, softens—she is pleading now. And then she says, "War?" and starts laughing.

"Why are you laughing?" He opens his eyes and focuses on the wall in front of him, as if Aisha was standing there.

"Because I imagined you fighting," she says, still laughing.

"What do you know?" Taher scoffs. "You should know your place!" He hisses, trying to keep his voice down.

"What do I know?" she says with the same defiance as always. "I am getting good grades so I can study medicine in Germany. Just like father wanted us to do. And you are wasting your life," she yells.

He can imagine Aisha's eyes getting wide. He can imagine her sitting on her bed in a small room filled with books and all the art their mother left them. Watercolors with landscapes from Turkey—rickshaws on the streets of Istanbul in the rain. People and buildings in blue and gray. Minarets on the background of a sky as blue as the waters of the Sea of Marmara. And then, their father's books—mostly science and math—huge volumes, some in German, some in Latin. He knows she cherishes them as much as the watercolors.

"I don't have to talk to you," he says, and hangs up.

Refugees

Ahmed is leaning over a young boy, when he and Taher hear the sound of car tires stopping suddenly on the tamped sand in front of their tent. The tent houses a hospital site in a refugee camp in Jalozai, close to Peshawar.

Exhausted from hours of work, both move slowly. They hardly speak.

Ahmed sits down next to a table. "I'm tired," he says, covering his face. "I can't see anyone else. That's enough." He looks at the young boy's slim body. "How many did we see today?" he asks, sighing.

"Two hundred forty-seven, including the boy." Taher is precise, he is the one who keeps the count.

After a short while, Ahmed comes back to the boy on the table. "It's poisoning," he says pressing the boy's round belly gently.

Taher is here to help, but also to learn.

"From what? He probably hasn't seen food for days," Taher says and wipes the boy's forehead.

"From the water, as usual." Ahmed squints twice as if trying to keep his eyes from closing.

At that moment the flap of the tent sweeps open.

"Where?" They hear the panting voice of a man carrying another man. "Where can I put him?" He keeps his feet spread apart, trying to maintain his balance under the weight. "We can't see anyone else today." Taher tries to stop him.

"It's us!" the man says. Tomorrow you are going with us!" His voice reminds Taher of the phone conversation he had two days before. "To Peshawar!" the man says, breathing fast. "You have to see Salman." He points to the man he is carrying. "Otherwise, he won't give us a break tomorrow."

"Over there," Ahmed says, pointing in the direction of boxes filled with medical supplies.

The man approaches the boxes and tries to kneel and lower his comrade but is unable to do so. He looks around helplessly. Salman is groaning, and when asked if he is able to stand, answers, "No, I can't." The man carrying him pauses for a moment and then yells, "Somebody help!" Several armed mujahideen enter the tent. One of them, handing his Kalashnikov to another, helps to lower the moaning man onto the floor between the boxes.

"You can take him back," Ahmed tells Taher, nodding toward the boy. "Tell them someone needs to stay with him, and if the fever rises, let them come here to get more medicine."

Taher embraces the limp body and lifts it. The boy's left arm falls to the side and moves through the air in an unconscious arc. The boy's shallow breath doesn't even raise his chest. Only the white moons of his eyes, moving rapidly under his half-closed eyelids, reveal the remains of life.

"His parents died in the ruins, in the minefield explosion, and his grandfather, the one who brought him to the refugee camp, died a week ago. This is what I've heard," Taher says sadly, going toward the door. "But he has an eight-year-old sister."

"Ask her to stay with him . . . maybe not . . . I don't know." Ahmed gazes at the man between the boxes.

Salman is propped up on his elbows. His pants are cut along the sides all the way to his thighs, exposing swollen knees. He is panting heavily, wiping his forehead, sweating despite the winter cold. He transfers the weight of his body to one side and wipes his forehead. The skin on his knees is as thin and translucent as parchment, glossy and tight, exposing boiling lava underneath. The pants, cut along the sides, resemble hanging sheets of peeling flesh. He tries to find a more comfortable position without any success. His swollen knees don't allow him to bend or straighten his legs.

"Give me something," he says finally, looking at Ahmed. "Give me something." He nods and looks at his legs.

"How did it happen?" Ahmed touches the reddened skin. "And when?"

"I have no idea how I got it." Salman shakes his head. "But it has been like this for the past two weeks. I can't walk. I can't even move them now."

The rest of the mujahideen, listening to this conversation, lower their Lee-Enfield rifles and Kalashnikovs along the wall of the tent, turning the place into a gallery of weapons. Their movements are slow. One after another, they sit on a faded piece of rug placed close to the door. They remove their jackets, their hats and turbans. Their weatherbeaten faces reflect signs of a long journey.

"Has anyone looked at this?" Ahmed barely finishes the sentence when thunderous laughter shakes the tent.

The unexpected display of emotion surprises him. He stops his examination and looks at the group of men. They are all excited, talking about something, gesturing and laughing. Some even interrupt the task of unrolling their turbans, allowing the long pieces of fabric to hang from their shoulders, raising their arms in animated movement.

"He was wailing!" someone from the group says, gesturing toward Ahmed. "Howling like a wolf!" says someone else. "Salman, tell him what you did!"

Even Salman, recalling the first visit to the doctor, can't stop laughing. He lies on the floor and covers his face with both hands.

"And like this!" shouts someone from the group, cutting the air with his hand in a stabbing motion. "And like this!" He repeats the movement. "And like this!" he says one more time.

The rest of the mujahideen join him in laughter and demonstrate the stabbing motion.

"Can I get an answer here?" Ahmed tries to interrupt them while laughing along.

Salman props himself up on his elbows again and describes the earlier visit to the doctor.

"A week ago," Salman starts as the laughs of his comrades slowly fade. "No, it was five or six days ago. We met a doctor on our way, in Darra. You know, in Darra you meet somebody not knowing exactly—they come from all over the place—you never know . . . He stabbed me with a needle," he points to his knee, "to extract some liquid."

"In Darra, you can buy a kilo of brown heroin for a hundred bucks!" Someone from the group attracts Ahmed's attention again.

"So what?" Ahmed asks.

"What do you mean, 'So what?' What do you mean?" yells the other man. "You send it in a truck to Karachi," he continues with excitement. "And from Karachi to Europe, and from Europe through Gdańsk to New York." He waves his arms in the air. "In New York, they sell it for one million bucks. A million bucks!"

"A million bucks?" Ahmed opens his eyes wide. "It means we don't charge enough. We need to raise the price. We need the money now more than ever."

"We must!"

Someone else nods in approval.

"What about the knee?" Ahmed returns to the sick man.

"What about it?" Salman doesn't understand.

"So did he get out the liquid?" Ahmed touches the tight skin on Salman's knee again.

"What liquid?" The man bridles. "Not even a drop! There is no liquid."

"And he stabbed him like this for nothing!" The mujahideen return to their story.

"Yeah, and he screamed and screamed." Roars of laughter cut the air again.

"The doctor was right to try." Ahmed's words quiet everyone immediately.

"No! No needles!" His screams follow Ahmed, who is receding between the piles of boxes.

"Don't be scared!" His comrades enjoy the spectacle. "He will just poke you like this!" The stabbing motion cuts the air once again.

"It's not funny!" Salman yells at Ahmed. "I don't want this! Do you hear me? I don't want this!" he pleads.

Ahmed, without paying any attention to the sick man, opens a box and retrieves a long syringe.

"Take me away from here!" Salman's screams break through the laughter of his comrades.

"It will hurt like hell, but after that you will be able to move your knees again," Ahmed informs him, kneeling on the ground.

"Take me away from here!" the sick man jokes in resignation.

Ahmed touches the swollen knee, examining all the sides carefully. Then he says, "Move him there," pointing to the table.

All the mujahideen get up as commanded, and although only two of them transfer Salman to the table, all of them walk there in a quiet procession.

"Hold him down on both sides," Ahmed says. "Hold him down on both sides." He places a rolled rag between Salman's teeth and instructs him to bite down.

When the needle is pushed slowly into his knee, Salman twitches like a jerked string and gives a muffled scream.

"Pus and blood," Ahmed says, as a brownish-gray fluid fills the syringe. "Quite an infection." He retrieves the needle slowly.

Salman's forehead, covered in sweat, shines in the beam of headlights coming from a tear in the tent's wall. He breathes heavily. Ahmed empties the syringe and then returns to his patient, whose arms are intertwined with the arms of his comrades. He examines the other side of the knee and plunges the needle in again. The patient groans. Tears run toward his ears. The syringe fills up with the same substance.

"This knee is done," Ahmed announces, pulling the needle out.

Salman's muffled cough brings him close to vomiting. His face reddens, and veins pop off his neck. One of the helpers removes the rolled-up rag from between his teeth.

"Let's take a break before the second one," Ahmed says, looking concerned.

"No, let's be done with it," Salman argues without hesitation, panting and moaning.

Ahmed repeats the procedure on the other knee and then administers an antibiotic.

"You are lucky I have this," he says handing Salman the rest of the pills. "You have to take them all. Don't skip any, unless you want another doctor to do this." Here Ahmed's hand cuts the air in a stabbing motion, resulting in a thunder of laughs.

"I won't forget," Salman says, smiling. "Never again."

*

Taher sits in front of the tent, across from the boy he just brought in and the boy's sister. Both children are covered tightly in colorful quilts, delivered yesterday by the Revolutionary Association of the Women of Afghanistan.

"What's your name?" he asks the little girl.

"Aisha," she whispers, sinking deeper into her quilt.

"That's my sister's name, too," Taher says.

The little girl and her brother are protected from the winter by a makeshift tent of blue tarp fastened to two crooked sticks.

"Stay with your brother, Aisha." Taher leans deeper into the tent and hands her a bottle of water. "Just wet his lips from time to time, and the rest is for you. It's clean. You can drink it."

The girl reaches for the bottle, but her eyes are still on her brother's face. His half-closed eyelids don't reveal any signs of life.

"When will he die?" she asks quietly.

Taher hesitates for a long moment, looking at Aisha, at the boy, and then in the distance between the rows and rows of tents. "I don't know," he whispers finally, looking at her tiny wrists. "When was the last time he ate?" he asks.

"Everyone dies," Aisha says but doesn't look up. She takes a corner of the red headscarf gently in her fingers and covers her mouth. The tiny round mirrors on the bright border of her sleeves flicker with little sparks.

"You can tell me," Taher tries to encourage her. "When did you last eat?"

"I don't remember." She freezes, closing her eyes.

"Where are you from?" He hands her a piece of flatbread.

"Jalalabad." She presses the bread to her cheek, and then inhales deeply, holding it close to her nose.

"Eat," he says. "This bread is for you, eat."

She looks at him as he walks away between the long rows of tents marked with signs: "United Nations High Commissioner for Refugees."

Taher walks slowly, stopping from time to time, engaging in conversation with children along the way. Those with hens in their arms are busy putting the birds under blankets for the night. Others are falling asleep cuddled in the warmth of their sheep. He talks to elders gathered in circles around thin ribbons of smoke, coming from small niches in the ground, from under teakettles.

Empty, bright yellow plastic bags from the International Food Bank accent the narrow paths between the tents, where wind blows in chilly gusts. Pieces of clothing on makeshift lines wave like praying flags toward the massive mountains. Under a tarp, two women wail softly, rocking their infants to sleep. Their hands, whitened with flour, wear the smell of memories—golden fields of wheat bowing to the wind; the earth warmed up by the campfire; white dust rising above their hands, busy with fresh dough; children falling asleep easily. The twilight is slowly descending above the refugee camp, like a piece of dark fabric falling over their silenced lives.

*

Earlier that day, the same women had asked for a bit of flour, hoping to survive yet another day.

"Give a handful. Just a handful," the eldest woman was begging, holding her arms up over her furrowed face, wet with tears.

A dense crowd besieged the back of a truck, swaying in the low sun like a black ocean readying itself before the storm. The smallest children, in the arms of staggering women, cried.

"Quiet, quiet." Mothers' voices were softer than breath.

"Give me milk." A three-year-old girl touched her mother's breast. "Milk!" she cried.

"I don't have any milk." Her mother embraced her tightly. "Tomorrow . . . wait until tomorrow."

"When will it be tomorrow?" the girl screamed toward the sky. Her tears formed clean paths on her dusty face.

The crowd pressed forward, preventing the truck from leaving. An hour earlier, single mothers had left with prayers of thanksgiving after receiving their portions of flour, oil, and *ghee,* buffalo butter. The food stamps for single mothers were scarce passports, saving only the chosen lives.

"We don't have any more flour!" the man on the truck yelled above the heads of the crowd. "You will have to wait for the next transport."

"Our children are dying from hunger!" the eldest woman yelled back. "It's winter! We are dying from hunger!" She wiped the scattered flour from the edge of the truck's floor. "There, there—under the wheel," she pointed her daughter to a place she couldn't reach. "Under there!" She pointed again.

"We can't help you!" the man on the back of the truck screamed at the top of his lungs. "Move back! Move back!" He waved his arms. "Let us go!"

Following his scream, the crowd floated in angry waves. "How can the world let us die here? On this strange soil?" the old men cried. They were the only men in the camp, too old to fight the enemy in their own country. Their toothless jaws, underlined with long white beards, chewed many other unspoken words. Their sunken eyes, harboring quicksilver drops, couldn't find rest even at night. Blue, brown, and white *burqas* swelled in the gusts of wind, like trapped birds, unable to ascend toward the destined horizons behind the white-peaked mountains. And the children watched carefully—their hair filled with road sand; their throats dry with dust; their bare feet roughened, coarse like a piece of old wood.

"I hate all the world," a little girl whispered to a little boy.

"I hate all my enemies," he whispered back.

*

Taher stops in front of a gray piece of tarpaulin raised on two sticks and anchored to the ground with two rocks. Underneath it, a veiled woman sits with a baby in her arms. She rocks the baby rhythmically, back and forth, back and forth. Her blue burqa, covering the little body, reveals only its motionless, statue-like face—a thin, disappearing crease of mouth. A bright stream of soft sand grains, brought on a breeze, runs along the baby's nose and fills up the niche of the eye socket, forming a tiny pool, swaying in the woman's rocking, back and forth, back and forth.

A shallow dream of anticipation wraps the barren land of the refugee camp in Jalozai. Naked trees on the outskirts soar towards the sky, cutting the mountain range in the background in the design of their branches. On the edge of the farthest horizon, behind the tallest mountain peaks, the last light of the day fades into the darkness.

"The baby was dead," Taher announces, entering the medical tent. "Ahmed, she was rocking a dead baby."

"We are all going there, Taher. If God allows." Ahmed doesn't stop rearranging the boxes. "And the baby will never experience . . . " He leans over an open box. " . . . all of this."

"But she was rocking it, as if in a trance, as if she was dead herself." Taher sits down on the floor between boxes.

"Maybe she already *is* dead—or will be tomorrow." Ahmed doesn't stop his work.

*

The first light of the day brightens a new landscape. Along the roads and soft hills on the background of silver mountains—as if formed by wind gusts—the soil runs in long wavy streaks of reds and charcoal. The truck loaded with boxes slowly approaches the city nested in the walls of the mountains. The air smells of baked brick and diesel fuel.

"How much longer?" Taher asks Salman, opening his eyes. "Where are we?"

"Almost there," Salman answers, smiling.

"How are you?" Taher asks, looking at Salman's bent knees.

"Much better." Salman rubs his knees. "In two, three days, I will be able to run the mountains!"

The truck staggers along the bumpy road for a while before it stops at the bazaar. The air here is thick with scents of fried food and burning logs.

The mujahideen make their first necessary purchases— flatbreads, onions, and cooking oil. "Now we can survive the day," they say, laughing. "Sweet tea," Salman says, walking slowly with the help of a stick. "I need sweet tea to survive," he laughs. "No, *you* need your *knees*," someone else jokes. "To fight the Russians, you need your knees!"

"Gongs! Gongs! For any occasion!" An old man invites all to purchase his goods: knick-knacks and trinkets, good luck amulets and toys.

A small piece of paper with a note, "Rugs at affordable prices," hangs above the head of a man whose eyes are blackened with charcoal. "Here only!" Another note, with a blue arrow pointing down, invites craving eyes.

"Bandoliers! Bandoliers!" An energetic man waves his hands in an inviting gesture toward the mujahideen. "And hot sweet tea for the newcomers and guests." He smiles broadly, stroking his long white beard.

After a while, the same man serves the mujahideen the promised tea from his mother's Russian samovar, in his house, just around the corner from the bazaar. No one refuses his hospitality. "Everyone has to take a rest on a long trip," he says, nodding his head and serving his strong black tea. He understands, without any explanations, that the mujahideen are on their way to Afghanistan, to fight the occupying force. "Let them be punished for our suffering!" he says.

The mujahideen, gathered in a small room, sharing bread dipped in oil and drinking sweet tea, listen to his life story. No one interrupts while he talks about his wife and three daughters, killed back in Afghanistan. No one asks questions when he talks about his return to his parents' house, here in Peshawar.

"Anyone who can escape, escapes. If I had made the decision sooner, I would still have my family. Many survive by going up the mountains with Massoud. Many, from the villages of the Panjshir Valley, owe their lives to his war tactics. He knows how to fool the Russians. I didn't make the decision soon enough," he sighs deeply. "In other countries, life is in demand. In Afghanistan, it's death." He is nearly whispering. "The war is profitable for those who invest in it."

He touches his chest and strokes it softly. "A man can get used to anything. It's better to be able to get used to anything. We have to agree on a war that kills us, in order to save our lives." Two quicksilver drops twitch under his eyes. "The Russian mines rip off our genitals, sometimes a leg, but they never kill. Yes, they prefer to injure than kill, especially our children, because the wounded need help. You can't fight if you have to take care of the wounded. Especially our children."

He reaches for his tea. "The mines fall from the sky," he continues after a pause. "They come like bugs. And they change their color when they hit the ground. You can't even see them, not on sand or grass, not on clay soil or rocks. Invisible. Some are hidden in toys. Dolls for children. And they always bring them at night. And then the next morning we find our children with no legs, no arms, dying from loss of blood. Some of the children get blinded by mines, eyes burned out by the blast. I heard about new mines disguised in plastic. Undetectable. Hidden in wristwatches and pens. Most were found north of Kabul, in the Panjshir Valley. Many people live there." He strokes his beard with a shaking hand.

"Crossing the border into Afghanistan equals death for most. Afghanistan has become a place of death." The quicksilver drops run down his cheeks, leaving two tracks. "Our land is full of death, already waiting for the generations to come. Already waiting for those who are not born yet." He clasps his hands and becomes silent.

More and more people appear in the bazaar. Little boys, refugees from Afghanistan, play on the streets with half-broken kites, following the mujahideen and imitating their moves and gestures. They want to be them, to grow up fast and become heroes of the mountains—lionhearts known for their strength, wit, and incomparable bravery. Sometimes the boys run after the white and red pickup trucks, screaming, waving their kites, and imitating the swaying motion of the mujahideen. Sometimes the boys stand around on the street corners, listening to conversations, absorbing what they hear with awe and admiration, especially the stories about successful skirmishes with the Russians. Those stories, repeated over and over, become legends of victory. The boys also wait for the handout of flatbread they will take back to their mothers and younger siblings waiting on the outskirts of the city.

Veiled women from the mountains, displaced by the war, separated from the world and abandoned, wander the streets absentmindedly. Only some of them show their faces marked with sorrow—empty eyes underlined with charcoal and void of desire. The elders meet in mosques to offer their prayers and ask for blessings. They find consolation in chanting the Holy Words, '*La Hah Illa Anta Sobhaneh Innyi Kont Men El Zalemin*. There is no God but God. God, forgive me my missteps."

*

"*Skurwysyny! Skurwysyny!* Sons of bitches!" Someone screams as Ahmed and Taher enter the foyer of the Dean's Hotel. A young man, with light blond hair and big blue eyes, sitting in the company of others, screams in a foreign language.

"Who is this?" Taher asks.

"A foreigner. Like the rest of them," Ahmed says, gazing toward the group gathered around the fireplace, surprised how many are still up. It's late, long past midnight.

They join the group and listen to the animated story of the blond man. An oversized mirror in an elaborate golden frame reflects the man's slouched back and the shining ballroom floor in the background. After long hours of shared stories and legends, all faces of the gathered wear signs of fatigue.

"My name is Abdullah." The words with their intriguing accent fill the air again. "It wasn't my name from the beginning."

Some people, coming from the veranda, join to listen to the blond man.

Abdullah raises his hand with a shot glass, then stops for a moment, as if suddenly remembering something. Surveying the room with a slow gaze, he adds, "And that's the truth!" He lowers his head in a bow. Strands of blond hair fall over his forehead, reaching his eyebrows. "We Poles tell the truth! Always! Straight talk! Always!" The incantation of his words evokes discreet smiles. "We Poles are known for the truth!" He raises his finger toward the ceiling. "Straight from the heart!" He bangs his chest vigorously with his fist, triggering a rapid cough and a forced deep bow forward. "You like it or not," he adds, banging his knee in turn. "I know," he says, gazing around. "I know I'm drunk right now . . . " He staggers. "But tomorrow," he continues, wagging his finger, "I'll fight those sons of bitches who killed my mother!"

The fireplace hisses, sending out dozens of sparks. The gathering becomes silent for a long while. Two Western women—most likely journalists—leave for their rooms on the first floor. Two waiters snooze in armchairs in the corner of the room.

The Hotel Dean is a popular place for British and American reporters, Red Cross workers, and other international organizations supporting Afghan refugees. Writers from abroad, spies, and all of those bored with their lives and looking for adventure, come here. The legendary architecture of the place, combining the Victorian style with the spirit of the city, attracts guests from all over the world. The apartments of the hotel are surrounded by lavish gardens. The spacious rooms, comfortable bathrooms, glassed-in verandas, and fireplaces have become a symbol of distinctive, yet familiar, taste for many throughout the years. The ballroom, the stylish antique chandeliers, and the grand piano from 1897, labeled "Made in Germany," give the travelers a sense of luxury, longed for in a journey far from their own country.

"So, what's your name?" someone directs the question to Abdullah.

"Abdullah," he answers forcefully.

"Yeah, but the real one," asks someone else.

"That's the real one! The realest one!" Abdullah buries his face in his hands and, shaking his head, starts crying. "My name is Marek Kowalski." He is crying out loud. "I mean . . . that was my name . . . before . . . I converted to Islam." He sighs and stops crying suddenly, as if cutting off the spasms with a sharp knife. "That was the name I was born with." His words in Polish, English, and Pashtu interweave almost seamlessly. "But now I am who I want to be. My name is Abdullah, and I am going to kill Russians because they killed my mother!"

"Have a drink." Someone fills his glass. "Your story is true and moving," someone else comments. "True and beautiful." Generous words of praise lift the spirits of all. "And you have a right to revenge."

"Yes, for my mother, I have!" Abdullah nods. "And now I'm going to sleep." He passes his glass to a man on his right, slaps his knee, gets up, makes a deep and long bow, and as if leaving a stage, he waves to his audience, directing himself to the staircase shaded in darkness.

"Poles have a soul," says someone, following Abdullah with his eyes.

"And such a story," adds someone else. "You know—"

"Let's go to bed. It's well past midnight," someone interrupts.

"No, just let me finish my thought," the man insists. "I think Abdullah was right. If the Russians hadn't invaded Afghanistan, we would be sitting right now in Poland. I am sure. When was it? Four years ago? 1980? They would have invaded Poland."

"That's possible."

"I am sure," the first man continues, "if not for the fact that they were engaged here, they would have the resources to go there."

"And we would be sitting in a hotel in Poland right now," the second man says.

"*I* would. I've been a war reporter for fifteen years now." The man has the last sip of his drink. "But I heard that they were not Russians, really. They were Polish police."

"The ones who shot his mother?" The second man is curious now.

"Yep, they were Poles shooting Poles." The war reporter confirms his statement.

"It doesn't really matter, I suppose. He wants to kill Russians. Let him do it."

"Yep. And let him have the reason he wants to have," the reporter adds. "Tragically romantic, and romantically tragic," he concludes, getting up from his seat.

*

Marek's story as told that day:

My Mama woke me up with a kiss on the cheek. That's the way she always did it. First, I would feel the soft kiss, and then I would smell her chamomile hair. Usually, she didn't have to support herself on her hands, leaning to kiss me, but that day, I remember, she used both hands, on both sides of me.

"Mama, are you okay?" I asked, opening my eyes.

"Oh, I'm just a little tired," she said, smiling. "Your brother is growing fast in my belly. He's getting heavy." She kissed my other cheek. "Brother or sister, I meant to say." She smiled the sweetest smile ever.

She added "sister" because I was dreaming of a brother, and she didn't want me to be disappointed in case it was a girl. "We want a healthy baby," she used to say to me. "I am a girl, and we play very well together, don't we?" And that was the best argument she had, because it was the truth. Playing with her was heaven. Always. We played by the river, where schools of tadpoles shimmered in crystal waters, above the golden smooth rocks of the bottom. And in the forests, where soft moss invited our hands. And on the beach, where white sand turned into ingenious fortresses with numerous corridors and dozens and dozens of carefully crafted portals and windows. And in the village, where we plaited the manes of Grandpa's horses, whispering soft words into their ears, pretending to be the Indians from a book we had just read. And in the orchard where everything smelled of pinkish-white flowers of the early spring. And in Tatry Mountains, on a long trip to Gievont Peak, where we rinsed our feet with water from tin canisters. And even on a train, where we were robbed, and someone stole my favorite kite. "Don't worry, sweetheart," she said. "We will make you an even nicer one as soon as we get home." She wiped my tears with a handkerchief. "With the Wawel Dragon in the center. How about that?" I didn't realize that the memory of the most beautiful words of love I had ever heard would become the words of the most unbearable pain in my life.

There was so much compassion in her, so much love. For everyone, not only for me. Even for strangers, and most of all for my father. Even when he would come back home drunk. Sometimes we could hear him on the staircase, talking to the neighbor a little too loudly.

"Mister Mietek, I made a good deal today; that's why I am a little bit soused." My father repeated the same sentence for years, and my mom believed that one day there really would be a "good deal."

She would open the front door and ask both of them to come in. "Mister Mietek, would you care for some tea and a fresh baked bun?" she would say. She knew Father needed an audience sometimes, and she didn't want him to bother our other neighbors.

"Marek, it's five thirty. You have to get up," she said that day.

There was the smell of oatmeal coming from the kitchen. This is what I had for breakfast every day, oatmeal and a soft-boiled egg, while looking out the window at the trees along the riverbank and the morning trains passing by in the distance.

In the winter of 1970, the snow covered the world around my house in a different manner. Everything became unrecognizably quiet, even the church bells sounded in a different, muffled tone. I liked to go for walks by myself. And I always went to the river, even when it was covered with ice. I would just go there and watch the trains on the other side. Enormous locomotives moved silently in thick, white clouds of steam and high fountains of snow, shooting up on both sides of the plow in front. There was nothing more beautiful on earth than the snow thrown up by the plow, it was higher than the locomotive itself—the force of the engine cutting through meters of snow, with no sound except for a very gentle huffing (unless, of course, they used the whistle). The thrown snow created perfectly arched, smooth walls on both sides of the plow, jumping up and running along the sides in a huge letter *V*. I dreamed of standing on the train tracks, in front of the train coming toward me, and seeing the perfectly shaped V, soft, written in cursive—massive banks of snow and the silence. I always wondered how come it moved so silently. The snow changed everything. The snow muffled the world. My mother knew how fascinated I was with the trains. She used to warn me often, "Stay away from the train tracks."

The day before, she said something else. Maybe because she noticed my interest in trains had become stronger. Maybe because I told her I would like to go on the other side of the river one day and just look at the trains up close. I don't know. But that day the vice prime minister, Stanisław Kociołek, announced on the evening news that agreements between the workers and the government had been reached, and shipyard workers in Gdynia should go back to work the next day. After the news, she told me never to go near the train tracks. "Death is waiting there," she said quietly. Her eyes became round like two coins, gray like the deepest waters of the ocean in my favorite book. I told her I wouldn't go, and I gave her a hug from the side. She was sitting on a chair with her arms on a table. I hugged her from the side because there was no place on her lap for me anymore; it was taken by my brother in her belly. I always thought, *my brother.*

Sometimes she would let me listen to my brother's heartbeat. "Put your ear here," she would say, pointing to a spot on the globe she was carrying. And I would stop breathing, with my eyes closed and my ear pressed to her belly. Then she would embrace me tightly, one hand on my back, the other on my head. "Let's see if we can synchronize our hearts," she would whisper. We waited, all three of us. And then we could hear a wave or light or maybe the wind, and our hearts would become one.

My Tata, my father, was always on the sidelines. Busy taking care of us, as he used to say. On the sidelines, for us. He often made trips to see a family that lived on a farm. He would stay with them a few days and then come back with loads of delicious sausages, pork loin, or sometimes he would come back with nothing. Mama never complained. She never spoke reproachfully. Even when he was drunk, crying, and apologizing for his sins, I never knew. "Forgive me!" I remember him begging through his wailing as he threw a bunch of enormous lilac branches under my Mama's feet. "Forgive me, my dearest Juliet!" Then he would bow for a long moment, with one hand on his back, the other one at his heart, squeezing the white shirt in his fist, and then he would leave the apartment. Mama would just smile understandingly.

I asked her once if Tata was an actor. She said, "Yes, he always was." Maybe that's why I never asked myself what I wanted to be when I grew up. I knew I wanted to be an actor because she loved the theater more than anything else.

That day, my oatmeal was different. I remember how surprised I was to see it. "Flies!" I screamed. "There are flies in my oatmeal!" And I was ready to cry when my mom said, "Raisins." She rubbed my back. "Flies in the winter?" she said, dispelling the rest of my doubts. Raisins were a delicacy, appearing in my house only in winter, before Christmas, in an annual food package from our family in Germany.

After breakfast, while brushing my teeth, proud of myself that I didn't need to use the little stool that had become a prop of the past under the sink, I could hear my mother putting on her shoes. "Oh, I am panting like a locomotive," she said to herself.

She used to put her coat on in front of the narrow mirror in the hallway, fixing up her shawl and hat. That day, she found that her coat was too small. She couldn't button it over her stomach. She grappled with it for a moment and then said, "I will freeze to death today."

"Why don't you put an extra sweater on?" I asked her, zipping up my jacket.

"Great idea." She smiled, ruffling my hair.

I heard her wrestling the wardrobe door in the bedroom, and then she came back wearing her favorite green angora sweater. I combed my hair, and we both left for the train.

Tata wasn't home. He had spent the night at his sister's in Gdańsk because he had left late from his parents' and missed the last train home. We were supposed to meet him at the inter-city train station in Gdynia-Stocznia. "At six-fifteen in the morning," my Mama said on the phone. They just wanted to see each other before work that day.

The inter-city train arrived quietly but without throwing the snow to the sides. *It's not the same,* I thought to myself. On the train, an old lady, offering her seat, asked Mama to rest. "Oh, no, thank you. That's not necessary," Mama responded while a young man in a Marine Academy uniform got up quickly. "Madame, please, take my seat." Mama took the offered place. "Thank you," she said to the young man, taking off her hat and shawl. "It's so hot in here," she whispered into my ear.

Usually, I would sit on her lap, but since the space was occupied by my brother, I had to stand. I was counting on the fact that when he was born, we could both share her lap. Me on her right knee, him on the left one. I wondered how families with more than two children share their mama's knees on the trains and buses and concluded that perhaps the father goes with them everywhere.

The doors of the inter-city train hissed every couple of minutes, as they opened for the passengers. "Open Sesame! Close Sesame!" I whispered into Mama's ear every time I heard the sound. She smiled, wiping her forehead with the back of her hand.

Everyone on the train talked about the speech Stanisław Kociołek had given the day before. You see, back then they didn't have any other means of communication except for the TV news, so no one was able to notify the workers that that morning, the gates to the shipyard and the Gdynia-Stocznia station were surrounded by army and police. No one knew that orders had already been given, and they contradicted Kociołek's speech. People on the train were saying in a unified voice, "Thank God! Thank God!" All of them were grateful to God, reminding me of my catechism classes, and the strong conviction of the priest who taught us to believe that Poland is the chosen country, and Poles are the chosen people. The representatives of God on the earth. I felt blessed.

Mama didn't notice when the inter-city train stopped at the Gdynia-Stocznia station, and only Miss Marylka, who was forcing her way through the door and on her way, noticing us, said, "Miss Julia! Gdynia-Stocznia!" Mama jumped from her seat. "Oh, I was deep in my thoughts! Thank you."

The round clock on the platform showed six fifteen. Mama stopped in the middle of the platform and looked around.

"Look for the bright yellow jacket," she said to me.

"Why?" I asked, surprised.

"Tata has his yellow jacket on from Uncle Henry. From Germany. Remember?"

Oh, yeah, I thought to myself. He had gotten this gigantic yellow jacket in the food package from our family in Germany. He even joked that he looked like a canned fish advertisement, especially with the too-long sleeves rolled up. I remember how eagerly he had gone through the pockets, hoping to find some change. "You never know," he had said, laughing. "Maybe they have hidden something here." He had raised his voice and his eyebrows in a way I thought meant something I couldn't understand.

Soon another inter-city train arrived, on the opposite side of the platform, from Gdańsk. The doors hissed loudly and a crowd of people spilled onto the platform.

I remember we were going toward the stairs because Mama said, "Let's go up there. It will be easier to spot Tata in the crowd, looking down from the bridge," she said, pulling my hand.

All that happened afterward exists in my memory as a thick pulp. I can't see it as it happened. I just see what I felt. Somebody yelled, "Jesus Christ, they're shooting!" People ran in all directions. Screams. Some men jumped back into the train from Gdańsk, forcing their way through the hissing door. On the other side of the stairs, a woman was lying on the platform with her legs spread wide apart. I remember Mama squeezing my hand hard. It hurt, but I didn't say anything. We were standing there paralyzed, unable to move. Then I saw the yellow jacket. Up on the bridge where we were heading. Far away. Closer to the sky than us. Many metal stairs, and the metal bridge. Railings. "Władek!" Mama's voice was strong. "Władek!"

Tata didn't see us. He was looking at something in the distance we couldn't see, behind the fence. Then I saw people on the bridge falling down. Just next to my father. Close to him. They were shooting at the people on the bridge, from both sides of the train station. No one could escape. There was nowhere to go. I couldn't see who was shooting. I could only see those falling down on the bridge, on the platform. Some tried to hide behind the concrete platform. Mama let go of my hand and, throwing her purse, hat, and shawl next to my feet, started running up the stairs. Holding her belly with one hand and the railing with the other, she ran, screaming, "For God's sake, Poles, stop shooting!" I remember she said, "Poles."

I looked at her from below. How hard it was for her to run up the stairs—the wings of her open coat flapping to the sides with every forced step. I felt guilty for suggesting the extra sweater that morning. I was thinking to myself, *Mama must be sweating right now.* I could feel myself sweating with her. But all of it was one—beyond time, beyond space. Thoughts, words, and pictures.

I saw two men with guns behind the fence. They were wearing the uniforms of the Polish police. Only later did I realize that in fact they were the Soviets, since some of them ended up in hospitals and didn't speak any Polish. I saw them pointing their machine guns toward the bridge, toward the stairs. My Mama raised her arms up in the air. The wings lifted up slowly, flap, flap. Her scream cut the air like a sharp battle axe. "Gentlemen, please, don't shoot! My husband is there!" These were her last words. I don't remember the shots. There was no sound. Everything became silent. The locomotive heaving in the high snow on both sides of the plow. Her long hair waving slowly when she fell on her back, down the stairs. I see the pale morning sky behind her hair. Falling and falling forever. Down the stairs. On the snow on the stairs. On the tracks her feet left in the snow just seconds before.

Mama was buried at night. They called us about the burial in the middle of the night, and we were not allowed to talk about it with anyone. Ever. All I remember is snow around the wet dark soil of the grave and the red lights of the Soviet agents' cigarettes in the darkness, surrounding us. Circling her grave and us. I see them now, those red lights going on and off. That's all I can see. Nothing else.

I want to kill those red lights. I want to kill them once and for all. For her.

Little Omar

Blessed is the man whose strength is in you, whose heart is set on pilgrimage. As they pass through the Valley of Baca, they make it a spring; the rain also covers it with pools. They go from strength to strength; each one appears before God in Zion.

Bible, Psalm 84:5-7

Muhammad is the Apostle of Allah, and those with him are firm of heart against the unbelievers, compassionate among themselves; you will see them bowing down, prostrating themselves, seeking grace from Allah and pleasure; their marks are in their faces because of the effect of prostration; that is their description in the *Taurat* and their description in the *Injeel;* like seed-produce that puts forth its sprout, then strengthens it, so it becomes stout and stands firmly on its stem, delighting the sowers that He may enrage the unbelievers on account of them; Allah has promised those among them who believe and do good, forgiveness and a great reward.

Qur'an 48:29

Drifting, airy snow fills the space between the entrance to the cave and the silver chain of mountain peaks on the horizon, where a gray dawn is making its way through the night. Little Omar, kneeling on the flat rock, is bringing his forehead to the ground in a monotonous motion. A tiny set of ribs, expanding and contracting with every breath of his prostrations, is visible through his thin white shirt. His bare feet rise and fall with the rhythm of his prayer.

Allah-a Akbar, Allah-a Akbar, Allah-a Akbar, Allah-a Akbar,
Ash'hadu an la illaha ill'allah, Ash'hadu an la illaha ill'allah Ash'hadu
anna Mohammed ar-rasulAllah,
Ash'hadu anna Mohammed ar-rasul Allah,
Haya al salah, Haya al salah,
Haya al falah, Haya al falah,
Allah-a Akbar, Allah-a Akbar,
La illaha ill'allah.

Other mujahideen come out of the cave for the first prayer of the day. One after another, fallowing the ritual ablutions with water, they gather around Little Omar, spreading their praying mats facing southwest, in the direction of the Valley of Baca, in the direction of the Holy Stone, Holy Ka'aba.

The Holy Ka'aba sits in the center of the quicksilver lake made of pilgrims. The quicksilver lake sits in the center of an ocean that spreads through the yard and arcades all the way through the streets of Mecca, and from there through valleys and mountains to the farthest and smallest settlements on the edges of the world, all the way to the cave where Little Omar kneels on the flat rock. The waves of pilgrims in prostrations—foreheads pressed to the ground—connect with him in the everlasting journey of transition and birth, transition and death.

In the middle of the yard—surrounded by three levels of arcades filled with echoing steps, under the dome of a lavender sky between minarets soaring with thousands of lights, among glass buildings of the metropolis and soft valleys punctured with white and sepia-colored houses—exist the mystery and the answer. The perfectly symmetrical black walls of the Holy Ka'aba, bordered with golden words of the Prophet, reach to the sky in perpetual renewal of the people's covenant with God.

The soft snow melts on the foreheads of the mujahideen. Their hands reach up to the sky, summoning the heavens to embrace the scarred earth. Their rhythmic words flow toward the Holy Ka'aba in a lament unified in faith.

As they finish the first prayer, Little Omar lifts up his arms and says, "Everything comes from the Holy Ka'aba. It is the beginning and the end. We come from the Holy Stone, and we go back to it. It is our life's destiny." He lowers his forehead to the ground and presses his lips to the flat stone. The mujahideen get up, nodding their heads. "Young and wise," they whisper among themselves. "Child and adult at the same time," they say.

They are still talking when they hear quick steps. It's Hamid, running towards them, waving his hands. All of them, except for Taher and Ahmed, rush to the cave.

"What's happening?" Taher asks Little Omar, who is folding his prayer mat in a hurry.

"They saw them. In the valley," Little Omar answers and immediately disappears into the entrance of the cave.

"Who?" Taher asks.

"The Soviets," Ahmed answers.

The preparations take just a couple of minutes, and the mujahideen are ready to descend into the Panjshir Valley. Armed and anxious, they move fast in a single line, following each other. Their shallow and fast breaths are forming a white mist around their heads. The narrow path winds down on a rocky bed, forcing them to be cautious and focused. They whisper, exchanging what Hamid shared with them. "Battalion. They said battalion." Taher hears a voice behind him.

"There are not enough of us! How many of us? Eleven?" Taher whispers into Ahmed's neck.

"The others—Massoud's people—are waiting in the valley already," Ahmed whispers back. "We are not alone."

For a moment, the narrow path disappears above a steep rock, and then appears again behind a sharp turn. Light snow is still falling slowly, softening their steps and voices. In front of them, a thin line of shimmering reds appears above the distant horizon, and the contours of the valley emerge from darkness.

"Just stay in the back." Little Omar delivers a message from their commander to Taher and Ahmed.

"Okay." Ahmed makes a space for Little Omar to pass him.

Ahmed and Taher are just visitors from outside, supplying the mujahideen with antibiotics, money, and sometimes arms. They aren't expected to fight, but they are here to witness.

"I can't tell if I'm more scared or more curious," Taher whispers to Ahmed's neck again.

"Curious!" Ahmed answers without hesitation. "And this is how you must see it always," he adds with conviction.

Moving fast, Little Omar disappears from Taher's view. His petite figure moves nimbly around the others, very different from them. He says he is thirteen and small for his age, a statement no one believes. Eleven, some speculate secretly. Both Taher and Ahmed know that Little Omar is the youngest mujahid they have ever met. His slim body, not much bigger than the Kalashnikov on his shoulder, seems to be everywhere—on lookout behind the high rock, leading the praying group, sharing a meal with others, and gathering the most strategic information.

*

Little Omar, just like Taher, memorized the Holy Qur'an when he was just six years old, and—just like Taher—likes to quote the chosen verses for his family, friends, and comrades. Standing on the flat rock with his face turned in the direction of Mecca, above the heads of the gathered, he recites with courage—words bringing hope, belief in the victory of good over evil, peace over occupation, and truth over falsehood.

"Little Omar," Mohammad, the commander, had said to him during the first meal with Taher and Ahmed. "Why don't you show them your Qur'an?"

"It's not for everyone to see," the boy answered, lowering his gaze to the ground.

"Let them see," others said. "Let them see how we fight here. Let them see your Qur'an." The boy didn't move.

Taher left the circle of mujahideen for a moment and then returned with something in his hands.

"And this is how *we* fight," he said, unwrapping a small book, Ahmed's Qur'an from the prison. The book circulated from hand to hand, slowly and in silence. Everyone understood. "Whose blood?" they asked, running their fingers over the stained pages. "Torture." "They set wild dogs on you?"

Their faces were sharpened with amber and blue light from the paraffin oil lamps. Patches of sunny waves shimmered on the high walls of the cave and moved with the gestures of arms and hands—sometimes, slow and steady; sometimes, fast and furious. The shadows of *shalabas* moved like open wings. The same soft light disappeared from time to time in dark and long corridors. Dissolved in golds and reds, traveling a long way just to return with echoing sounds.

"Occupiers are like sharks!" Familiar voices recalled the distant past. "Bloodsuckers!"

"We need to fight for our freedom!"

"For the dignity of our ancestors and our children!"

Mohammad turned the pages of Taher's Qur'an for a long time, and finally came across a small picture from the newspaper.

"Who is this?" he asked, bringing the picture closer to light.

"That's a Palestinian boy," Taher answered.

"You can't even tell it's a boy," Mohammad said quietly.

Mohammad gave the picture to Hamid. Hamid looked at it with bewilderment and passed it along. The faded piece of newspaper made its way through the group.

"And who is it?" someone else asked.

"It's a four-year-old boy killed by Israelis," Ahmed explained. "He became a symbol for us, a part of our Qur'an in the prison."

"But the world doesn't want to know this," another voice rose from the group.

"Palestine, Afghanistan . . . " Mohammad looked into the fading fire of the lamp. "We can count only on ourselves. Suffering brings us closer to God," he added softly. "Suffering and sacrifice. And most of all—death."

Little Omar turned the pages slowly, one after another, running his fingers along brown spots and frayed edges, until he came to *Al-Fath,* The Victory. He stopped. Then, putting his right palm on the open book, he said, "This is my Qur'an." He passed the book to the commander and started unbuttoning his shirt. No one moved. Everyone was silent. All eyes were fixed on the tiny body of the boy who claimed to be thirteen. Everyone waited. The shadows on the cave walls froze into an enormous monolith built upon the shapes of the gathered. When the white shroud of Little Omar's shirt fell from his shoulders, they saw his Qur'an tattooed in perfect cursive on his chest.

> *It is He Who sent down tranquility into the hearts of the Believers, that they may add faith to their faith; for to Allah belong the Forces of the heavens and the earth; and Allah is Full of Knowledge and Wisdom.*

The Holy Words of *Al-Fath* were suspended on the fragile shoulders of a child, a leaf of translucent parchment on a blue web of pulsating veins. "This is my Qur'an," said the boy, looking at Taher and Ahmed. "This is my Qur'an," he said, putting his hand over his heart.

*

It stops snowing right before they reach the riverbed. They move silently toward the meeting point below the village, close to a long line of naked trees. The chain of Hindu Kush is rising in the mellow light of the early morning.

"We are all going to die," Taher whispers to Ahmed when they finally stop.

"They aren't expecting us," Ahmed answers. "And we don't really know if anything will happen."

"What do you mean?" Taher covers himself with a blanket.

"If the odds are bad, they said we won't attack." Ahmed lowers himself under a tree.

"I don't know which is better." Taher sinks into his covers.

"To be cautious," Ahmed says forcefully.

In the early morning light, the wide, blue-green waters of the Panjshir River glow with pale silver scales. Above the scales, a gentle fog appears and disappears around the silent mujahideen. Covered with blankets, they are awaiting orders. Some check their guns. Others move their lips in silent prayer.

Hamid comes back after several minutes.

"They came in low." His breath is fast. "They're on the riverside."

"How do we know?" Mohammad, the commander, asks.

"When it was still dark, their cigarette lights were seen at the riverside." Hamid is breathing heavily. "They are in the open."

"Where should we go?" the commander secures his Kalashnikov on his shoulder.

"Massoud wants us there." Hamid raises his hand and makes a long arc in the air. "At the double row of trees." He points towards the mountains.

"How many?" Mohammad asks and mobilizes the others with a nod of his head.

"A small portion of a division," Hamid says, following him. "From Kabul."

"How do we know when to attack?" Mohammad asks his last question.

"Immediately." The answer comes fast. "They are already there." He points in the direction of the river.

When they reach the double row of trees, weapons lowered, they are eager to engage. "Be cautious and vigilant." Mohammad gives his final orders. "And you—stay back," he says to Ahmed and Taher, pointing his finger at them. The moist air from the river carries a heavy scent of animals and smoke from the nearby village. A lone dog howls in the distance, piercing the silence of the early hour.

When the air thickens with gunfire sounds, Taher curls up in his blanket next to Ahmed, and time condenses with waiting and shallow breaths.

"That's us!" Ahmed listens intently, his eyes focused on something far away.

"How do you know?" Taher wants to believe.

"I don't know." Ahmed's gaze is fixed. He is present and absent.

*

Soviet soldiers—dozens of them—pierced with bullets, lie along the riverbank. Their uniforms are unbuttoned. Bits of crackers cover their bare chests. One of them holds a half-opened can of meatloaf. Its golden sauce drips drop by drop, sinking into the white flesh of his hand. Another is holding an empty thermos. A wet patch on his stomach gives off a warm mist. Someone else is holding a still-burning cigarette, the dying light cupped in his palm. Pocket knives and shattered cans of condensed milk sit in white syrupy pools. Unexpected, motionless silence holds the last echo reverberating in the valley, a blow bouncing off the massive mountain wall.

The Soviet commander is lying on a bed of rocks in shallow water. His arm is floating on the surface, pointing in the direction of a red ribbon coming from underneath. The ribbon is running downstream, dissolving in the distance. His light blue eyes reflect the first rays of the morning sky. The shot that killed him is buried deep in the stillness of his body.

The mujahideen circle among the dead, collecting shoes and weapons. Some collect boxes of crackers, cans of meatloaf, and neatly folded brown papers filled with tobacco leaves.

"He fell like this!" someone says, re-enacting the fall over the soldier's body. "And then like this!" He turns over his lowered shoulder.

"They don't usually have any money," says another one, going through the pockets of the dead.

"Sometimes they do."

"His uniform is brand new."

"Sent from Russia just days ago." The first one laughs.

"Sent with a shaved Christian." The second joins him.

After a while, they both stand over the body of a young Soviet soldier whose pale blue eyes are fixed on the only cloud in the sky.

"Anybody speak Russian?" yells the first one, looking around.

Several mujahideen turn toward him. Someone drops a box of crackers. "You scared me!" says the man who dropped the crackers, to the loud laughter of his comrades.

"Anybody speak Russian? He has something tattooed on his chest."

"Hamid," answers someone else. "Hamid knows Russian. He is from Tajikistan."

"Where is he?" asks the one bowed over the Soviet soldier. "Call him!"

Hamid rushes toward the little crowd gathered over the body. "Move!" He pushes his way through. "Move aside!"

"I can't see anything," he says, kneeling next to the dead soldier. "I need more light!" The crowd retreats slowly, one step at a time, allowing the early light to slide inside the tight, human ring. Hamid is silent for a long moment, trying to decipher the words tattooed on the Russian soldier's chest.

"So, what does it say?" asks someone impatiently.

"It's a fragment from the Book," Hamid says, moving his index finger along the soldier's chest.

"The Book?" asks someone in a *pashtun* hat. "He is one of us?" His words carry grief.

"Yes, from the Bible," Hamid explains, studying the words.

"The Bible is the Book. He was one of ours!" says someone else.

"Yes, the Bible *is* the Book, but he *wasn't* one of ours!" Strong disapproval comes from the back of the crowd.

"How come?" says the one in a *pashtun* hat. "He is one of ours if this comes from the Bible. He says it comes from the Bible!" He points at Hamid.

"He is Christian!" yells someone from the back. "Christian, not one of us!"

"He said from the Book!" the one in the *pashtun* hat turns around and yells toward his opponent.

"No, he can't be one of ours," says someone close by. "Tattoos are forbidden by Islam. He isn't one of ours."

There are laughs and screams in the crowd. "He is one of ours, just shaved!" Everyone wants to join the debate. "Like a woman!" Mujahideen from the far back ask more questions. "Maybe ours, but queer!" Someone screams at the top of his lungs. "No, worse than that. Christian! He is a Christian!" Several others stroke their cheeks and laugh.

"*Khawal!*" Someone from the back yells in Arabic.

"*Khawal?* What does it mean, *khawal?*" asks someone else.

"*Khawal* means queer in Arabic."

"Who is he?" The next question in Arabic cuts the air. "*Kafer* or *Mo'men?*"

"What's he saying?" Someone is speaking in Pashtu. "What is the Arab saying?"

"He's asking if the Russian is a non-believer," someone translates. "*Kafer* is a non-believer."

"What about the other word?" Laughs cut the air again.

"If he *is* a believer!" The translator becomes impatient. "*Mo'men* means believer."

"*Kafer! Kafer!*" the Arab yells again, raising his hands over his head. "*La'an Allah Al Washem w'Al Motaweshemma!*"

"What is he saying? What is he saying?"

"He's saying that God curses those who tattoo themselves." The translator is growing more and more impatient under the pressure of all the questions.

"What does the Arab know? Nothing!" someone objects. "Nothing!"

"*Rabbena Harram El-washm!*" the Arab smiles broadly at the crowd. "*El Washm Haram fee El Islam.*"

"What is he saying now?" Someone points a finger at the Arab's chest. "And tell him to shut up!"

"He is saying that God disapproves of tattoos and that tattoos are forbidden in Islam!" The translator starts to laugh. "And *you* tell him to shut up!"

The mujahideen are still screaming and laughing. Some of them take off their Pashtun hats; some of them take off their turbans.

Some fold and unfold the blankets they still have on their shoulders. Some put their weapons away. Questions and answers fly in Pashtu, Dari, and Arabic, but just the last one needs to be translated.

"But what does it mean?" Mohammad asks Hamid. "Shut up, everyone!" he yells toward the crowd. "I can't hear anything!"

Hamid traces the words on the Russian soldier's chest, translating slowly. The words are written in perfect Cyrillic. He repeats this motion several times before he is ready to read it.

Живущий под кровом Всевышнего под сенью Всемогущего покоится, говорит Господу: <прибежище мое и защита моя, Бог мой, на Которого я уповаю!>

Псалтирь 91

The commander shakes his hands in the air impatiently. "Translate," he says. "It means . . . " Hamid translates slowly:

> He that dwells in the secret place of the Most High rests under the shadow of the Almighty. I will say of the Lord: "He is my refuge and my fortress, my God, in Him will I trust."

> Psalm 91

"He is one of ours, after all!" The man in the Pashtun hat raises his hands triumphantly.

"Who says he is?" Voices of the opponents rise quickly. "He is talking to *his* God, not ours!"

"He is a shaved non-believer!"

"Ours!"

"Christian!"

"Like a woman!"

"Our God!"

"His God!"

"Almighty means *our* God! Our God only!"

*

The chilly air from the river echoes with noises running downstream. In the distance, a small hamlet is waking up. The day is opening with a wide window of shimmering light from the snow-capped mountains and the soft sheen of blue-green waters. Narrow ribbons of pale smoke rise from the flat roofs between the high mud fences and touch the sky, glowing with gold. Rows of naked mulberry trees cut the horizon with their bare branches. Rocky roads climb through soft hills along the hamlet toward the high mountains of Hindu Kush.

"Little Omar!" A piercing sound cuts the air. "Little Omar!"

"What happened?" Mohammad looks at the running man. "We can't find him!" the man yells, making signs, explaining they are looking for the one with the tattooed chest. "Little Omar! We wanted to know about Kabul's—"

"Did he go out to collect the information?" Mohammad is trying to remember something. "Anybody see Little Omar?" His voice rises above the heads of the mujahideen. "Anybody?" His voice flies toward the smoky golden web above the distant hamlet.

"Little Omar! Little Omar!" Other voices join the search.

"I saw him!" Marek Abdullah, the only man from Poland fighting in this war, comes out of the river. His sandals are soaked with water, the bottoms of his pants dripping. "I saw him. He was killed," he says, breathing heavily.

He comes to the rocky edge, shaking the water off his legs. The white and gray pebbles darken with the moisture. Mohammad and others approach him in silence.

"I saw who killed him," Marek Abdullah says, lowering his weapon. "He did." He points toward the dead Russian with the tattoo. "He killed Little Omar, and then I killed him," he says, still holding his hand up in the air. His eyes soften with pain. "I was aiming here," he says, pointing to his chest. "I was aiming into his heart." He makes a circle. "But I missed," he adds and starts walking toward the body. Mohammad and the silent crowd follow him. "I shot him in the neck." He touches the dead soldier under his ear. "He fell to the ground . . . "

"I saw him fall," the mujahid who first inspected the body says hesitantly. "I was there."

"How do you know it was our Little Omar?" Mohammad asks but doesn't look at Marek Abdullah. He doesn't want to see the truth in Marek Abdullah's face. Hope is still strong in him.

"Everybody knows him," Marek Abdullah says. "Everybody knew him," he corrects himself. "Because of his Qur'an." He crosses his chest in a slow motion.

They don't have to wait long before they see a long procession led by Taher holding the limp body of Little Omar. The left arm of the boy is swinging in the air in the rhythm of Taher's steps. The boy's white shirt is shining with a silver glow coming from the river. Ahmed walks next to Taher, holding Little Omar's weapon and his jacket. The procession is heading toward the crowd gathered at the dead Russian.

Both groups face each other in an eerie silence, in the valley of the blue-green waters and soft hills, in the girdle of high peaks on the horizon, in the fullness of the morning light. Nobody says anything. All are motionless, looking at the boy's body. His eyes are focused on the distant sky. His wavy dark hair moves in the gentle breeze. Half-opened lips, shoes tied in a double knot, shirt open with a patch of spreading redness on his chest.

"He is not asleep," Mohammad says finally, coming closer.

He takes the blanket off his shoulders and places it on the ground. Taher kneels and lowers Little Omar's body. The mujahideen encircle them, kneeling next to one another. Some still hold their weapons; some hold their hands to the sky in a quiet prayer. Some cry silently.

"I can't believe it." Taher starts to sob. "I can't believe it," he says, still holding the boy's body.

Ahmed kneels next to him and, putting down Little Omar's belongings, says firmly, "You have to believe and remember."

"I can't," Taher cries out.

Ahmed embraces him tightly, the same way he used to when they were children. Now, both of them cry.

"His spilled blood will stay with us forever," he whispers into Taher's ear. "His life and death will never be forgotten."

Then he takes Taher's hand and puts it on Little Omar's heart. "Put your finger in his wound, and you'll believe," he says, easing his grip. Taher lowers his head to the boy's chest. He grips the boy's shirt, and shakes in long spasms. He cries for a long time, bringing others with him. Finally, he raises his head and kisses the boy's chest. Under the wound, the perfect Arabic cursive says:

... *that they may add faith to their faith; for to Allah belong the Forces of the heavens and the earth; and Allah is Full of Knowledge and Wisdom.*

Mohammad closes Little Omar's eyes and kisses his forehead. Placing his hand on the boy's chest, he calls for a prayer.

Little Omar's face turns pale quickly. His lips become dull with deepening shadows. His chest falls into darkness. Unattainable, swallowing the Holy Words.

Time stops with the prayer—in the foreheads lowered to the ground, in the eyes marked with heaviness, in the hands raised to the heavens, toward the river and the mountains. From the blackening wound in the boy's chest through the highest peaks to the edges of the world, all the way to the quicksilver lake in the middle of the ocean where the Holy Stone, Holy Ka'aba, stands and unites them all.

Escape

They have looked each other between the eyes, and
There they found no fault . . .
On the hilt and half of the Khyber knife, and the Wondrous
Names of God.
—Rudyard Kipling, "The Ballad of East and West"

Taher's Dream

The sun, spilling out in carmine and gold streaks, is receding slowly behind the horizon, where sharp mountain peaks sink gradually into the soft sunset. Sandy ribbons of roads climb between mild hills and, connecting a few hamlets on their way up, disappear in the distance, where miniature plots of land weave autumn and winter colors—a reminder of life spread across the land.

The first caravan on the Silk Road is moving from east to west. Camels and horses, their strong necks gilded in the sun, weighed down with exotic wood and ivory, are set in tedious motion. Tired carriers communicate with silent hand signs. Their big white turbans cover their faces tightly, leaving only a narrow slit with dark and glowing pupils.

In small cages, they carry live animals—bright parrots and pink-muzzled, rowdy monkeys. Sleepy prisoners turned into slaves ride in bigger cages. Their sweating bodies shimmer in the late light in a shade of burnished brass. Motionless snakes sleep next to them in wicker baskets.

In huge green trunks, they carry paper and gum arabic. In yellow ones, leathers and decorative saddles wrapped in bright, patterned fabrics. In red ones, Chinese silks, jewelry, and precious stones—corals, pearls, and amber. In the bulging vessels, they carry flacons of medicine and spices, ampoules of perfume, and the priceless musk of Tibetan and Chinese deer. In small barrels, decorated with a symmetrical design, they carry exotic fruits, raisins, and hashish.

The caravan heads toward Herat, where the goods, after changing carriers, will travel farther west, through Baghdad, Damascus, and over the Mediterranean Sea to Byzantium.

Purple rocks, sitting in burnt amber soil, measure the distance of the second caravan, heading in the opposite direction. This caravan passes landscapes flowing in slow motion—fields hung with the smells of lupine and thyme, descending toward valleys of fig and mulberry trees.

Every day, the golden brightness of the full sunlight descends steadily into the reds of sunsets only to give way to the cobalt firmament of the nights, beaded with flickering silver.

The second caravan is approaching Herat from the west, where goods are transferred and sent to India and China.

Giant shields, encrusted with colored semi-precious stones and fastened to the saddles of tall horses, flash in kaleidoscopes. Sometimes the horses, startled by the sight of desert snakes, rear on their hind legs, their teeth and eyes flashing white in the darkness, the wings of the shields opening. The horsemen, lifting up their leather thongs, cut the air with a swish.

In huge brown trunks filled with hay, they carry bronze dishes. Smaller trunks contain glassware wrapped neatly in white linen. In skins, they carry wine, and half-circled black bags hold colorful vials filled with fragrant oils.

Both caravans approach their destinations with perseverance, day and night, in the scorching heat, in the cold, in hunger, in thirst.

And then, Taher is dreaming of omnipresent whiteness. The defeated army of Alexander the Great is pushing its way back home. The earth is locked in snow and night. The cold pierces the boundless terrain, bodies of warriors, and horses. Translucent snowflakes fill the air, not falling, but hanging there, filling the space, suffocating all life. The warriors move slowly, one after another, in a wide circle. Always to the left, trying to warm up their hands with their fading breaths. Sometimes they stop and talk about landscapes

of light green valleys—vineyards and fig trees. Then the first horse
dies. They cut his belly open and warm their numb hands in the
stench for a while. For a while, its meat is warm. They don't look
at each other chewing greedily. Someone mentions Bucefalus, the
horse of their commander, just his name, one word, remembering
the beauty and strength of its victorious life. The blood clots on
their hands, freezing faster than their last breaths.

*

"Ty skurwysynie! Ty skurwysynie!" You son of a bitch! Marek Abdullah
screams, pressing his opponent to the ground.

"Nyet! Nyet!" No! The man under him tries to free himself
without success. *"Nyet! Nyet! Pyerestan!"* Stop it! His face, in a grimace
of despair, is pressed to the ground.

"Ty rosyjski skurwysynie!" You Russian son of a bitch! Marek sits
on the soldier and, twisting his arm behind his back, screams straight
into his ear, "You are first on my list! I will cut your throat!"

"Ja nye soldat!" I am not a soldier! the man pleads.

Taher, awakened suddenly by the noise, runs out of the cave,
where he witnesses two men of blond hair and light complexion
fighting and talking in a foreign language.

The world swims in slow motion—falling snow, voices quieted
by the silence of the space. The contour of the nearby rocks and the
distant horizon emerge vaguely from the nightly haze. The single
screech of a bird sounds in the distance.

The mujahideen, shaken from their sleep, still yawning, join
Taher. They watch the fight, bored, until someone asks, "Is he going
to kill him or not?" A thunder of laughs meets the question. Marek
looks surprised, still twisting the Russian's arm.

"It's Wołodia!" Hamid says, emerging from the group. "Wołodia!"
Marek looks at the group, not understanding anything.

"Ja nye soldat!" I am not a soldier! Wołodia repeats, trying to catch
his breath.

"He is one of ours. Russian, but one of ours," Hamid says,

smiling. "You can let go of him," he adds, placing his hand on Marek's shoulder.

Marek gets up slowly, brushing off his clothes, but keeps his eyes on Wołodia.

"Abdullah, that was full steam ahead!" someone yells, triggering new thunders of laughs.

"Steam is not everything." Wołodia gets up slowly. "You should lose some weight!" He hits his stomach twice. "Here!" He points to his own belly.

"It's a reserve for hard times!" Marek Abdullah pats his sides. "Just in case!"

"What are you all doing here in the middle of the night?" The commander comes at last from the cave.

"I was trying to take a leak," Wołodia says.

"You idiot!" Marek raises his index finger. "You were singing in Russian."

"Yeah, because I *am* Russian," Wołodia mimics Marek. "*You* are the idiot, attacking a peeing man. Look at my pants. All wet!"

"Make sure you don't catch a cold."

Another roar of laughter. Everyone has a good time reenacting the scene.

"Knee to his ribs! Knee to the ribs!"

"From behind! Like a man!"

"He wasn't peeing, he just peed in his pants from the scare!"

*

"I didn't see any difference between myself and the Nazis in Ukraine, my home country." Wołodia covers his eyes and stops for a moment. "Rolled-up sleeves, machine guns, burned villages."

The mujahideen gather around the food and listen to the story of the Russian deserter. They dip pieces of flatbread in a common dish of oil, eat onions and turnips. They don't ask any questions, knowing the story needs to unravel in its own way. They listen and nod with acceptance. Hamid translates from Russian into Pashtu, sometimes confirming he got it right, sometimes waiting for Wołodia to conquer his own memories.

"The government lied to us about the invasion of Afghanistan," Wołodia carries on. "They said we need to liberate Afghanistan from American imperialism. But I was shooting Afghan children and elders, not Americans. The children and elders were dying from landmines, and our commanders were saying, 'That's *Dukh*, let him die. He is the enemy! Let him rot!'"

Wołodia bursts out crying. The mujahideen lower their eyes.

"The governments in your countries never tell the truth." Taher's voice, interrupting the silence, is strong and clear. "They want you to believe that your cause is noble, because morale is stronger if you think that you are on the right side of history. Otherwise, you would be barbarians attacking the innocent."

"Don't be naïve, Taher." Wołodia wipes his face. "What government doesn't lie? For the common good of its people? But really against its own people? Are you sure that *your* governments don't lie?"

A long and heavy silence falls over the gathering. No one says anything, no one moves. All gazes are turned down. Only long shadows flicker in the light of the kerosene lamps.

"There is a significant difference you don't see." Ahmed finally comes to the rescue. "Religion in our countries changes everything. Underlines everything, is part of everything. Like breathing," he continues with passion. "It changes everything."

"Really?" Wołodia doesn't twitch. "I'm not sure." He lowers his voice. "I've lost my faith. I saw too much."

"For us, real life begins after death," Ahmed says forcefully. "And that's the main difference."

"Life after death? No kidding!" Wołodia's sarcasm causes a stir among the mujahideen. "I would like to see life *before* death. Any life. Have you seen life so far? Anyone?" Wołodia's voice rises and his eyes scan the cave. "What did *I* see? I saw Russian soldiers under fire, praying, 'Mommy, mommy, take me back, take me back.' They don't have life. They don't even have memories of life. School? Childhood? First bicycle? Books and pencils? No! Only mountains."

His voice rises up. "Only mountains, machine guns, and dry rations of food. And those who deserted, like me? They are chased by helicopters and killed. My brothers are forced to kill us. They kill us. Chase us and kill us. Russians killing Russians in Afghanistan. From helicopters." He raises his arms. "From fuckin' helicopters. I was lucky to escape. Many were killed."

"We are fighting Jihad, and that's the difference," Ahmed interrupts him. "That's the fundamental difference."

"No, Ahmed. No. You are blinded, the way I was before I saw it with my own eyes." Wołodia looks at Ahmed. "Promoting democracy, liberating the oppressed, or Jihad. They're just different names for the same process."

"No, they're not." Ahmed rises from his seat to face Wołodia.

"They are. There is no difference! No difference whatsoever! And you will learn it very soon if you stay here."

"I will stay, and I already know what I needed to learn, Wołodia." Ahmed wags his finger. "I can't believe you don't understand the difference. How can you even live like this?"

"Who said I'm alive?" Wołodia lowers his voice. "I just said I'm not. You are not listening, Ahmed. You are not listening, and that's why *you* are the one who doesn't understand." Now he wags his finger at Ahmed.

"My religion gives me strength and purpose. That's why it all makes sense to me!" Ahmed says.

"Ahmed." Wołodia's voice is calm. "A war is a war. And only that, nothing else. Ever. War is destruction. It's nothing but destruction. It's death. War is always a defeat for everybody. For those who win and for those who lose. War brings only loss. For both sides. Only loss." Wołodia closes his eyes as if reaching to the unreachable place in the deepest corners of his mind. "This is my world, but this is also your world, Ahmed. You just don't want to see it. You are fooling yourself."

"No, Wołodia, *you* are fooling yourself. Let me show you my world," Ahmed says, taking off his shirt. "This is my world, Wołodia," he says, lowering his head and exposing long slashes of deep wounds running along his spine. "And that's something you don't understand," Ahmed says. "For us, for Muslims, it's always a victory. My wounds are my victory. This is something you can't comprehend."

"I know pain, Ahmed. I know sacrifice. That's why I know that your world is my world. Killing is killing, and nothing else. We are twins, Ahmed." Wołodia turns his eyes away from Ahmed's back. "There is no victory in killing. Killing someone is killing yourself. We all are twins. When I kill you, I also kill myself. Maybe not the body, but who cares about that if you are dead already. It's almost better to die after you kill someone. We humans—all humans—are twins. When one dies, the other dies too, even if the body still moves."

"There is a difference, and I will tell you why. Because when we Muslims win, then this is called victory, but when we lose and die, then this is called victory as well. We are victorious in every outcome. Either by winning the battle or by martyrdom." Ahmed's words are slow and clear. His eyes burn with fire. "Every outcome is honorable for us. And that is why God is great!"

"When you kill someone," Wołodia starts slowly, looking at the mujahideen, "when you kill someone," he repeats, as if making sure everyone can hear him, "you also kill yourself. Trust me." He stops for a moment. "This is something you don't understand, Ahmed," he adds softly. "There is no going back to the time before killing. There is no way of forgetting or moving on. The killing stays in your skin, and it becomes your every single breath for the rest of your life! You live in the death you inflicted until you yourself die, but even then, it's not over, unless," Wołodia raises his index finger as if trying to have the absolute attention of everyone gathered, " . . . unless you can shield your own children from the death you carry in you after killing someone. But I don't think it's possible. I think you simply pass it on to your children."

"I would kill only if this was the way to help my people," Ahmed answers. "I would kill for a bigger cause."

"This is what I'm saying. You make it impossible for them to have a better life because you've killed. There is no better life for anyone through killing. This is what I've learned through killing. And this is what you still have to learn. Maybe through killing as well."

*

"We were all hungry," Wołodia says quietly. "We didn't see food for days. But we had vodka. Always. We used to start drinking in the evening, and it would go on until midnight. Every day. And then things happened. Suicides, killings. War changes everything. It erases the memory of life before. What stays is only the war. Nothing else. I would like to forget, but I know I can't. It's in my blood. Like a virus. It kills me, and it leaves me alive.

"One day, our commander shaved Misha. He said that Misha's hair was too long. Misha didn't twitch. Didn't say anything. After the commander was done, Misha went silently to a mirror. I remember his wild eyes. The mirror was broken and Misha's reflection in it showed many eyes. Many wild eyes. After that, he walked up to the commander silently, and shot him three times. Then he shot himself.

"There was a young boy who was beaten every day. They didn't like his birthplace. He tried to hide, but never succeeded. Some men beat him until he was unconscious. These men were from my village. We went to the same school. We used to steal apples from an orchard together. One day, the young boy tried to run away, but he didn't think of doing it at night. I still remember the swooshing sounds of the helicopters. They said he was too tired to run. They saw him fall after they shot him. They left his body there.

"That day, we were all hungry. Hungry and drunk. Then it must have been the middle of the night—I remember the cold and darkness—those guys from Russia were leading. There were five of us. Three from Ukraine and two from Russia. Sasha, Losha, and I from Ukraine. Two Kolas from Russia. We called them Kola One and Kola Two.

"They said they could find the compound we were looking for. They said they'd made this trip a couple of times before. They said they knew where *Dukhi* stored their food supply. Flour and chickens.

'We will have a fat goose!' Kola Two was singing. 'Chicken and goose washed down with vodka!'

"We were walking fast. The Russians knew the way. Even in the middle of the night. I didn't expect to meet anyone. I thought we were going to steal something quietly. That's all. I thought there must be a hole in the mud fence or something. I thought maybe eggs. Chicken.

"Kola One knocked on the door of the mud house, but no one answered. He knocked several times. Louder and louder. Finally, he yelled that if they didn't open, we would shoot them all. I didn't see any other mud houses around. But it was dark.

"After a while, the door opened and an old man, with a white beard reaching down to his waist, looked at us and said, 'Please, leave us. We have no food.' He had such small round eyes. They looked like two little holes in his head.

"But it was too late. Kola One pushed him, and we entered the house. 'We don't have anything to eat,' a young girl said, backing up, covering her mouth with a scarf. 'And what do you call this?' Kola Two asked, showing a pouch of flour he found in a back room.

"As he stepped toward the girl, he tripped, and the bag of flour fell out of his arms. A white stream of powder cascaded down, leaving a fine dust floating in the air around his arms. 'You bitch!' he screamed at her. 'Look what you've done!' They both looked at the floor between them, where the flour was covering their shoes.

"From the darkness of the room, two other girls, both younger than the first one, ran toward the door. No one had noticed them before. They were young; their heads were not covered yet. Their faces were lit with the faint glow coming from the windows. They reached the door, jumped out, and ran toward the fence. Their bare heels flashed on the run. They didn't get far. Kola Two's machine gun reached them. One fell on top of the other.

"The old man raised the dry sticks of his arms and attacked Kola Two, but received a hard blow to his head from a rifle butt. His white turban soaked up the blood quickly. I remember that we were all very surprised to discover, later on, that there was a fourth girl, probably somewhere outside the house, who saw us kill the two girls that were running toward the fence. She reported on us. None of us noticed her. Her testimony brought us so much trouble. Investigations. Questions and more questions. She identified us immediately. She told the investigators about the old man, too. She either saw Kola Two killing him through the open front door or she saw the old man's body after we left. I don't remember exactly where we all were. All of it happened so fast. I think it all happened at the door. Kola Two shooting the girls. The old man attacking him. I vomited looking at the white, soft substance of his eye running down his cheek. I never got used to the blood and all of this. It makes me sick. It always did.

"After the old man and the two girls were killed, only the girl who said that they didn't have anything to eat was left. Kola One and Kola Two ripped her clothes off. She was twelve, maybe thirteen. Her eyes were withdrawing slowly. She was waiting. I still remember her beautiful skin glowing in the darkness, the color of polished brass.

"All of it was coming to me through a fog. And it stayed like that in my memory. Just flashes of reality. Pictures. Thoughts. Voices. And the girl. Her beautiful almond-shaped eyes and wet eyelashes. Her long hair was glowing in the weak light like a soft aura. She had beautiful, delicate hands. White moons on her fingernails. She saw me looking at her. We made eye contact. I think that was the moment when she realized I wasn't one of them. She realized it before I did. Or maybe she helped me to realize the truth.

"After that, after she looked at me, everything became even more painful. Unbearable. That split second of something connected us. Right there. While I watched. *She could have been my wife in a different world*, I thought to myself. *The most beautiful wife ever. In a different world, she would embrace me gently and kiss my eyes. In a world that doesn't exist. Why doesn't that other world exist? Why?*

"When Kola One and Kola Two were done and left the room, I approached her. I kneeled next to her. She opened her arms toward me. I couldn't stop trembling. I lowered myself next to her. She embraced me gently. She stroked my hair. *"Ubiy mne,"* she whispered into my ear in Russian. "Kill me," she said in the softest and sweetest voice.

"Kola One came back and kicked me. I jumped to my feet and hit him. 'You son of a bitch!' I screamed. 'You son of a bitch! You got what you wanted! Now fuck off!' That's all I said before I felt a blow to my ear, then warmth. I knew I was falling, and I knew I couldn't do anything about it. I had no idea how long it lasted, but when I opened my eyes, the girl was dead, shot in the heart. *This is my world,* I thought to myself. *This is my world.* I kneeled next to her and cried. When I embraced her, she was weightless. Like an angel. Her blood soaked into my uniform, her open heart into mine. I couldn't let go of her.

'I want to live in a different world,' I cried into her ear. I could swear she embraced me back. I could hear her voice.

'You already do,' she whispered and smiled at me. And that was the moment when I decided I had to leave. I wasn't afraid of the helicopters anymore."

*

The mujahideen approach the village, talking about their life before the war. Hamid describes his favorite foods in great detail.

"Nobody, nobody could ever prepare *gabli pilou* as well as my mother." Hamid closes his eyes and shrugs his shoulders as if hugging his memories. "The rice was tender, but not soggy. The meat was soft, but not mushy. And the raisins, almonds, and pistachios gave it this nutty and sweet aroma that reminded me of everything dear to my heart."

The mujahideen laugh. "You talk about food like a woman," someone says, mimicking his shrugging shoulders. "Sweet, sweet," someone else repeats in a high-pitched voice.

"You can laugh." Hamid isn't offended. "Today we will have, if we are lucky, bread and onions."

"That's men's food!" Marek Abdullah says, laughing. "I can fart my way through the night again!" The mujahideen are amused.

"Hamid, what else?" the commander asks in a longing voice. "What else did she make?" He makes a smacking noise. "I have to prepare myself for the feast of bread and onions."

"Before the war," Hamid continues, "There was *montu.*"

"What's that?" asked Marek.

"A nice and tender meat, it's steamed, I think, or maybe fried, and then it's rolled in dough and deep fried in oil. It's a special Tibetan delicacy. My mother knows how to make it just right, so the meat is very tender and not dry."

"Tender, tender!" someone laughs again.

"And the best samosas."

"Samo-what?" Marek asks again.

"*Samosas* are pierogies," Hamid explains.

"Pierogies?" Marek jumps. "That's Polish food! Pierogies are Polish. They were Polish, are Polish, and will be Polish forever!"

"*Samosas* are different," Hamid says.

"What are they then?"

"They are stuffed with boiled vegetables, yogurt, and mint sauce."

"I would need lots of vodka to flush this one down," Marek says to roars of laughter. "I hope she won't serve that today."

"Today we can expect dark tea. Sweet, if we're lucky," Hamid continues. "Maybe bread, oil, and onions. If we're lucky, that is."

"What else is Polish?" the commander asks Marek. "Give us something very Polish."

"Well." Marek stops for a moment. "That would be *bigos.*"

"Be-what?" Hamid returns the friendly sarcasm. "What's that?"

"That's the food of my dreams." Marek closes his eyes and presses both hands to his heart, amusing everyone.

The mujahideen stop, giving him some space to perform. "Go ahead, *bigos*. Go ahead." Hamid's encouragement is genuine.

"In short—it's like heaven!" Marek outstretches his arms and turns his face toward the sky.

"Yep," someone says. "And in detail?"

The mujahideen form a semicircle around the performer.

"One head of chopped sweet cabbage into the biggest pot you

can imagine." His hands make a movement of placing something into an imaginary pot in front of him. "Two jars of sauerkraut. To the pot!" His arms move swiftly. "One-liter jars are the best." Additional explanation comes with a flat palm slapping the side of his mouth. "And then the best of it—after the cabbage gets soft— sausages, any kind you have handy, chopped in cubes or slices, like this." His hand makes a cutting movement. "Hot dogs, *kabanoski*, yum, *krakowska parzona*, yum, yum, *polska*, Polish sausage."

"Too many ingredients." Hamid waves his arm.

"I'm just getting started . . . " Marek blinks twice and moves his head back, forming a second chin and bringing back the roars of laughter. "Next, smoked meats. Whatever is available at the time of cooking. Chicken breast from last night's dinner. Or a leg. Lamb leg? Fine! Duck leg? Fine! Both legs? Fine!" His hands sweep the air, throwing all the ingredients into the pot. "And dried wild mushrooms. The ones you harvested yourself in the nearby forest. This is life! And, prunes!"

"Prunes!" Hamid yells. "You must be joking."

"That's all he does!" the commander points out.

"No." Marek lowers his arms sadly. "I'm serious. The prunes give it a bittersweet taste. Especially if you use prunes with the pits—the pits add the bitterness."

"Okay, we believe you! What next?"

"You cook it for hours."

"Do you get to eat it too? Or you just cook it and cook it?" Laughter follows.

"You can keep it in your fridge for weeks."

"Yeah, then you *really* need a lot of vodka to wash this one down!"

"And that's the beauty of it!" Marek bows, ending his performance.

After bursts of laughter and quick comments, the mujahideen are back on their way to Hamid's house. Powdery snow fills the air around them, settling on their beards, turbans, hats, and the blankets covering their shoulders, shrouding everything in a fine tapestry of shimmering web.

The day is ending with a dim light behind the horizon when they finally reach the hamlet. They pass long mud fences along the compounds, climbing between the fields—frozen, waiting for spring. The place, spread between leafless trees, pulsates with thin ribbons of smoke coming from low chimneys.

"It's there." Hamid points toward a compound, and the mujahideen turn left, following his sign. All of them rush suddenly as if hurried with hunger or simply relieved to be reaching their destination.

A valley below them—silent and broad—darkens in the receding lines of lights and shadows, heralding a quiet night.

When they finally reach the gate of the house, Hamid takes his Kalashnikov off his shoulder and yells to the group, "Welcome to my home." As he smiles broadly—his face lit up with excitement—they hear the all too familiar sound: a single shot. The mujahideen freeze in confusion. Hamid stops and then rushes to the front door. All follow.

"Nooo!" A loud howl rips the air. "Nooo!" Hamid's father screams.

*

Six weeks ago, a woman knelt in front of a man. There was a faded rug on the floor. Its flowery design resembled patches of pale land and spring valleys. The man sat on a pillow, with his back against the wall.

"I beg you to kill me," the woman cried.

"No!" The man turned his gaze to the side. "No! And this is my last word."

"We have no other choice." The woman touched his face gently. "It has to be this way." She stroked his cheeks, wet with tears.

"I said no." The man's chin trembled. "No one needs to know. No one needs to find out." He tried to find convincing words.

"*I* know." She covered her face and gave a loud cry. "I know, and that's enough."

"Then just forget about it." The man covered his face. "Just forget what happened."

"How can I forget?" The woman raised her arms. "I will never forget their humiliating eyes. And their dirty hands touching my belly. They said I was too pregnant. They said I looked like a cow. They laughed. They saw me naked. Don't you understand? I can still smell them. I can smell the Russians! Day and night. I can't sleep. I am already dead. How can you expect me to live like that? I want to die. I have the right to die," she said, lowering her voice. "I have the right to die, and you have the right to live in dignity, with your honor preserved for your children."

The man put his hands on the woman's belly. She started crying louder. Her long black hair spilled around her shoulders as she lowered her gaze and reached to meet his hands. She pressed them tightly to herself for a moment and then moved quickly away from him.

"You are carrying my son," the man said quietly. "I want my son to be born."

"Then I'll wait," she said, leaving the room.

*

Hamid lowers his Kalashnikov, ready to fire, and jumps into the room. Stops. His father is kneeling over his mother. "No, no, no, no," he repeats quietly, holding her hand. His father's rifle lies on the floor.

Hamid lowers his gun and kneels.

"It was an accident. My God, it was an accident," his father cries. "I was cleaning my gun, and she pulled it accidentally."

Hamid's mother is dying. "Ommi," Hamid whispers. She looks at him.

"I'm sorry . . . " Her lips move silently.

He takes her hand. "Ommi," he whispers again.

Her long hair on the floor forms a wide circle of waving rays around her head. A black pool of blood spreads under her body, soaking into the rug, absorbing pale flowers, leaves, and branches, one at a time, one at a time—moving with the rhythm of her fading breath and carrying her life away.

"Ommi," Hamid says for the last time.

Her gaze turns inward, into the unreachable place. And all becomes nothing.

Beautiful Life

Who shall live and who shall die?
Who shall be born and who shall come to an end?
Who by fire and who by water?
But prayer, repentance, and deeds of loving kindness
avert the evil decree.

—Yom Kippur prayer

When Taher enters the lobby, two workmen kneel in an open elevator and tell him that it's out of order for the next ten to fifteen minutes. By the time he climbs to the fifth floor, he is out of breath and waits a moment before he knocks on the door. He knocks twice and then he hears a child's cry and a woman's voice.

"Oh, hi," the woman says, opening the door slightly. The child in her arms stops crying for a second. "Please, wait." She releases the chain and opens the door for him to enter. "You must be Taher," she says.

"And you must be Irene," he says, entering.

"Marek called just a couple of minutes ago and said he'll be a bit late. Sorry." She leads him into the living room. "One of the copy machines broke down again, and they needed it fixed right away. You know he fixes copy machines and faxes at the Center."

"Yes, I know. He told me on the phone."

"Please, make yourself at home," she says, rocking the child in her arms. "He is sick." She points to the child. "But *she* isn't. Yet, I should add," she rolls her eyes, smiling at the same time, and then she points to another child sitting in a playpen. "I gave him Tylenol ten minutes ago. He should fall asleep, hopefully soon. Did Marek tell you we have twins?"

"That was the first thing he told me on the phone," Taher answers. "Marek is very proud of being a father."

"I think he is," she says, smiling and kissing the boy's forehead. "I have lemonade and orange juice," she says, leading Taher to the kitchen.

The boy starts crying again.

"I'll try to put him to sleep," Irene says. "Please, help yourself to a drink. There are cookies in the jar." She points to the table.

"I'll be fine," Taher says, pouring lemonade.

"If he falls asleep, we might have some peaceful time to talk." She smiles as she leaves the kitchen.

Taher looks out the window and reads the signs. *Dunkin' Donuts. Law Office of Larry Dobry. Pizza and Pasta. Shima Fine Japanese Food Restaurant. Anagenesis, Society of Epirotes. Insurance and Travel. Royal Nails. Schrier Optical, Varilux Professional. Beer, Lotto, Quick Draw, Phone Cards, Stationery, DVD and Movies, ATM.*

A line of people waits at a Halal food stand. *Blacks and whites craving an Arab meal.* Taher nods to his thoughts. *Coming from around the planet.* Faces and faces. Different hair. Round heads and narrow eyes. Full lips and purple gums. White eyelashes and sky under translucent eyelids. Many colors, many shapes. Long fingernails and Puma running shoes. Dark braids with red and yellow heart-shaped beads. Eyeglasses and beards. Cranes and strollers. The world is condensed here. People below him are joined in indescribable oneness—*in a strange, unfitting unity*—he thinks.

Above the shops are apartment buildings—city life piled in vertical rows. *Floors and ceilings, floors and ceilings.* People live one on top of another, with their goldfish and dogs. With cats on their desks, on top of stacks of books, among patches of artificial light.

In the south corner, a window fogs with shower mist, and the white shape of a curtain swings in a fast motion. *Someone is leaving.* Across the street, a young woman in a white window frame waves her arms. *With anger? Disbelief? Disappointment?* And a second person retreats into a darker part of the room. *Separate, disconnected lives of people living together. Strangers to one another.* A feeling of unsatisfying repletion washes over Taher. *Nourished but weak.*

People on the street below pick fruits and vegetables at the stand from green boxes filled with rainbows cascading all the way to the pavement—shades of greens, yellows, purples, oranges, and whites. They choose their fruits carefully—touching, smelling, taking them, or putting them back. They close their eyes, evoking the taste through the skin's softness or roughness, through the density of the flesh below their fingertips.

A little girl jumps in the door of a flower shop, pointing to the balloon above, and her mother reaches for it. Both of them glow in the soft light of the late afternoon. With their smiles and matching summer dresses, they are happy among the carpets of flowers surrounding them at the entrance of the shop. The mother bends at her narrow and strong waist, picks yellow roses and shakes the water from the stems. Dark patches of water appear on the sidewalk around her feet.

Below them, the earth is covered with concrete and asphalt, enclosed tightly in an endless shroud. *Locked up by the harsh decree of modern man.* The earth is suffocating, removed from life without air and sunshine, separated from rain. Its soil—deprived of seeds—is barren. *Nothing will sprout, nothing will grow to bear fruit.* Nothing will ever reach toward the crystal-clear sky.

Taher closes his eyes and the images—invited and longed for— arrive instantly. He sees the boundless spaciousness of the Hindu Kush. He takes a deep breath, and the air of distant winds fills his lungs—from the world cupped by valleys rich in lupine and mulberry trees, where soft hills, shaded in carpets of dwarf greens, climb up in hundreds of waving ribbons to the silver and white peaks set in the sky, flowing between sunrises and sunsets, the same and different each day. Where flatbreads and spring water nourish the body with warmth and lightness, for all people the same. *For the same people, the same.* The world of nature is exposed to man in an untailored way from the beginning of life, all in a primordial union of the elements—the presence and order of a power greater than anything else. *God.* And unity.

Taher opens his eyes. *Nice, simple kitchen. A jar.* He lifts the lid and reaches for a cookie. *Chocolate chip,* he notices, and takes a bite.

As soon as the taste enters his senses, his navel tightens with nausea. He parts his lips and looks around for a trashcan. The trashcan he spots in the corner seems too far away. He spits the bite into the sink and lets the water run for a while. *Killing with sweetness.*

He comes back to the window with a bitter aftertaste in his mouth. *Too much is never enough. Doesn't sustain anything. That's the paradox of the Western world.*

The walls of the living room are covered in bookshelves. *Idiota* by Dostojewski, Taher moves his finger along the spines, *Collected Poems* by Czesław Miłosz, *Mr. Cogito* by Zbigniew Herbert, *Kobiety i duch inności* by Maria Janion.

In a wide space between the bookshelves, Taher stops in front of sepia photographs. They show people marching on the street—a caravan of men, women, and children carrying suitcases, backpacks, and bundles. Their eyes are absent or fearful, he can't tell. Some carry babies in their arms. All of them wear an armband—the Star of David.

Taher is about to pull a book from the shelf when the little girl in the playpen starts to cry. *Not this*, he thinks, pushing the retracted spine back. She is facing him with both arms outstretched. *Forget about it*, he thinks, looking at the two streams of mucus hanging above her upper lip.

"Up," she says, moving her hands in a rushing motion.

"No!" Taher whispers as loud as he can.

The little girl rests her chin and her hands on the edge of the pen and smiles.

"Diaper," she says, her high voice curling up when she points between her legs.

"Hush." Taher places his index finger on his mouth.

The girl's lower lip curves in a horseshoe, and her eyes fill with tears.

"Up, up!" she cries.

Disoriented, Taher looks around the room, and hands her a stuffed animal he has spotted on the floor. She shakes her head angrily.

"Up, up!"

"Oh, shut up," Taher pleads with her softly, lowering his face, "Your mom is trying to put your brother to sleep." He points to the hallway.

The little girl gazes in that direction and says, "Makkie, Makkie."

"Makkie?"

"Makkie dere." She points to the hallway.

"Oh, your brother's name is Markie," he says, "and yours is Julie." *Like your grandmother, your father's mother.* He looks at her bib with a name embroidered below a smiling sun. "Are you Julie?" he asks, moving his eyebrows high up.

Julie looks at him in amazement, opening her mouth. The streams of mucus grow, reaching her upper lip.

"Lullie," she says, smiling, "Lullie me." She points to her bib.

Taher pulls a couple of tissues from the box on a table and hands them to Julie.

"Wipe your nose," he says, waving the tissues in front of her face.

She grabs them clumsily, flutters them in the air, and with a mischievous smile, drops them to the floor.

"Down," she says, looking at them.

"Not down," Taher pulls another tissue from the box. "Like this," he says demonstrating what she needs to do.

Little Julie listens, turning her head to the side.

"Got it?" Taher hands her new tissues.

She takes them slowly and following with the same slow motion, places them on her mouth. Before Taher is able to say anything, she closes her eyes and blows her nose with all her might. In a split second, a handful of mucus is suspended between her hands and her mouth, revealing just half of a smile.

"Oh, no!" Taher covers his face with both hands. *Irene, hurry!*

He gets up and heads toward the hallway but is stopped by Julie's soft cry.

She stands there helplessly holding the tissues close to her shiny face.

He comes back, and leaning forward over her tiny body, says, "Why do people have children? Julie, I am too old for this! And too

young! I hate this! I came to visit your father, not to wipe your ass!"
he hisses over her.

"Ass! Ass!" Julie repeats and opens her arms again. "Up, up,"
she pleads.

Taher reaches for a handful of tissues, separating himself from
what he has to do.

"I hate you, Julie," he whispers, wiping her face gently. "I hate
children. They are weak, dirty, and loud. And stupid."

"Oopit, Oopit," she repeats, looking him straight in the eyes.

She lets him wipe her hands, finger after finger, opening her tiny
palms wide. She giggles and laughs. She observes his movements
and face, listening tentatively, reaching deep inside Taher.

"Done," Taher says, looking into her eyes. Her eyes are light
blue and as clear as crystal water. Two tears, still hanging on the dark
line of her eyelashes, reflect a longing he recognizes—a plea with no
hope. *Something familiar and something strange.* She smiles, revealing six
little teeth, four on the top and two on the bottom. He wipes her
tears with a fresh tissue.

Julie grabs his sleeve. Taher tries to pull away. Once, twice. "Let
go now," he says. Her little fingers lock in the opening above the cuff
of his shirt. She doesn't give up.

"Up," she repeats the plea, turning her face towards him.

They stay there, connected by her baby will, unprotected and
strong. She seems to trust him with no hesitation. *Children are easy to
kill,* Taher thinks, and new images rush in—the refugee camp from
ten years ago. He remembers the boy and his sister Aisha, who asked
when her brother would die. He remembers the mothers cradling
their babies and elderly men hunched over small fires between the
tents.

Suddenly, Julie's little hand loses its way in the cuff opening and
travels up his arm. Taher pulls fast but is forced to a painful stop.
The little fingers clench his forearm hair. "Oh, shit," his lips move
silently.

"Up," she says and raises her other hand up.

He leans forward, over her, and embracing her softly, picks her up.

She is weightless. As she leans on his chest, her arm moves deeper into his sleeve. He feels her baby skin—soft and tender—melting into his. There is an unexpected comfort in this strange nearness. She smells of lavender oil and bread. He feels the softness of her baby hair on his cheek and he slowly gives in. The sounds fade into silence.

"Dada, Dada," she says, grabbing his nose.

"I'm not your dad," he says quietly but doesn't move, allowing her to touch him in her own fearless manner, inviting her curiosity.

"Da, da, da, da," she repeats, tightening her grip.

Taher closes his eyes, allowing Julie to come even deeper—to the place abandoned for years, but never forgotten—where everything is the same from the beginning of time, where we are connected to one another and to all that comes and all that passes. Where memories stored in words, pictures, and scents form the innermost place—sometimes called home, other times called the soul—that can turn with ease into unexpected tears of joy. Where Julie is his sister.

"I am so sorry." Irene's voice breaks the silence as she takes Julie from Taher. "She is such a little bully, always getting what she wants. Her brother, Markie, is different—sensitive, thoughtful, and quiet." Irene doesn't stop talking. "I'm sorry, did she hurt you?" She looks at Taher with concern.

"Oh, no, no." He sniffles and wipes his eyes. "Something got into my nose." He laughs. "Allergies, perhaps," he adds.

Irene places Julie back in the playpen and gives her a bottle of milk.

"She's hungry," she adds, rolling Julie to the side, and placing her against the padded wall.

Julie closes her eyes and, holding tightly to the bottle, sucks the nipple with a smacking noise, enjoying every drop with the same intensity.

"Please, sit down." Irene points to a chair behind the coffee table. "I have some Polish delicacies you must try," she says, opening a little cabinet.

"Marek talked a lot about Polish food in Afghanistan." Taher is glad to change the subject.

"What else could you talk about in a place like that? Girls?" she laughed, opening boxes of sweets.

"It's a different culture." Taher lowers his gaze.

"Oh, sorry, I was just joking. I didn't mean to offend you." She sits down across the table from him. "I know you live in Germany now. You study medicine there, right?"

"Yes, I do, but some things never change," he says defiantly.

"Good for you. It's nice to be innocent in today's world."

"It's not innocence. It's a choice of priorities, I suppose."

"Priorities?" Irene doesn't cover her surprise. "What's more important than family?"

"Exactly . . . " Taher says forcefully, but doesn't finish, feeling the thought die out in misunderstanding.

"So." Irene looks at him, waiting. "You have to look around before you make your decision. Right?"

"Well, sometimes it's better if more experienced people guide you."

"You mean arranged marriages?"

"Yes."

"You seriously think that's a better way?"

"Sometimes."

"Well, come to think of it"—Irene stares into the sweets— "sometimes it really does seem better. I have so many divorced friends," she adds, placing a small plate in front of Taher.

"Well, come to think of it," Taher moves the plate slightly to the right, "sometimes it's *not* better."

"I guess there is no guaranteed recipe for anything in life—and especially for big things like marriage." She serves him some cookies and chocolate. "We should just live and enjoy every moment as much as we can." She looks at him and smiles. "Life is too short not to enjoy it with a full heart."

"I wish I could agree."

"The choice is yours, isn't it?" She smiles again.

"Sometimes I wonder," he answers without conviction.

"I think the coffee is ready." She leans back and listens for sounds coming from the kitchen. "I'll be right back." She jumps up and quickly leaves the room.

Taher looks at Julie. Her hands are curled up. For a moment, he marvels at her tiny fingernails, translucent above the pink baby flesh. One hand is holding the nipple of the empty bottle. A drop of milk is still hanging on her lower lip and tiny pearls of sweat at the top of her forehead are marching up, dissolving into her soft blonde curls. Little nose and puffed cheeks are marked with a soft blush. Her eyes, slightly open, reveal the narrow whites of her restless eyes. *You silly creature.*

"I was just thinking," Irene says as she comes back, holding a tray with two coffee cups. "I was thinking about my grandmother, and how we don't really know anything, how we don't really influence anything in our own lives. How life takes over, I mean the circumstances of life, because we don't have a choice, or we're not in a position to make a choice. I don't know what it is exactly, but I think you're right."

"I am?" Taher raises his eyebrows. "Aren't we going to wake her up talking?" He points to Julie.

"Oh, no, she sleeps like a rock. Not like Markie."

"What were you saying?" Taher takes the cup she hands him and places it on a table.

"I was saying that thinking about my grandmother's life is repulsive and amazingly beautiful at the same time, and also strange. My grandmother insisted that she made choices, even at times and places she didn't really have any choice."

"Repulsive and amazing? That's a very strange combination." Taher takes a sip from his cup. "Thank you for the coffee. It's exactly what I need after the long flight from Hamburg."

"Her life was very strange. I would say the most extreme example of strength in weakness or the most extreme example of how much we can or can't really choose our destiny."

"What happened to her?"

"It's a long and sad story. I'm not sure if you want to hear it." Irene takes a bite of a cookie and pauses as if trying to decide the course of the conversation.

"I want to hear it. It sounds interesting already."

"You'd better make yourself comfortable, then." She laughs her light laugh. Taher is quickly getting used to it.

"Okay." He leans back in his chair.

"My grandmother used to say, 'Life is complicated and simple— it's what we do with it. It's always our choice between *black* and *white.* "

The words "black" and "white" make him think of his father. The room shifts sideways—the present and the past collide to form a brand-new tense, thick and solid like a rock. The woman sitting on the other side of the table seems to be from his past and seems to know exactly who he is.

"My grandmother was Jewish. Did you know?" she says.

Taher moves in his seat. The room shifts sideways again. He hadn't expected this and is trying to understand why he feels close to this woman he has just met.

"Her name was Miriam. Which, by the way, is the original Hebrew form of Mary, and Mary is originally an Egyptian name. Did you know that? It means love."

Taher freezes for a moment, realizing the conversation is slowly becoming something he hadn't expected, a monologue he can't access. He thinks of Marek and tries to reconcile the Marek he remembers from Afghanistan with the one married to Irene.

"She was born in Lublin, Poland. There was a huge Jewish community before World War II. She was seventeen when her entire family was transported to Auschwitz. To die. It was 1944. You know there was a concentration camp, right? It was called Auschwitz Birkenau."

Yeah, there's one in Gaza. No ovens, though, Taher thinks. "Yes, I've heard about it," he says.

"Sometimes people don't believe it ever happened, so I always ask," Irene says and takes another bite of her cookie.

"Anyway," she continues. "The story of my grandmother is too strange. Some people don't believe it. You know, Jews don't want to hear about it. I've made many enemies with this story. No one wants to hear the truth, or I should say, no one wants to hear that kind of truth. Even the family never talks about my grandmother. Her brothers and sisters—she had two older brothers and two older sisters, all of them are dead now—pretended she never existed."

"Did she die in the concentration camp? Was she murdered?" Taher asks and crosses his legs.

"Oh no, none of them died in the concentration camp. They all survived. She actually saved them. No, they would never admit this is how they survived. They never admitted the extra portions of bread and soup they received, thanks to her. And when two of them got sick, they were treated with antibiotics. Believe me, the Nazis didn't help the sick in the concentration camps. They would rather send them to the ovens. Do you know they burned the bodies in the ovens? First they killed them in gas chambers and then burned them in ovens, millions of Jews, Gypsies, Poles, homosexuals, disabled people, and the mentally disabled."

"I know that," Taher nods.

"Her brothers, sisters, and even their father renounced her after the war. They burned family pictures to make sure she would disappear from their lives forever. They wanted her to disappear from their past, from their memories also. How crazy is that?"

"Why? What did she do?" Taher asks.

"How they hated her." Irene goes on without answering his question. "She didn't disappear, and today I have her photographs. And she's there, you see? On the wall. Here. Look at the middle picture. The most beautiful girl in Lublin. Her blonde hair was long, wavy, and very shiny."

Taher looks at the picture with a sigh of resignation.

Irene, spare me the details, just tell me the story, and let's be done with it, he thinks, but says nothing.

"She was a dancer as a little girl and wanted to study medicine at Jagiellonian University in Kraków. The war changed everything. The women on her right are her sisters, and the two men on her left are her brothers. The father is behind. You can see his shoulder. Their mother died before the war. My grandmother believed we should love no matter what. Never an eye for an eye. Always love. Kind of a Jewish Mother Teresa."

"What time is Marek coming?" Taher interrupts her.

"Soon," she answers, but doesn't stop. "When my grandmother Miriam was sent to Auschwitz, she was seventeen and engaged to her high school sweetheart. They were supposed to get married as soon as the war ended."

Taher uncrosses and crosses his legs again.

"They were so in love. Do you see the other picture? The one on the left? There he is. His name was Adam. They exchanged hundreds of letters and poems during their high school years. I have some of them."

Taher reaches for a sweet and then takes a sip of his coffee.

"I don't even know why I'm sharing all this with you, Taher, maybe because Marek talks about Afghanistan sometimes. I can imagine war brings people close quickly."

"Maybe," Taher says and drifts off into his own thought. *Why did Marek get married?*

"My grandmother told me that when they arrived at Auschwitz, the sky was dark from the smoke coming from the high chimneys. She said people were disoriented and terrified. Many cried. No one understood what was happening until they were asked to leave their belongings on the platform, and the families were separated. The Nazis asked the young and strong ones to step to the right, and the old, weak, sick, and children to the left side. In that moment, they understood they had been brought to hell."

"There are many hells, you know, Irene," Taher interjects.

"And that was when she met Hans. Hans was one of the German officers overseeing the new transport that day. When he saw Miriam, he immediately took her to be his maid."

"What do you mean by maid?" Taher asks and looks at her, focused and waiting.

"My grandmother told me that she was too scared to even look at him, but she said to herself, in her mind, *'You, be nice to me.'* That's all she could think of. *'In the midst of hell, be nice to me.'*"

"Was she putting a spell on him?" Taher asks.

"She cooked for him, she cleaned his place, but most of all, she played the piano and read and discussed books with him—literature, philosophy, poetry."

Did she—? Taher thinks, but again, says nothing.

"You see, she had taken piano lessons since she was four years old. Hans loved the piano but couldn't play very well. He appreciated classical music, and she played for him almost every evening. How awkward. Imagine Beethoven's "Für Elise" in such a place. He even bought books for her. They read together, out loud. She said sometimes she would play the piano, and they both would cry. They both knew the hell must end because hell always ends."

"Not really. This sounds like a fairy tale, not a concentration camp," Taher says, and takes another sip of his coffee.

"I know!" Irene says. "This is why I'm telling you the story is crazy. I'm telling you that she was able to create life in the middle of hell."

"How would the Nazis allow something like this?" Taher asks.

"Of course, no one knew. None of the other officers, none of the prisoners. It was strictly between them. He said to her once, if he needed to hit her in front of the other officers, to make a point, he hoped she could forgive him. She said she would."

"What about her family?"

"That's the whole point! Through Hans, she was able to help them. This is how they all survived! They thought she was a whore, but in fact, she was saving them from the ovens."

"This is impossible!" Taher says.

"I know! That's why no one believed her, including her family, the family she saved! She told me they were both prisoners there. Hans and she. But who would see a German Nazi officer in Auschwitz from such a perspective? Now you understand why the story is so unbelievable."

"If Hans had the power to give them antibiotics, why didn't he help them get out of there?" Taher tries to challenge the story.

"I asked her why he didn't just let them all leave the camp. She said he couldn't do it, but he could help them to survive. Maybe he kept them there to make sure she stayed with him?"

"If that was the case, you can't call it love, right?" Taher looks at her and waits for her to agree.

"I don't know. All I know is that they survived. Her fiancé

survived, too, but committed suicide a couple of years after the war.

"Did she tell them what happened?"

"She couldn't be open with all of this in the camp, but it wasn't so difficult to figure things out. I remember she said to me one day, 'They were jealous of me sleeping in a bed, having regular, full meals, clean water to drink and shower with, and living in a place that was suitable for a human being. I was jealous of them having each other, because I didn't have anyone when they all turned away from me.'"

"You are not telling me that they didn't sleep together, right?" Taher looks at Irene again, waiting for her to agree.

"According to my grandmother, Hans never touched her until she wanted him to, and she started wanting him to when they all abandoned her. I don't know if they fell in love, or were just hopelessly lonely. She used to say there is no difference between these two. Anyway, to make the long story a bit shorter—Hans was my mother's father."

Marek-Abdullah, you've lost your mind, man. Taher thinks, but again says nothing.

"He died in a POW camp in Russia in 1952. That's all she knew about him. My mother married a German. And I'm their only daughter. So, according to Judaism, I'm really Jewish," Irene says, looking at the photographs on her wall.

"*Are* you Jewish?" Taher says, following her gaze to the wall.

"I'm not, because we were never religious. I mean my grandmother wasn't, my mother wasn't. So here I am—a woman named Irene. My first language was Polish. I was born in New York City, and I adore my Polish husband." Irena smiles and reaches for a cookie. She takes a bite and looks at the edge left by her teeth. "Taher, am I boring you?"

"No, I am still processing the wild story of your grandmother," he says, and takes another sip.

"The wildest part of my grandmother was her view on the 'chosen people.' You see, she thought Jews misunderstood the message God sent them through Moses. She believed that Jews were the chosen ones, not because they were Jews, but because they were human beings."

"What does that mean?"

"She used to say to me, 'Irene, we were chosen to receive the message of a human-like God, a power we possess, not as Jews, but as human beings.'"

"I don't get it." Taher puts his cup on the table.

"'And we, the Jews, were chosen to receive the message because we were the ones who were suffering. Pharaoh already knew about it and used it to his own advantage against his people as well. We were the slaves because we didn't know we didn't have to be the slaves.' My grandmother strongly believed that, throughout the ages, Jews forgot what was expected of them. And what was expected? To share the message with everyone! Not only with other Jews, but also with every single human being. She said we were expected to teach everyone a lesson that said, 'You, a human being, were created in the image of God. Use that gift and pass it on to your children and your grandchildren. You possess a power greater than any other creature on this planet—you can create anything you want.'"

"Irene, tell me you don't believe this!"

"God said, 'You were created in my image.' So, use it! How would God use this power of free will? He would create love and peace and happiness and prosperity for everyone. Did we, human beings, do that?"

"Don't be naïve, Irene."

"Did we share the message of power we possess? Did we choose to be gods like God and create all the goodness? It's so simple! Be grateful. Create peace. Prosperity for everyone. There is enough for everyone to be happy. Create love. Love each other." Irene stops talking and takes another bite of her cookie. "My God, I'm not saying anything new! All the same, all the same," Irene says, looking at Taher, chewing.

"It's just not true. Look how people live in the refugee camps all over the world. How do you think they can get out of these camps? Can they do it with wishful thinking? Can Palestinians part the sea and walk out of Gaza?"

"Taher, just think about it. Maybe my grandmother was crazy, but I really believe that a person who discovers God's power in himself or herself becomes humble, and this humility brings clarity, and from this clarity they can desire only goodness. For all humanity."

"That's wishful thinking."

"Just imagine what God's power means."

"We don't have God's powers!"

"Just imagine it for a second. If you could achieve anything just by wishing it upon yourself, would you choose to kill your enemy, or would you choose to change him into your dearest faithful friend? What would you choose to have? A dead enemy at your feet or a faithful friend?"

"That's cute, but impossible."

"My grandmother said to me, 'I will tell you the secret. Use it and share it with everyone. First, be very careful what you wish for. Second, practice a feeling of gratitude every second of your life. Third, every night before going to bed, say this little prayer and teach it to everyone you possibly can.'

> For the wellbeing of all on this planet
> I am filled with gratitude
> I am filled with gratitude
> I am filled with gratitude

"She said, 'You can attract all the things you want, as long as you are sure you want what you ask for.'"

"How can you believe this nonsense? Do you know how many children are dying from hunger, disease, and conflict this very moment? Their wanting can't change anything. Do you know what *you* want, Irene?"

"You know, Taher, I thought about it. What *do* I want? I want my family to be healthy and happy. That's all. What else? Maybe one more thing. I want us to be together forever. I know that's silly, but I can't imagine my life without Marek, or Julie, or little Markie. If something were to happen, you know, a car accident, or something, I hope we all go together, and no one is left with sorrow, like my grandmother."

"I certainly don't agree with you," Taher says, still meaning her wishful thinking.

"Don't feel bad about it. Most people wouldn't agree with me, and that's why we are where we are as humans—constantly fighting each other."

They both pause and reach for another sweet.

"You know, she also said that there would be no peace for Israel or Palestine, because they don't believe that peace is possible."

"I might agree with her on that one," Taher says, swallowing.

"She said, if they would believe, then it would happen. Instead, they stock up on arms—this is the way they've chosen to live."

"Nonsense. Palestinians didn't have a choice," Taher says, and shakes his head.

"Jews didn't have one either, Taher." Now, Irene shakes her head.

"Okay, even if that's the case, their wishful thinking won't stop them from going to hell," he says.

"No, not necessarily," she says, lifting her arms. "If they could only help one another. They *are* brothers, after all—twins from the same womb—as my grandmother would say. She said there was one Jew who wanted to share this message with the rest of humanity. His name was Jesus, but we all know what happened to him. And what a sad thing, what a sad story, she would say. God sent him with a message of love. He was killed by the Romans, and those who became Christians made themselves prisoners in churches instead of freeing themselves from churches. Why? Because they rely on their churches instead of relying on what is within, on the message of the heart. They want the church to do the work for them, to take the responsibility. It can't be done this way."

"Help!" Marek calls, squeezing himself through the door with loads of baby diapers.

"Oh, I totally forgot about the diapers!" Irene jumps up and goes to the door. "Thank you, honey."

Both of them laugh and give each other a long welcome kiss. Marek is still holding the packs of diapers that display a baby's face and a red banner reading, "Extra Value," and Irene is embracing him and the packs.

They stand in the open door, joined in a private moment.

"How do I look?" Marek steps into the living room, smiling.

"Like you don't have your Kalashnikov." Taher stands up, laughing.

"I tend *life* now." Marek drops the packs on the floor next to Julie's playpen and approaches Taher with open arms.

"It's so good to see you," he says, giving him a hug and patting him on the back.

"It's good to see you too." Taher returns the affection.

"My God, how long has it been?" Marek asks.

"Ten years exactly." Taher smiles. "You have a nice family." Taher looks at Irene, who comes closer and touches Marek's elbow gently.

"Yes," Marek says, embracing her and kissing her forehead.

"Dadda, Dadda." Little Julie, wide awake, is standing up in her playpen, reaching toward Marek. "Up, up," she repeats, smiling, revealing tiny pearls of teeth.

"Here is my little princess." Marek reaches for her.

"Wash your hands," Irene whispers, trying to take Julie from him.

"Okay, we will go to the bathroom to wash Daddy's hands, okay?" Marek kisses Julie. "We will be right back," he says to Taher.

"Wash, wash." Julie's words mixed with Taher's—"Take your time."

"I'm telling you." Irene smiles, spreading her arms in a helpless gesture, shrugging her shoulders. "Family life is different. Have you ever read Swedenborg? I studied literature and taught a bit at a community college before the twins were born."

"I don't believe I have." Taher looks perplexed.

"I don't remember exactly if he was talking about perfect marriage, or perfect family, but I guess one leads to another. Anyway, he said that if it's perfect, then it's heaven."

"Heaven?"

"Yes, he said it's the closest thing on earth to heaven. It's like the taste of heaven on earth. Swedenborg meant the perfect union between a man and a woman. And the fruits of this union are children, of course, if they have children. Well, not everyone has to have children."

"Do you think you have this heaven?" Taher looks at her.

"Taher, I know I do." She stops for a moment. "I know I do," she answers, lengthening her spine as if energized by her own words. "Yes, I do have it." She looks him in the eye. She is motionless, full of grace and peace. Suddenly Taher notices details he hadn't seen before—the softness of the skin of her neck, a small silver pendant—a cross, a heart, and an anchor.

"It's not what you think," she says touching the pendant.

"Oh, I don't think anything." Taher looks at his cup.

"The heart is love for all that's beautiful in life. The anchor is Marek, Julie, and Markie. And the cross is wisdom. I don't consider myself a Christian. I don't see myself in any religion. I have regard for all of them. I just like Jesus, or I should say the version of Jesus from the Gnostic Gospels. I think he was an extraordinary human being. He was perfect. Jesus for me is the ultimate wisdom I would like to possess." She smiles softly.

"He wasn't bad, I have to admit." Taher smiles back. "We Muslims regard him as a great prophet too, you know."

"Hmmm." She nods, stroking her pendant.

"We're back!" Marek stands in the door holding both children. Little Markie is yawning, his cheeks reddened and eyes still half asleep. Julie is busy pulling on Marek's ear. "I think Junior needs to be changed." Marek leans forward, handing him to Irene.

Before Irene is able to take the boy from her husband, they hear knocking on the door, and then children's voices arguing and screaming.

"Oh, it must be Susan," Irene says, taking Markie to the foyer.

"Susan?" Marek calls after her.

"Yes, we want to do our hair," Irene calls back.

The foyer fills with voices of a woman and jumping children. "Mine, mine!" one child screams.

"Let go! Let go!" another answers. "Children, children, please, stop it! That's enough." A woman's voice tries and fails to stop the argument.

"I found it!" the girl persists.

"Yes, but I saw it first," the boy fights back.

"If you can't share, I will have to put it away," the mother says.

"That's not fair!" both of the children answer in unison.

*

The park is quiet. Only from time to time, someone passes the bench where Marek and Taher sit with their meal—hot dogs, French fries, pretzels, and Coke purchased from the concession stand.

"This reminds me of Afghanistan." Marek says and wipes his mouth with an open hand. "Fresh air, simple food, and nature around."

"You were always a joker," Taher says, and laughs. "No fresh air, nothing simple about this genetically modified and highly processed stuff we are having, and I don't really see any nature here. Nature is raw, not artificial like this!"

"You're wrong," Marek says, and reaches for his Coke.

A group of children on roller blades passes them, screaming. Their voices fade as they roll away.

"Wizard!" A single word resonates in the moist air of the evening.

"Magic was invented by the rich of the West." Taher's gaze and his index finger follow the path of the children.

"Why?"

"Because in places where childhood is unspoiled, there is no need for miracles." Taher points to the lake. "Just like this."

"What? I don't get it," Marek says and takes a sip of his Coke.

"Calm and steady. Then you reflect on the clouds and trees and all of it. You just listen, and it comes straight to you." Taher closes his eyes.

"What does?" Marek stops chewing and looks at the lake and then at Taher. "What?" he repeats anxiously.

"It comes from God, I mean. I miss Afghanistan." Taher leans his head on the back of the bench and closes his eyes.

"Yeah, me too, the sunsets and fighting, but shit, I don't miss the lack of drinking water and the pain in my kidneys."

"I mean, the life," Taher says, keeping his eyes closed. "Why did you get married?" he adds.

"Do you have something against marriage?"

"Nothing, except that it changes a man into a husband."

"What do you mean?" Marek dips his hand into the bag of fries.

"People here are preoccupied with so many things that they are completely disconnected from who they are and how they relate to the world around them. Just compare it with Afghanistan. Simplicity. Connection with earth, with oneself, with God. No need for miracles."

"Well," Marek puts aside the bag of fries and reaches for his Coke. "Poverty, starvation, lack of education. Sorry, Taher, I miss the mountains more than I can say, but the reality is—" He doesn't finish before Taher interrupts him.

"Education?" Taher sits up and stares at Marek. "What are you calling *education*? Regular visits to a shrink?"

"Don't oversimplify, Taher." Marek points to the lake. "Manmade, like everything else in this world, and it works."

"Don't complicate, Marek. Life wasn't supposed to be manmade, but God-made."

"Afghanistan, you say? But here, there is no enemy." Marek stretches his legs.

"No enemy? Everyone is an enemy of himself here," Taher says, getting up and starting to pace. "Just look around you. Greed. Overconsumption. Killing the planet. Advertisements for toilet paper. Sex. Money. Power. This is the wrong life." Taher turns to face Marek and spreads his arms. "Don't you see it?"

"I love Irene, Taher. I love her more than I can say, and I love my children. I would die for them at any moment of my life. Life is good for me."

"You don't remember anything we went through?" Taher says and lowers his arms.

"I do, and that is why I love the life I have now."

"What's good about it? Changing diapers? Sex with your wife?

Getting up in the middle of the night for a crying child? Going to work every day? Worrying and worrying? For what? To have things? To have toilet paper?"

"All of it and more. Including the worrying part. I feel I am in the right place...or something." Marek looks at Taher and tries to find the friend he left behind years ago. "I never really thought about it. I just enjoy living now. I can't imagine life without Irene and the kids. They are my everything. The beginning of me in them. I think of my mother often when I see Julie. The same eyes, the same energy. All of us as one, together and not alone. Irene filled the void my mother's death left in me. Remember, killing Russians in Afghanistan didn't help me. And when we met Wołodia, then I was done with killing for good. He helped me to understand why, with more killing, more of me was missing. With Irene, everything makes sense. Killing the Russians, nothing did." Marek falls quiet and looks at the lake.

"All for the body and nothing else," Taher says, sitting back down and looking at the lake, too.

"Taher, I go to the mosque now and then. I know I am more than just the flesh."

"Marek, you are just flesh right now. I see it clearly. All those ideas of freeing the world from—"

"From what, Taher? Tell me from what." Marek stands up and starts pacing back and forth. "This is life. Life is about living every day in peace with yourself. I have it now. I found it in the midst of changing diapers, holding my children, and making love to my wife. I found it here, in this park, while strolling down the paths with them and just taking all of it in, here. Taking it in here. Here!" He hits himself in the chest twice. "And you know what you do? You talk about Afghanistan in this romantic, unrealistic way. You are a romantic, Taher."

"*I* am? *You* are!" Taher points his finger at Marek. The surface of the lake is still, stretched between the lavish green of the shore, suspended between the sounds of birds, rustling leaves, and children playing nearby.

The sounds around them hum in an orderly incantation. First comes the sudden swoosh of wings parting the waters as ducks plunge in at full speed, then the sound of a bouncing ball. The high pitch of an infant cry is followed by the soft voice of a mother, "Hush, baby, hush." Old men laugh over their memories, "One hundred thousand bucks!" And two girls share poems by Rumi. They are sitting with their knees under their chins, their bare feet with bright red toenails are propped on the edge of the bench. One of them reads out loud—

> A pure heart, open to the Light, will be filled with the elixir of Truth.

They laugh and continue reading.

> Love was from the beginning of time, and love will
> be for all eternity.

"Listen, listen to this," one of them says, waving her hand and then tucking a long strand of hair behind her ear.

> We may know who we are or we may not.
> We may be Muslim, Jews, or Christians
> but until our hearts become the mold for every heart, we will
> see only our differences.

"Beautiful, just beautiful," says the other girl. They sit on the bench, but their belongings are scattered on a quilt nearby, among other items—two notebooks with red ribbon bookmarks, a collection of poems, *A Book of Luminous Things*, ankle bracelets, Diet Cokes, red apples, and potato chips on a paper plate.

And then there is a sound like rain on tin rooftops as a group of boys pass by on roller blades. They are followed by a group of bikers—tight yellow tops and black shorts, mirrored sunglasses. For a moment, the air reverberates with their panting as they push uphill. On the lawn near the lake, two golden retrievers jump high to catch bright tennis balls. Topless teenage boys throw Frisbees and boomerangs. Their torsos glisten in the hot, humid air. Young mothers place freshly prepared food on picnic tables with care and dedication—cheese sandwiches, hard boiled eggs, tuna salads, bowls of strawberries, blueberries, and dwarf apples. They have brought the food in a large picnic basket with a red and white checkered lining.

Suddenly, from behind a cluster of lush trees, a rowboat appears on the lake. It glides, cutting the water smoothly, leaving a wavy trail behind. A little boy on the boat screams, "Daddy, look, look!" The man on the boat shades his eyes with an open palm and turns to look at the center of the lake. The boy raises his arm with a stone and swings it with all the strength of his small body, leaning forward over the edge of the boat. The man, his father, catches him—one hand on the boy's chest, the other on his back. Both laugh.

Taher watches the scene, the waves made by the stone—how they rush from the center toward the shore, toward the boat, toward his feet, and thinks of his father. The memory of his own childhood is far away and very close. He can feel it bouncing around in his head, trying to find a place to land and settle.

"Don't you feel like life is sort of going in circles?" Taher says, looking at the boat, his gaze mesmerized and absent, drawn deeply into the unseen, where memories resurface like smoke, with no clear explanation.

"Like what?" Marek looks at him and then at the lake, searching for clues.

"Like repeating the same paths or maybe seeing that we all repeat the same paths, really. I don't know what I mean, exactly." Taher stares at the same point in the distance. "Sometimes I feel that we all really live the same lives, like we are the same, kind of twins," he says dreamily, still looking at the boat and the little boy.

"I know what you mean, like Julie and my mother."

"I suppose, something like that. But something else, too, something like loss. Like we lost something essential somewhere on our way to adulthood. This reminds me of my father," he says, pointing to the boat. "You know, sometimes I feel like life is a chess game," Taher says after hearing the two old men laugh. "We make some moves. There are consequences. People fight each other. One dies. The other lives." He pauses for a moment and then continues, "and it always seems that one has to kill in order to stay alive. Only one side can win, right?"

"Funny you say that." Marek lifts his chin and looks at the sky. "My dad and I used to play chess almost every day after dinner. It was like a ritual—dessert and chess. My mom's cheesecake and the wooden white and black pieces on the chessboard always came together. My father always played black, I always played white, and whoever won, we would say: 'Today the evil wins'—that was black—or 'today the angel wins'—that was white. I always felt that the game had bigger, sort of universal implications."

"Like you were writing human history with your game or something?" Taher asks, but still thinks about his own father and the familiar feeling that washed over him at the sight of the boat and the lake. For a moment, everything connects and forms a monolithic piece—the little boy on the boat, his own memories, and Marek's story.

"We *were* the microscopic example of human history, if you want to look at it that way." Marek smiles at his own words. "Well, as a child, I truly believed that all my moves on the board were bringing concrete results in real life. You know—" He chuckles. "As if . . . every evening after dinner we decided, with the outcome of our game, what would prevail on earth for all of humanity. That's how I felt."

"That's funny."

"I can still remember how peaceful I felt after winning, beating the evil. I always went to bed with a strong conviction that I was safe and that the world was safe, thanks to me."

"Yes, to feel that kind of conviction again would—" Taher says, but doesn't finish.

"But there is something else." Marek turns to face the lake. He starts slowly, remembering something difficult. "My mother used to say that killing the opponent in chess makes you die also—because there are no more moves left for you either. The end of the game is the end of life for both sides, she used to say," Marek says and looks at Taher. "Does that make sense to you?" he asks.

"Winning is winning, that's it," Taher says.

"But the game is over, you have to admit."

"Yeah, but otherwise, there would be no game." Taher looks at the lake and freezes, as if seeing something for the first time.

"Why did you get married? Like, really—" Taher asks.

"Because, in the darkness, sometimes I can see her wings." Marek's gaze turns inward, far away from Taher and the park, far away from the lake and the soft light reflected on the water. Marek's eyes are looking but not seeing. Taher—silent and mesmerized— waits for the story.

"I swear, she has big white wings. The tips of the feathers are golden. They sparkle in darkness, like stars. When she lies on her left side, they fold behind her back. I've seen them many times in the middle of the night, when I'm coming back from the bathroom. I swear they are real. I've seen her so many times like this—naked, with her knees slightly bent, with this fabulous curve of her hip, and her tiny waist—palms folded together under her cheek. And the wings reaching over her head and coming down all the way to her feet. The feathers are soft and kind of alive. As if each one of them is separate but also a part of this glowing whiteness at the same time. I don't know how to explain it exactly."

Marek falls silent and covers his face. He is revealing his deepest secret for the first time. He is relieved and ashamed, but he knows that Taher is the only person—like a twin brother—who can understand this.

"Marek, are you okay?" Taher whispers, touching Marek's shoulder gently.

"I know it's impossible, but I know I've seen the wings many times," Marek whispers.

"You can talk to me about it anytime, you know."

"I know," Marek continues. "I never told anyone—"

"I know." Taher's voice pulls Marek in.

And what it brings stands in their memory, undimmed by what surrounds them at the lake. They look at each other and know without a doubt what the other is thinking—the images seem to come out of their minds and connect in the space between them. They both feel it—the closeness of the days when they dipped flatbreads in a peasant clay dish filled with green oil. There is the clay dish. There are their fingers dripping with oil. And the long trips in the mountains—long winter days. And caves. And silence shared in solace. There is the time of sudden loss and the time of great hope. And then the vast landscape illuminated with colors rich and vibrant—gold and carmine, silvered with the sharp edges of the mountains, or softened by rolling green hills. And then there are the sunrises that didn't resemble anything else in the world, as if God had chosen the place for himself to dwell in and enjoy. And then there are the images of exhaustion—snow falling for weeks, and the words of the Qur'an shared five times a day. And then—there are the sounds of machine guns and the fear of death, and the echoes and echoes of steps.

Naim

"Of course, death means a lot. The important thing is to know why."

—*Ghassan Kanafani*

"Everyone should remember I died pure of heart."

—*Shahid*

Three years later, Taher and Ahmed walk fast with Naim along narrow alleys that are sinking quickly into nightfall. The light behind them recedes softly, and the contours of the houses they pass are losing their details fast. The air is filled with faint smells of smoke and freshly baked bread.

"We're almost there," Naim says, looking straight ahead. "They should be waiting for us."

They pass a huge pile of rubble, a rupture in a row of small houses. It is filled with tall grass bending gently in the breeze coming in from the fields behind. They pass everyday things, reminders of life's sudden endings—a red crossbar of a small bicycle, shredded car tires, the green back of a chair, and a dark bedframe still holding the heap of a mattress's white entrails. Along the way, some of the tall walls over their heads are ruptured by explosions. Twisted arms of metal rods hold pieces of concrete and brick, hanging in midair like abstract art. Between them, stairs lead to nonexistent rooms. Locked doors guard nothing in the sky-filled spaces. They pass houses crumbled into a mass of silent loss—endings too sudden.

"What's that?" Taher sniffs the air, lifting his chin.

"A car," Naim answers, without slowing down. "Exploded, still burning over there." He points to the alley on the left. "There was a fight with the Israelis today."

Taher looks there but can't see anything. The dusk has swallowed the shapes already, leaving only the closest surroundings visible.

The fading light withdraws into long shadows, slithering along the chipped walls of the houses. Patches of disappearing illuminations wander between the white sheets on a short laundry line, slide down onto the toys left behind—a blue ball and a one-eyed plush bear. In the niches and nooks, they sink into the blackness of the barren soil.

The three men turn into an alley that winds over cracked plates of concrete through a narrow passage between high walls.

"Watch your head," Naim says, squeezing himself into a small opening without a door. "Follow me."

They enter a small, confined space with a ceiling that hangs just above their heads.

"Here you are!" Naim says into the darkness of the room.

"We've been waiting here for ages," a male voice with a heavily accented Arabic says from the darkness.

"This is Taher and Ahmed," Naim says into the dark. "They were late. Smuggling across the border is never punctual." He gives a short laugh.

"Where did you come from?" asks a female voice, also with a strong accent.

"From the east, from Egypt," Naim answers for them. "Ahmed and Taher are our saviors and heroes. They bring money and antibiotics. Thanks to them, we can buy weapons. The medicine they bring has saved many lives already."

"We are doing our small part," Ahmed says. "You guys are on the ground. You are the heroes."

"This is Greta from Germany and Jean Paul from France. They are with the International Solidarity Movement," Naim says.

Gradually, their eyes become accustomed to the darkness. Greta is tall and thin. She is wearing jeans, a corduroy jacket, and a black and white checkered *keffiyeh* around her neck, on top of her long blonde hair. Jean Paul towers over her, hunching forward. His long, wavy hair forms an unruly cloud around his forehead. Both of them are wearing orange vests with silver reflective stripes across their chests.

"Hi," they say together and chuckle.

"*Salam*," Taher and Ahmed answer. "We can barely see you, but we can hear you very well," Ahmed adds, laughing.

"Okay, let's go. We don't have much time before the curfew." Naim signals for everyone to follow him outside.

Back on the street, they go through another scattered neighborhood. They pass walls covered with white graffiti, still visible in the low light of the evening: "Long live the Intifada," "Long live Hamas," "Long live Jihad." Silent faces of women in open windows recede into the shadows of rooms behind them. Young boys with toy guns stand in an open door and greet them with curious eyes and smiles. A woman on a small balcony rocks her infant. They pass more houses turned into rubble and tall cylinders of old car tires piled up and encircled with wire fences. Behind the fence lie more abandoned objects—cabinet doors with chipped glass knobs and piles of mattress stuffing boiling over deep cuts in the fabric, a wooden horse with one rocker, white parts of furniture, window frames and doorframes, burned car frames—skeletons leaning into nothingness.

They walk quickly, in silence—Taher, Ahmed, and Naim with heavy backpacks, Greta and Jean Paul with signs that read: "International Solidarity Movement," and "Justice and Peace." They walk to Naim's house—located on the outskirts of a refugee camp—where they'll spend the night. The only sound they hear as they pass the refugee camp—where shacks made of cardboard form alleys among patches of tiny gardens—is their own hurried steps.

Stepping in through the front door, Naim warns, "Watch your step and—"

The room on the first floor is prepared for their visit with food displayed on a round tablecloth in the middle of a worn carpet adorned with bright pillows. There is fresh baked bread that still gives off a warm smell of home, *zaatar* with olive oil next to it, and a big bowl of salad—fresh tomatoes, onions, and cucumbers.

"We knew you would be late, so Yasmin baked the bread just a little while ago," an older man says, smiling broadly. "Smuggling through the border can't be timed precisely. We have learned that many times. How did it go?"

"It wasn't bad," Ahmed answers. "They didn't search the truck, so we were lucky, but crossing the desert took us longer than we thought. The Bedouins knew their way around, and the Israeli soldier who got us through the border knew what he was doing. He was paid well. But still, we weren't able to predict the time at all."

"Hmm," the older man nods. "You are young and strong." He lowers his gaze. "It's easy for you, even if you have to wait."

"Yeah, Grandfather, everyone is young and strong at one point in their lifetime, and should take advantage of it when they still can," Naim says, as they all sit down around the food.

The room becomes silent for a moment. Everyone understands Naim's cutting words, but no one wants to engage.

"What's this?" Jean Paul asks after a while, dipping his bread in olive oil and pointing to the small dish with green powder and sesame seeds.

"It's *zaatar*," the grandfather answers.

"What is it?"

"Just dip your bread in it," Naim's grandfather says. "It's ground thyme, sesame seeds, and sumac."

"What's *sumac*?"

"This red sour thing. Is it an herb, Naim?" The grandfather looks at silent Naim.

Naim doesn't answer.

"Maybe your sister can answer this for us," his grandfather says quietly. "Yasmin, is sumac an herb or a vegetable?"

"Grandfather doesn't want you to die," Yasmin says softly to Naim, kneeling next to the old man.

The room becomes silent again. Greta sucks on a strand of her hair. Her big blue eyes stare absentmindedly into space. Jean Paul tries to pull his unruly hair behind his ears. Both Taher and Ahmed look at the floor. Yasmin puts her hand on Grandfather's shoulder and says to Naim, "And I don't want you to die, either."

"If not me, then who?" Naim looks at his sister. "You?"

"Stop it." Yasmin squeezes her grandfather's shoulder. Her dark eyes are wide.

"Not Grandfather," Naim continues with force. "His generation had the chance in Deir Yassin, but chose to flee."

"That was different!" his grandfather says. "In 1948, we were the first village to be attacked. No one knew what would happen." He pauses.

As soon as he finishes the sentence, the house is shaken by a nearby explosion. Taher and Ahmed jump. No one else moves.

"That's why we are here," Jean Paul explains, smiling broadly.

"To stop the demolition of houses," Greta adds, still nibbling on her hair. "They usually start early in the morning; that's why we sleep here, to be ready when they come." Her words are punctuated by intense gunfire.

"But why are they shooting?" Ahmed asks.

"Just for fun," Jean Paul answers. "To keep us up all night long, I suppose, just to torture us with sleep deprivation." He and Greta give a short laugh. "But they're not very successful."

"No, they shoot to let us know that they're still there and won't leave," Naim adds.

"No, they shoot because they're scared. Just like us. They are kids, scared kids," the grandfather says softly.

"They're not scared." Naim looks him in the eye. "They butcher our children. They have helicopters. They have a well-equipped army. We have nothing. We are the ones who are scared. And that's why we have to fight them the way we fight them."

"I'm against suicide missions." Taher's words surprise everyone. "If that's what you're talking about, that is."

"You're from Egypt. You don't get it," Naim bridles.

"Convince me." Now Taher's words are interrupted by gunfire. "Let me play devil's advocate," he says.

"If I won't go, who will?" Naim says impatiently.

"Okay, but why *you?*" Taher asks, pointing at Naim.

"Why *not* me? I ask *that* question, and I don't see a reason why not. That's all." Naim spreads his arms.

"You didn't answer my question."

"I won't, because your question is not my problem. My problem is the opposite question, 'Why *not* me?'"

"Okay, just try to answer my question and see what comes up."

"I can't. This question is not my reality. The other is. And let me tell you something, Taher. One day, the question will change for you too. You will ask yourself—'Why *not* me?' The day will come. Mark my words." Naim smiles. "We all go the same route here, all of us. And if you are one of us, you will get it one day. You will feel liberated from everything and connected to everything and everyone you ever loved. It's heaven."

"Heaven?" Taher snorts.

"Yes, the peace of mind you gain. It's heaven." Naim smiles, sighing deeply.

"Okay. Let me ask you—what comes from killing yourself, even if you kill your enemies at the same time? I will tell you what. From killing comes nothing. Nothingness."

"My killing is not about killing. And that's what you're not getting." Naim's words are calm. He gazes slowly around the room, connecting with the silent faces turned toward him. "My killing is about dignity, about integrity, about freedom for my people, about preserving my heritage. It's *against* nothingness. Do you know what nothingness is? Nothingness is Deir Yassin, that village that was wiped off the map forever. Why? Because someone wanted it that way. I am trying to reverse it. I'm reversing history. I am bringing the memory of Deir Yassin back to life. If no one does it, they will never be remembered, like they never existed. The murdered ones need a mark to remember their end. It has to be remembered because it needs to be understood by the future generations. So, my killing is about life. I'm not killing to destroy. I'm killing to bring something to life, back to life."

"You don't see other ways of 'bringing to life?'" Taher isn't ready to give up.

"Do you? Maybe somewhere else in the world there are other ways of 'bringing something to life,' but not here, not for us. What do we have to fight with except our bodies? Nothing!"

"I don't know." Taher lowers his gaze. "I'm not saying that I have all the answers." He dips his bread in oil and allows the heavy drops to trickle for a while over the yellow surface before touching the *zaatar.* "I've seen death in my life," he starts slowly.

The gunfire stops. Everyone looks at Taher. Greta is still nibbling on her hair, and Jean Paul rubs his knuckles. Ahmed is motionless, waiting to hear what is said. Yasmin is still close to her grandfather, her hand on his arm. For a moment, the room is still in silence. Taher puts aside the piece of bread he has been holding and continues his tale.

"I saw that killing makes life fragmented. Just pieces and pieces that no one can put back together. Nothing whole and nothing connected. Everything is separated from everything. I don't see a solution in killing." He looks at the floor in front of him, as if mesmerized by the tablecloth. "I feel that killing brings only retaliation, which means more killing. We kill ourselves, and they kill us. Think about it: by killing ourselves, we create a narrative of victimhood for them, instead of showing the world that *we* are the victims, that we are the defenseless ones."

"Why are you dwelling on it if you don't have a different solution?" Naim interrupts. "And why do you say 'we'? You have nothing to do with it."

"I don't know."

"If the villagers from Deir Yassin had not run the way they did, maybe Deir Yassin would still be on the map today." Naim doesn't look at his grandfather.

"It was early morning. I was still in my pajamas," his grandfather says. "One hundred and thirty of their commandos attacked the village. There were maybe seven hundred and fifty of us, a small place. It was a massacre. Mostly children, women, and elders were killed. About two hundred and fifty. I saw many of them being killed. Like animals." He wipes away tears. "People didn't expect anything like that. They didn't fight. They weren't prepared. For the first time in my life, that day, I saw adults more scared than children. That was what scared me. For the first time, the adults didn't know what to do. Their eyes were wild with fear." He stops for a long while and then continues. "My mother pushed me under the bed, and I stayed there until the next day, looking at her body just a few meters away from me, on the kitchen floor, motionless."

"Exactly!" Naim cuts in. "They didn't fight. They were scared. They fled. That's why there is no Deir Yassin on the map today, and no one knows, and no one remembers. Where is the memorial? Did you see it? It doesn't exist! Like the place never existed. Like the people weren't killed. Like it never happened. It's a disgrace to all humankind."

"You don't know what you would do in their place," Taher says, and picks up the piece of bread he had dipped in *zaatar*.

"Who are you?" Naim's eyes widen. "Which side are you on? You are not playing the devil's advocate, you *are* the devil. Are you a collaborator?"

"No, I'm not. I'm helping Ahmed. I'm not saying I understand everything." Taher's voice softens.

"You will one day, and you will take a side. I'm sure of it. And it will be our side, because there is no other choice for us." Naim dips his bread in oil and gently touches it to the *zaatar*. "Taher, let me tell you something." He reaches for the next piece of bread. "And this is for you, too." He points his finger at Yasmin. "The math of history is very simple. Someone has to die. We have to die because our grandparents wanted to live, and we have to die so the next generations can have a life."

"I want to protect our lives without dying," Taher says quietly.

"How?" Naim snorts. "Don't be naïve! What choice do we have?"

"There must be a way of living without dying. A different way," Taher adds.

"Where did you learn that?" Naim snorts again.

"Taher studied medicine in Hamburg for four years. It rubbed off," Ahmed jokes, but no one is amused.

"I'm from there," Greta protests. "I agree with Taher. Killing yourself doesn't give you what you want. It only gives the Israelis an excuse to kill more."

"That's why we protest peacefully," Jean Paul adds. "We don't want you or anybody else to die."

"And who said I am going to die?" Naim unfolds his arms. "Most likely I won't, because I'm talking about it. Those who do it are silent. They don't talk about it."

"The *way* you talk makes it clear." Yasmin sits down next to her grandfather. "It's just a new way, a new tactic to make us believe that you won't do it."

"Your logic is clouded. It's full of holes, Yasmin. There is no other, no better way. That's all I am saying," he says, reaching for the salad.

"And by the way, you look like a Jew. I thought you were a Jew," Taher says to Naim.

"And that's why I would be the perfect candidate." Naim looks at Yasmin. "But I am not saying anything."

"Yes, because it's supposed to be a secret," Yasmin says, frowning, serving salad in a small bowl to her grandfather.

"Sir," Greta asks the old man. "Tell us more about the day when you were attacked." She reaches for a cup of tea, her hand shaking slightly. "Tell us what you remember."

The grandfather puts his salad bowl aside and closes his eyes. Two kerosene lamp flames flicker in the far corners of the room. The bare walls are peppered with bullet holes and white patches of plaster—the crooked roads of a shattered life in a refugee camp.

"I was thirteen years old. I remember it was a beautiful day." The grandfather keeps his eyes closed. "The almond trees were blooming. The little kids spent their days running around the orchards. The air was thick with the sweet smell of flowers. It was heaven on earth until *they* came, until they burned the bodies in the quarry. That was when I learned about the smell of burning human flesh. It lingered in the air for weeks. Some nights, I can still remember that smell. We had olive trees, lemons, oranges, tomatoes, and kusa."

"What's *kusa?*" Greta asks, sipping her tea.

"Squash," Yasmin answers, handing her a bowl of sugar.

"They destroyed over four hundred villages. Hundreds of thousands of people became refugees. People who were afraid that Deir Yassin would be repeated, so they fled. You see, Naim?" He opens his eyes and looks at his grandson. "We fled the village, but stayed in the country. We didn't die. We became refugees on our own soil. My older sister escaped to Tripoli. She left all her possessions. Her books, the books she loved so much! She thought that the war would be short, and she would come back. But she wasn't allowed to return, ever. And she was never compensated for anything. Sometimes I wonder if we did the right thing, or if she did."

"None of you made the right choice," Naim says. His words are sharp.

"You don't understand everything, Naim," his grandfather says calmly. "And you don't know everything, either."

"What don't I understand? What don't I know?"

"My grandmother was Jewish." The grandfather looks him straight in the eye.

"What?" Naim drops his piece of bread into the golden pool of oil.

"My grandmother was Jewish, and my grandfather was from Deir Yassin. My grandfather lived there all his life, just like many generations of his family before him," he continues. "And they were the perfect couple. My grandmother was the most beautiful girl in the village, and my grandfather the handsomest man." He pauses. "My grandmother talked about the Jewish people with passion. She used to tell me stories about their lives as if all the Jews were dead. As if they were part of an ancient history. She used to say, 'Biblical people without a land, biblical people without a spot on earth.' And when they started coming from Europe after the First World War, and then the Second, I felt like they were rising from the dead. I felt so lucky to be witnessing this miracle. My grandmother used to say, 'They are kissing the soil.' I had never seen anyone kissing the soil, but in my mind, they were all going down on their knees and bowing to the land that was taken away from them two thousand years ago. In their long black coats and hats." He pauses for a moment and then continues. "My grandmother didn't see it the way I did, and it took me many years to understand what she said to my grandfather in a letter she wrote to him."

He reaches inside his pocket and retrieves a folded piece of paper. He unfolds it carefully and, putting his glasses on, he reads—

My Dearest Muhammad,

I wish I could explain the world to you and to myself, but I feel it has become impossible. For all I know, I wanted this to happen. I wanted them to have the land that they carried in their hearts for a millennium. I wanted them to reunite with their place. Because for me, it is their place. Theirs and ours. I wanted to witness this exceptional reunion. I myself felt like I was reuniting with something bigger than me, something sacred and given as a gift from God, that so many of us waited for so long.

And so deserved! And so deserved, my dearest! After all the suffering they went through, it's all so clear to me. When I think about Auschwitz and the deaths of innocents in gas chambers. Their bodies turned into soap. Their gold teeth melted into wedding rings for others. Who would imagine, who would imagine that the human race was capable of this?

I didn't expect that their own Holocaust would spill over to this sacred land. I didn't expect that they would carry their Holocaust and pass it on to us. Because our suffering, one day, will become their suffering. This is how the universe works.

It almost feels like there was no other choice. History made a full circle when the lost children of the land came back to destroy the land they longed for. And now, we are paying the price. We Palestinians, and we Jews, over and over again.

Salam, my love,
Sarah

"My great-great-grandmother was Jewish, and I didn't know anything about it?" Naim looks at his grandfather in disbelief.

"You look just like her," his grandfather answers. "And you talk with the same passion. That's why I understand your anger and your sense of injustice. You are a romantic, just like Sarah."

Naim buries his face in his hands. No one moves. No one reaches for food. No one speaks. Some things must be left undisturbed to become real.

They sit in the pulsating shroud of flickering flame from the kerosine lamp. The waves of golden amber and translucent blues wash over them and climb up the walls marked with holes and patches that stand like history checkpoints. Each one of them is sinking deeper and deeper into their own thoughts, disappearing from the others, vanishing quietly and without a trace. Separate from one another, they see different worlds. One of them is in the desert, where the blazing sun is pushing sweat into his eyes. Someone else is flying towards the horizon that is disappearing and emerging from behind the mountains. She is surprised by the voices that seem close, yet undistinguishable. Another is sinking again and again, giving up to the earth his entire weight, unable to lift himself. Someone else is drowning, water rising over his head. He can see the white crests of waves arched above, all the way to the sky. Dwelling in different worlds of their minds, they all arrive at the same conclusion—life is one, and it has one aim: to unify.

Suddenly, they hear a loud knock at the door. Yasmin opens it and invites a young boy in.

"They closed the roads. Can I stay for the night?" the boy asks, stepping in.

"Yussef, you are always welcome," the grandfather says, smiling. "Are you hungry?"

"No, thank you, I ate at my friend's house," Yussef answers.

"Let's rest then. It's late." With Yasmin's help, the grandfather rises to his feet. "And tomorrow, Yussef, you can work as a guide. What do you say?

"I say, *inshallah*. God willing."

"*Inshallah*," the grandfather says, leaving the room.

*

"It's not far from here." Yussef wipes his nose on his sleeve. "Two more blocks," he adds, sniffling.

"How old are you?" Taher asks the young guide.

"Almost nine," Yussef answers, puffing out his chest and smiling.

"But I know everything about the resistance movement."

"What does that mean, 'almost nine?'" Taher laughs and pokes the boy on the shoulder. "Does it mean seven or eight and a half?"

"Oh, no, it means eight and three quarters." Yussef kicks a rock and hops twice. "In December, I will turn nine. Seriously!"

"I think you are so close to your birthday that you can say you are nine. Officially. I think you can say that. What do you think, Taher?" Ahmed asks, winking and smiling.

"I think Ahmed is right. You can say it officially at this point. And how come you know everything about the resistance movement?"

"Everybody knows about the resistance movement!"

"Yes." Taher looks at Ahmed and scratches his head. "But you said you know *everything*, that's different."

"I know," the boy starts slowly, "because of my friend Said," he says, kicking another rock, but differently. The bounce in his step is lost.

"What about him?"

"When he was killed by a rocket that hit his house, I decided to join the resistance movement. He was my best friend." Yussef touches his chest. "He was like my brother. Some people thought that we were twins."

"Said is a martyr," Ahmed says, touching the boy's shoulder firmly. "You can be proud of him."

"I am," Yussef looks up. "And I want to become a martyr too," he adds proudly.

"Does your mother know?" Taher stops and looks at the boy.

"She is against it," Yussef answers softly. "But mothers are always against it, and *after* they are proud to see their son on a big poster. Only heroes are on posters, you know. And I have four brothers, so if I die and become a martyr, my mother will still have four sons left," he says, smiling. The bounce in his step is back.

They turn the corner and immediately find themselves surrounded by a group of small boys running and screaming. "I killed him! I killed him!" the smallest one yells at top of his lungs, lifting up his chin. Their bare feet raise clouds of fine dust.

"With a bottle of gas!" yells someone else.

"Let every household give a martyr!" A strong male voice comes out of the megaphone. "One martyr after another!" The voice comes closer. "Every day, one martyr from every neighborhood. There is only victory or martyrdom. Be vigilant!"

A red Toyota pickup truck passes them slowly. On the bed of the truck stands a man with a megaphone. He reaches for a bottle of water, takes a sip, and then brings the megaphone back to his mouth. He wipes his forehead with the back of his hand and then screams—"Be a martyr!" When the pickup truck sways on potholes, the man spreads his feet wide and grabs the back of the cabin. When he notices Yussef, he waves to him and smiles. Yussef waves back. "Let every household give a martyr! Surrender is disgrace. There is only Jihad!" the man yells as the pickup truck drives away in a cloud of powdery soft dust.

"It's here." Yussef says and points to a low metal door.

They enter a dark hallway that leads them to the underground. They pass rooms that are either empty or furnished sparsely—a table with no chairs in one, a metal bed with a bare mattress in another.

In the last room, seven men in black face masks sit on pillows propped against the wall. They all hold rifles. Their face masks reveal only their eyes—glossy beads moving in search of something urgent.

When Ahmed, Taher, and Yussef enter the room, two of the men get up, and after a brief conversation, take their backpacks and leave.

The side walls of the room are covered in posters of martyrs. In the middle of the central wall hangs a calendar with a close-up of a young face with angelic eyes. Beneath the photograph is a bold line in Arabic and English—"Ahmed-Ahmed, the martyr of September."

The calendar is surrounded by handwritten notes:

My mission is in revenge
for the spilled blood of my brothers.
The blood of our women, the blood of our elders,
the blood of our children.
My mission is for the blood of a newborn Imam.
Jihad is the only hope.

Allah is Great.
My death is a revenge
For the death of my father
For the death of my mother
For the death of my brother
For the death of my daughter.
Allah is Great.
I am dying for the death of my sister
for the death of my brother
and my cousin.
I am dying to avenge
the death of my wife.
I am dying for my home.

"So, Yussef, are you ready?" One of the men in face masks approaches the boy.

Yussef shrugs his shoulders as if trying to cover his ears, and presses his knuckles together.

"I think I am," he answers quietly, smiling.

"You think?" the man places his weapon against the wall. "The freedom fighter has to be sure. Always sure and ready to die. You know this, right?"

"I am ready to die," Yussef says quietly, lowering his gaze, trying to stand up straight.

"Oh, no, you sound like you're not." The man places his hands on the boy's shoulders.

The boy looks up into the bright eyes in the narrow space of the face mask. The eyes blink twice.

"Do you know why you sound like you're not ready?" the man asks and squeezes the boy's shoulders.

"Because I am too young?" the boy asks, swaying gently from side to side under the man's arms.

"No, not because you are too young!" The man laughs.

"Why then?"

"Because you are too quiet!" the man laughs again. "You have to be strong and loud so everyone will see you!" He pats Yussef's cheek gently.

"Oh, okay." The boy smiles shyly.

"But first, I want to see if you're smart," the man says, leading the boy to two chairs in the middle of the room.

They sit down facing each other, and the man starts explaining his test.

"I will put my hands like this," the man says, extending his arms in front of him with his palms up. "And you put your hands on top of mine," the man adds.

Yussef, sitting on the edge of the chair, follows the request timidly.

"Okay, now I'll do this!" The man's hands turn up swiftly and hit the top of Yussef's hands.

Yussef pulls his hands back, laughing and grimacing at the same time.

"Did it hurt?" the man asks.

"No!" the boy says loudly.

"Good! Now, you hit me." The man extends his arms with palms facing down, waiting for Yussef to put his underneath.

Yussef's small hands disappear for a while under the cover and then come up in a wide arc, but miss the man's hands. The man is fast and knows when to pull his hands back.

All the men in the room laugh. Yussef places his hands under his thighs and smiles.

"You have to be quick!" the man says. "Otherwise, they'll get you before you can get them," he says, patting the boy's face.

"I will get them." The boy lowers his gaze and shrugs.

"Let's try one more time." The man extends his hands, palms up. As soon as the boy extends his hands, the blow comes down hard.

"Now, your turn." The man doesn't wait.

Yussef stands up, pushes his chair back, and takes his turn. He stays motionless and focused for a long while before making his move, this time successfully hitting the tops of the man's hands.

"Very good!" The man shakes the boy strongly, grabbing his upper arms. "Yussef, you are a very smart boy, and I think that you qualify to fight and even to die." The room erupts with congratulations. The other men in face masks clap and yell their approval. One of them screams, "Yussef!"

Yussef smiles, extends his spine proudly, and looks around the room.

"Now you can go home, and remember"—the man raises his index finger—"You can't tell anyone, not even your mother." He shakes his finger in the air.

"I know *that!*" the boy says loudly.

As soon as the boy leaves, all the men in the room remove their masks and put their weapons away. Two of them leave and after a while return with food—green bean stew and rice. The man who tested Yussef introduces himself as Hassan.

"I'm sorry Naim couldn't come, but I'm happy you're here," he says to Ahmed and Taher. "Let's sit down and eat. You must be hungry."

"I'm not hungry at all." Taher stares at him.

"Just sit down," Ahmed says quietly, touching his shoulder.

"No, I don't want to sit down, and I don't want to eat." He doesn't stop staring at Hassan.

"What's wrong?" Hassan asks in surprise.

"How can you do that?" Taher's eyes grow wild.

"What?"

"How can you send them to their deaths? Children." Taher's voice rises.

"Oh, is that what you think?" Hassan steps back.

"No, I don't *think* that. That's a fact. You send those children to die."

"What do you know about life in a refugee camp? And who are you to judge?" Hassan steps back again. He needs more distance to scan the newcomer.

"What you are doing doesn't help anybody." Taher steps forward. "It doesn't gain us anything."

"Don't you tell me what helps and what doesn't. I was born in a refugee camp. I live with the demolition of our houses. I live with women giving birth at checkpoints. I live with our ambulances being shot at by the occupiers. I live with people deposed of their land—the land that belonged to them from the time they can't even remember, from forever. I live every day with humiliation. Here, where you can't move without your identification card, and where you are jailed when your identification card is taken by their guards and not returned to you. I live around the wounded, the elders, children, women. I live around people jailed without a trial for years. I live in a place that is deprived of witnesses to come and just see what's going on. In a place that attracts college students from all over the world to protest in solidarity movements because no one else is interested. I live here, in the most blessed place on earth that became hell for us because of the occupation."

"I'm against sending children to their deaths, that's all." Taher moves back a step.

"And what do you suggest instead?" Hassan steps forward. "Begging for help from the UN? The USA? Where else? Arab countries? We have done that already. And if you haven't noticed, nobody cares! You need to get that!"

"I understand. I see your point of view, and it still doesn't explain why you have to send children to their deaths, and make the rest of us look like monsters."

Hassan's face becomes motionless. He approaches Taher, looking him straight in the eye. All the gazes in the room focus on Hassan's slim body—tight black T-shirt and black jeans. He moves like liquid. His well-defined arms twitch as he tightens his fists. His chest rises and falls with long breaths. He stops in front of Taher, just inches away from his face.

"Yes, we *are* monsters. All of us. We're monsters because we were born in hell." His face draws even closer to Taher's. "And we send our children to death because that's the only dignity we're allowed to have."

"Dignity?" Taher snorts. "What are you talking about? You're killing your own children to kill the occupiers! Where do you see dignity in that?" Taher's breath is fast. He faces his opponent and doesn't move.

Hassan pushes Taher with all his strength. "You, you're just a little boy from a nice neighborhood in Egypt. What do you know?

You're not even listening to what I'm saying!" He pushes him again. Taher steps back but doesn't give in.

"The killing will turn against you. One day, you'll see." Taher's voice is strong. His words come as an incantation, meticulous and forceful. He sounds convincing and that enrages Hassan.

He pushes Taher again, his anger growing.

"Stop pushing me!" Taher yells.

"No! You show me what you do when you are pushed over and over again, little boy from Egypt."

"Stop pushing me!" Taher yells again.

"No, you show me what you do, when you're pushed and pushed—" Hassan hits Taher's chest several more times.

"Stop it!"

"No!"

Then comes the blow. Taher loses his balance and falls. Dark blood starts dripping from his lower lip. It sinks into his white T-shirt in oval spots.

"Oh, you're bleeding," Hassan grimaces. "Poor baby. But it's all your fault. If you didn't have teeth, you wouldn't have cut your lip!" He lowers his face over Taher, who is sitting on the floor, touching his lip gently.

"Why did you do that?" Taher looks up.

"It was historically and politically motivated and justified. I am sure of that," Hassan says, his face contorted with disdain.

"You are an aggressive idiot, Hassan!" Taher gets up and faces Hassan. "You"—he points his finger at Hassan's chest—"you, Hassan, are an aggressive idiot!" Again, Taher's words come out as a forceful incantation. "You don't win by being an idiot! Idiots never win!"

Then comes the second blow. Taher lands on his elbows.

"What do you expect from someone who was jailed for seventeen years? I have my own Holocaust to share with you. Do you want to hear a story of my personal Holocaust? You well-fed, well-dressed, well-traveled, well-educated boy?" Hassan's body grows over Taher. "Do you want to hear how they knocked out my front teeth and forced me to swallow them, or would you prefer the part where they locked me in a cell the size of a coffin for months, and left me there in my own shit and piss?"

Taher gets up slowly and, wiping his lips, looks at Ahmed. Ahmed doesn't move.

"Killing comes from killing. I know that," Taher says slowly. "And that's why *someone* has to stop." He looks at Hassan.

"Not me." Hassan snorts. "You can stop all you want. I have to fight. That was the life I was given by the occupier."

"Don't try to explain everything away with the occupation." Taher's words are muffled. His lips are swelling fast. "You have your own choices to make."

"I'm sure. A whole variety. I just haven't learned about them yet. Why don't you teach me? Teach me about the Holocaust." Hassan nods as if calling for the beginning of a fight.

"You don't understand the meaning of Holocaust." Taher's words are more muffled than before. His lower lip spills over, swollen red and purple.

"You tell me, Taher, pretty boy from Egypt, you tell me what it is. I bet *you* know." Hassan spreads his arms and turns toward the men sitting against the wall. No one reacts. They all are just watching the scene.

"I know what it's *not*." Taher gets up slowly.

"No, you don't know anything." Hassan interrupts him and moves back. His entire body twitches like a pulled string. "A Holocaust is something no one can get over. It doesn't matter if it's personal or national. There is no other choice than to pass it on to someone else. It's too much to keep for yourself." Hassan's last words come slowly, with the same grimace of disdain. The men by the wall laugh.

"Yeah, you have to share it," someone else repeats to another eruption of laughter.

Taher stops.

I remember the graffiti on the wall. It was in English. ARABS TO THE GAS CHAMBERS! The concrete wall was built on rocks. I remember the lines in the wall left by the boards that held it before it became a wall. ARABS TO THE GAS CHAMBERS! All in capital letters with an exclamation point.

"Yeah, but it's nothing you want to share with your loved ones," someone else adds, laughing as well. "But you do it for your loved ones," Hassan says.

"You're all romantics." Taher looks around the room, then repeats again: "You're all delusional romantics."

"Is that good or bad?" someone asks, laughing sarcastically.

Taher looks at them for a long while. "It's bad. It's very bad," he says, touching his swollen lip. "It's bad because you've all become fascinated with abomination. Even if you were given a normal and free life, you wouldn't know what to do with it."

"The sane ones didn't help," Hassan raises his arms over his head and turns in slow motion, looking at his comrades, speaking to them as if from a stage high above. "They were all either killed or went crazy." He is still holding his arms up. "Now, we must follow the insane; maybe they can save the world for us."

"But killing someone is killing yourself, don't you see?" Taher says in a muffled murmur. "It always comes back and stays with you. Death comes back. There is no escape. By killing, you poison the blood of your children. There is no life after killing. Not for you. Not for your children. Not for their children. Ever. Killing someone without killing yourself is impossible."

Taher's words aren't words anymore, only the movements of his lips, now turned into a swollen pulp. Blood is dripping onto his white shirt. Streaks of red are running down his chest, one after another, one after another. No one can understand what he is saying, and no one cares.

*

When Aisha calls, Taher jumps and accidentally kicks the table. After composing himself, he looks around, embarrassed. Luckily, no one at the restaurant pays any attention to him. He is not used to carrying a cell phone in his pocket, and every time it rings, it startles him. He is sitting on a patio with a view of the Mosque of Muhammad Ali in Cairo. In the distance, the dome looks white, and the two tallest minarets are silver. In front of him is a plate with two pieces of *konafa*, a blue teapot, a sugar bowl, and a glass of black tea.

"Did I startle you again?" Aisha asks.

"I can't get used to it," Taher laughs.

"But it's wonderful, isn't it? I can call you from Berlin. Imagine that," she says, laughing, too. In the background, children's voices scream. One uses actual words: "Mine, give it back! Mine!" The other is just a high-pitched scream.

"How are they?" Taher asks.

"I'm losing my mind. Aya just started walking, so she is everywhere now, and Ata is trying to keep his toys away from her. It's a madhouse," she laughs. "Walter is coming back tomorrow from his business trip, and I already can't wait to hand them over," she says., the tone of her voice light.

"It would be nice to see the kids next month," Taher says, looking at the mosque. The structure seems to float above the hill.

"About that," Aisha says. "Can you bring me mom's watercolors? All of them, please."

"That would be too heavy. There are, like, seven or more—" he says.

"No, not the frames. Take them out and roll them up."

"Oh, I can do that, no problem," Taher says and takes a sip of his tea.

"You are the best brother, Taher," Aisha says to the screams of her son.

"You wouldn't have said that when we were twins," he says. "Remember, we used to fight like Aya and Ata."

"*Were?*" Aisha says, laughing. "What are you talking about?"

"I mean children. When we were children. Back then, I could feel you being my twin—or something like that," he says and looks into the distance, sipping his tea. "Now—" he pauses. The children have quieted down, and he can hear Ata, saying, "Aya, you can have this. Okay?"

"I will always be your twin sister, Taher," Aisha says quietly.

"I know—and also, I don't know. I can't feel it anymore. I can't find you in myself," he says.

They both pause and listen to the sounds around them for a moment.

"What about you, Taher," Aisha says. "How are you doing? Really?"

Taher starts to say something, but what he says makes no sense—disconnected words and sounds with no structure or essence follow the choppy line of his voice. He is trying to find the right words while also deciding if he wants to tell her the truth.

"Just say it," Aisha says, and Taher suddenly remembers that she has always understood him better than anyone else.

"I am thinking about going back to Afghanistan with Ahmed," he says.

"No, no, Taher, don't do it! Nothing good can come of it. Go back to medical school. Finish your degree." She is trying to be convincing, but her tone is not focused. Her attention is elsewhere. The children are screaming again. Taher imagines his sister waving her hand and bringing her index finger to her lips, but he knows that her children are too young to follow such a signal.

As he waits for her to calm them, something in him and around him moves. It's like a wave that rearranges things and leaves a new order. He feels himself disconnecting from Aisha—not because she said, "Don't do it," but because he said, "I can't feel it anymore. I can't find you in myself." With these words, he has created a new reality. The disconnection is not a rupture, he realizes. It is the conclusion of something very gradual. It's like a coastline that erodes a little bit every year, eating away the land, expanding the way of the ocean.

Tiny Mirrors

The men gather in the city square in small groups. They talk and gesture. They stroke their long beards and nod. Some toss coins into the cup of a dervish who came to their city the day before. Two of them stop next to a boy who is grinding ginger in a small dish. They draw circles in the air in front of their faces with their long fingers and describe the proper way of grinding. Some wait in a long line in front of the small shop of a shoemaker who mends the soles of shoes with wrinkled pieces of leather hanging on the walls of his shop. He works while his customers wait patiently.

A larger group of men besiege a tailor hunched over a sewing machine. The rhythmic movement of the pedal whirs dully and is interrupted only by the quiet whispers of the observers. The walls of this shop are covered with scraps of all sorts. The tailor raises his head from time to time to look at the crowd and then—with a smile—goes back to his task.

On the street corner, sellers of flour and herbs weigh their goods on mechanical scale pans, balancing them with stones. They watch their scales attentively, and while adding the products slowly, consider the instructions and satisfaction of their customers.

Taher heads to the post office. It is a one-story building that— except for numerous marks left by shrapnel—hasn't suffered any substantial damage during the war.

The inside of the building is darkened by a low ceiling smeared with gray streaks. The space is divided by barbed wire into two rooms—a narrow one for the customers and a wide one for the personnel.

Taher waits a long while for someone to show up, and then

he waits even longer to receive instructions and guarantees about sending money abroad.

"It may take a month," the man behind the counter explains gloomily.

When the man disappears through a door leading to the back, Taher approaches a small box at the end of the counter. The sign reads: *Poste Restante*. The box is full of envelopes from England, France, Poland, Russia, and other countries. Their yellowed surfaces and worn corners speak of the years they have waited for their chance. The various longhand letters, colorful stamps, and decorative borders on some of them have faded with time, receding into nothingness with little hope of change. *Are they destined not to make their connections?* Taher touches some of them. *The unknown fate of things and people.*

When he finally leaves the post office, he feels drained of all desire. He stands facing the street, taking a moment to decide what to do next. The street is dusty and hot, and the air is filled with the smell of diesel. On the opposite side, there is an abandoned photo shop. Taher crosses the street and stops in front of the window. He shades his eyes and peeks inside. One chair with green paint peeling off in long strips is standing in the middle of the otherwise empty room. A tarnished mirror on the wall behind the chair holds a newspaper clipping. An old camera on a crooked tripod (*the melancholy of sepia photographs*) stands next to the chair.

"You can't take pictures here," a soft voice comes from behind, "unless it's for a passport."

Taher turns around and faces an old man.

"That's the new rule here," the old man adds.

"Uhm." Taher looks inside the shop again.

"Some people take wedding pictures secretly," the old man says. "But who cares, really?"

The old man touches Taher's shoulder gently. "Follow me," he says, pointing to the shop next door.

The old man is a watchmaker. His thin, dried-out fingers patiently turn small objects over and over for many hours. His small, round eyes trace the tiniest details of the tiniest mechanism in search of misalignments. Every day he talks to himself for reassurance, bringing the objects closer to his eyes and then lowering them over a small table.

"Where are you from?" he asks.

"From Ismailia in Egypt," Taher answers, entering the shop.

"Oh, no," the old man says, pointing to Taher's suede shoes. "I was asking about your shoes. You are from somewhere in Europe. They look European," he says.

"Oh." Taher looks at his dusty shoes. "I used to study in Germany. In Hamburg," his voice breaks in surprise.

"Let me bring you some tea," the old man says, slipping behind a curtain at the back of the shop.

The small table in front of Taher is filled with dozens of darkened clock dials—faded Roman and Arabic numbers of many sizes and shapes. Small clay saucers are filled with springs, thin fragments of wires, and dozens of microscopic screws and bolts. Pendulums and once-colorful wristwatch bands, placed in long wooden containers, are fading and cracking with time. The shop is filled with objects forgotten and saved with no purpose.

Two incomplete clocks on the wall show different times. Next to the small window is a calendar with one date circled in red—September 11. The year is blackened out. A notebook—clearly signed by a child—rests on the narrow windowsill.

"I have a brother over there." The old man returns carrying a tray with a teapot and two small mugs. "Helps us sometimes, sending money. When I see someone like you, I always hope for some news from him." The old man stops and looks at Taher. "Nothing has come from him for a long time now," he adds without moving.

"I'm sorry. I don't have anything for you, or for anyone else. I haven't been to Germany for some time," Taher says. "I was just walking by your store."

"Have some tea." The old man hands him a mug and pours the tea.

They both sit in silence until a high-pitched voice from the street makes them both jump to their feet. They move to the open door and stand in a pool of light saturated with dancing speckles of dust coming from the outside.

"No, no," a young boy cries out.

On the street, a small crowd of children is gathered around a policeman. The policeman is holding the screaming boy by the ear. The screaming boy stands on his toes and flaps his arms around as if trying to fly away.

"It's not a kite!" the boy pleads. "It's not a kite!"

The rest of the boys in the crowd laugh. Some of them cover their own ears and jump on one foot. Others cover their mouths but still manage to comment on the scene and give orders. "Admit it! Admit it!" they yell. Finally, the policeman breaks both sticks of the frame he is holding and, giving it back to the boy, says, "*Now*, it's not a kite!"

"It's a life we never knew here," the old shop owner says, stepping back into the room. "Please, have some more tea," he adds, lifting up the teapot.

"No, thank you." Taher puts his palm on his chest. "I must be on my way."

"Are you going back to Germany?" the old man asks, retrieving a small envelope from a pocket in his *shalvar kameez*.

"Yes, but not soon." Taher hesitates for a moment. "In about a month," he adds.

"This will be safer with you than with them." The old man nods his head toward the door, and after kissing the envelope, hands it to Taher.

"No!" a familiar voice comes from behind Taher suddenly. It is Ahmed. He takes the letter from Taher and puts in on the table, on top of the piles of items.

"We must go," he says to the old man and leaves immediately.

"What are you doing?" Taher catches up with him on the street.

"No, I'm the one asking—what are *you* doing?" Ahmed stops and looks Taher in the eye. "Taher, what were you doing in there?"

"What?" Taher lifts his shoulders and spreads his arms.

"We are in Afghanistan after the war!" Ahmed says and gestures with both hands, bringing his fingertips together. "They're already spying on this man. Don't you get it?"

"How do *you* know?"

"Don't ask too many questions, or you'll never get to the training camp. If you want to get there, you must follow the rules! The new rules of Afghanistan! That's all I'm asking!" Ahmed puts an arm around Taher's shoulders. "Just trust me, okay?"

"Okay," Taher answers, nodding.

The city square pulsates with the same energy as before. The men gather in groups on the street corners and talk, raising their arms, nodding their heads, and stroking their long beards. A barefoot boy carries a basket filled with hay on his bicycle and two packages in brown paper fastened to his back. Another boy carries water in a makeshift yoke—two cans hanging on wires attached to a stick on his shoulders. A pickup truck full of men in shiny black turbans passes by, swaying over potholes, leaving clouds of thick dust behind. Only a very few women, accompanied by men, mingle in the streets. They carry baskets or infants pressed to their chests. Their burqas billow in the wind or rustle with their quick steps.

The horizon on the outskirts of the city vibrates in a crystal drop hanging above the ground. The air shimmers. Below the horizon, the deep brown earth sits in a delicate glow of white and gold that melts into the higher terrain of warm ambers. Beyond, rich greens climb up to the foot of the mountains, where they dissolve slowly into pale turquoise, moving up the blue and silver walls. Further up, the silver changes into sharp purple peaks. In the distance, scales of bright light flow down the blue-green waters of the slow river. Here, the world is a postcard, enticing seekers and vagabonds with promises of new, untouched places.

*

With their well-groomed black beards and eyebrows that arch when they speak, the leaders hold the attention of the room. Their dark eyes are underlined with black charcoal, as deep as the blackness of their silk turbans that give off a delicate vapor of European perfumes. Their attire is exquisite—snow white *patu* under long black *shalwar kameez*. Their wrists are decorated with solid gold watches. From time to time, when they speak, their manicured hands move gracefully. They speak with the authority of their ancestors.

> And reckon not those who are killed in Allah's way as dead; nay, they are alive and are provided sustenance from their Lord.

In the middle of the red carpet are trays and plates of food—lamb and rice with herbs and green beans, kebabs of finely cut meats, Turkish quince, Persian pilaf, Chinese noodles, Indian crumb cakes, and multicolored Russian and Korean salads. Deep fried pirozhki, garlic bread, flat yeast bread, and buns with coriander are scattered between the main dishes. Red onions with pomegranate seeds and white salads of cheese, almonds, and turnips give the place a festive feel. Melons, dried fruits, fried walnuts, almonds in sugar, and apples in syrups from all over the world, convey the luxurious life of the privileged.

The food is served by teenage boys, in a manner of subtle grace. They move quietly, communicating with one another only with their eyes and small gestures. No task is beyond them. Their hair is darkened with fresh henna, and their hands, decorated with elaborate ornaments, touch the dishes and platters elegantly, moving them swiftly between the guests. They pour sweet black tea and serve the desserts in a timely fashion.

"You need to have a firm understanding of the most important date," says the leader of the meeting, raising his index finger above his head. His gold watch flashes a brief, golden sparkle. "Remember February 23, 1998—the Fatwa was issued and signed by Osama bin Laden and Ayman al-Zawahiri," he adds, moving his plate away from him.

When al-Zawahiri's name is spoken, Ahmed whispers to Taher, "Told you he would be important one day."

When the speaker extends his arm over his head, he is immediately handed a worn issue of *Al-Quds al Arabi*. He spreads the newspaper in front of him, and after surveying the room with a long gaze, starts reading.

"First, for over seven years, the United States has been occupying the lands of Islam in the holiest of places, the Arabian Peninsula, plundering its riches, dictating to its rulers, humiliating its people, terrorizing its neighbors, and turning its bases in the peninsula into a spearhead through which to fight the neighboring Muslim peoples.

If some people have in the past argued about the fact of the occupation, all the people of the peninsula have now acknowledged it. The best proof of this is the Americans' continuing aggression against the Iraqi people using the peninsula as a staging post, even though all its rulers are against their territories being used to that end, but they are helpless.

Second, despite the great devastation inflicted on the Iraqi people by the crusader-Zionist alliance, and despite the huge number of those killed, which has exceeded one million...despite all this, the Americans are once again trying to repeat the horrific massacres, as though they are not content with the protracted blockade imposed after the ferocious war or the fragmentation and devastation that followed. So here they come to annihilate what is left of this people and to humiliate their Muslim neighbors.

Third, if the Americans' aims behind these wars are religious and economic, the aim is also to serve the Jews' petty state and divert attention from its occupation of Jerusalem and the murder of Muslims there. The best proof of this is their eagerness to destroy Iraq, the strongest neighboring Arab state, and their endeavor to fragment all the states of the region such as Iraq, Saudi Arabia, Egypt, and Sudan into paper statelets, and through their disunion and weakness, to guarantee Israel's survival and the continuation of the brutal crusade occupation of the peninsula.

The International Islamic Front for Jihad against the U.S. and Israel has issued a crystal-clear Fatwa, calling on the Islamic nation to carry on Jihad aimed at liberating holy sites.

The nation of Muhammad has responded to this appeal. If the instigation for Jihad against the Jews and the Americans in order to liberate Al-Aksa Mosque and the Holy Ka'aba Islamic shrines in the Middle East is considered a crime, then let history be a witness that I am a criminal."

The speaker gazes around the room again. He strokes his beard gently, as if not to disturb its shape. The room is silent. All look at him, absorbing the information. There is much to absorb and understand. The gravity of the meeting becomes apparent. Even after the speaker stops reading, his words stay in the air and echo in everyone's ears, hum in their bodies. Al-Aksa Mosque, Holy Ka'aba become the places of unity once more. Where the palms of the believers meet their chests, where the quicksilver lake sits in the eye of the ocean, far beyond the dome of the lavender sky covering the minarets soaring with lights, far beyond the glass buildings of the metropolis and the valleys filled with white and sepia-colored houses, the gathered in the room unite in strength and resolve.

"And let's remember that in our Jihad, we bring together our brothers from Afghanistan, Sudan, Saudi Arabia, Somalia, Yemen, Eritrea, Kenya, Pakistan, Bosnia, Croatia, Algeria, Tunisia, Lebanon, Philippines, Tajikistan, Chechnya, Bangladesh, Kashmir, Azerbaijan, and Palestine. We unite all of them, all of us together." The speaker strokes his beard again. "Do you have any questions?" he asks, and smiling softly—like a benevolent father—looks at the motionless faces.

A young man with soft facial hair clears his throat and asks, "How are the orders issued?"

"Orders?" The speaker's eyebrows slide up to form a thick M above his nose.

"Yes, so we know what to do," the young man adds, clearing his throat again.

"If you don't know what to do, you're in the wrong place." The speaker's eyes become dark. "We need only those of you with initiative, clear minds, and clear hearts. We need the brave ones. You need to come up with your own ideas, wherever you come from, whatever you can come up with. This is your own Jihad. Not mine. I have my own. We unite in Jihad by fighting our own Jihads." He stops for a moment and then continues. "However," he pauses, strokes his beard, "however, some of you might be chosen for special martyrdom missions, but this is a rare honor reserved for the best ones."

The room becomes quiet again. No one moves. All eyes, piercing and waiting, are focused on the speaker. He gives them the time to absorb his message, to grow in expectation and hope. He gives them time to savor his words—not to miss anything, to grasp every cue, to understand and follow, to become part of the bigger truth. Bigger than any one of them individually. Not only for this short sparkle called life, but forever, for eternity. That's what they all expect. That's what they all long for—to grasp and gain eternity.

"But it all depends," the speaker continues, "on the results of the training, on recommendations from your superiors, and on your own luck." He smiles warmly.

"But what about here? In Afghanistan?" someone else asks.

"We are still fighting some remnants of the Northern Alliance," he chuckles, "but I don't expect you to get into any fighting, unless"—he raises his index finger and shakes it the same way as before—"unless you are incredibly lucky."

"Insh'allah, Insh'allah," reverberates in the room. God willing, God willing.

"We are not afraid of bombs. We are not intimidated by threats or acts of aggression. We suffered and survived thanks to the grace of God." He raises his index finger toward the ceiling again. "We were not defeated by the Russians! Ten years of war! And we prevailed. Our enemies should prepare themselves for our answer! We are not afraid of them! We are ready for more sacrifices. More sacrifices in the name of the Almighty!" He shakes his fist. The gold watch throws new sparks around the room.

Allahu Akbar! Allahu Akbar!

"The occupation of Palestine and the Holy Lands in Saudi Arabia must end, and we, the defenders of God, will succeed." The speaker raises both arms, as if he is summoning the heavens to descend and join him in his crusade.

Now the room roars with applause.

"God didn't promise us an easy battle, but He promised to be by our side." He clasps his hands and places them on his chest. "This is our strength. Strength in God Almighty," he finishes, closing his eyes.

Everyone applauds again.

"We are a nation of martyrs," the speaker continues. "We are in love with death in the name of God!"

The room roars.

"Save your energy." He smiles, looking around. "You, the best of the best, save your energy." His eyes become soft when he smiles again. "Let us pray," he finishes.

*

Taher takes a deep breath. The air by the river smells of sweet dampness. On the other bank, a dense avenue of poplar trees obscures the view of the compound walls. The silence of the night is interrupted only by the murmur of cicadas, one and then two of them, then one again. A white ribbon of smoke rises into the air and points to the life shielded by the walls. Running parallel to the front wall, a well-trodden path leads to the fragment of a makeshift wooden bridge, where the laundry is done on most days.

He sits on a flat rock and looks at the river. The images of the world, reflected on the surface, wave to him—with every wave, a different shape for the same tree, a different line for the same river bank, a different shape for the same cloud, for the same sky. A different shape for the same rock. He watches the steady flow, the changes on the surface in the constant undulation where nothing can be saved, where everything follows the same path. Where is the connection? How do they compare? The tree and its images. How do different images relate to one another? How do the images relate to the tree? Images are like twins. How are the twins the same? How are the twins different? Where is the summit, where does it all come together? The lightness of the mind overcomes the body, the lightness of the body overcomes the struggle—absolute freedom, absolute lightness beyond time, absolute understanding and connection.

They are the same. Like twins connected in the same womb, but then separated at birth. Everything exists in me. The slope of the roof of my house in Ismailia, the broken fountain, and Aisha's voice. My mother's lips. The cloud mirrored in the lake. My small hand covering the cold rock that I throw far away from the boat. Father's arm around me. The smell of his skin and the roughness of his beard. Khaled's scream in Ahmed's voice remembering the scream. The dampness of the many corridors. The smell of Grandmother's bread. Little kittens clinging to Aisha's chest. And the words of my Qur'an above the heads of our guests in the garden. At the flower pools, where water sits on the plates of leaves in big bubbles. Sharks and rays in the Sacred Room. The wings of a falcon. Father. Life is a journey, and your thirst helps you reach the destination. The thirst can be your strength or it can become your death. The choice is yours. Where is the beginning of me? Where is the end?

*

"I can't go any farther." Taher coughs heavily, leaning forward.
"Of course, you can." Khaled stops to look at his comrade.

"My throat hurts," Taher says, kneeling. "It's dry." He coughs again.

"Wait, don't sit down," Khaled says quickly.

"I want water." Taher closes his eyes and lies on his backpack. His gun falls to the ground next to him. "How far to the village?"

"You asked that two minutes ago. I don't know." Khaled comes closer and with his body, blocks the sun from Taher's face.

"I want water," Taher repeats.

"Me too, but we can't stay here."

"I don't care. I'm exhausted." Taher's eyes remain closed as he speaks.

"You're not exhausted." Khaled sits next to him and then lies down. "I can tell you what exhaustion is."

"I know your story from the Cairo prison," Taher says, and coughs.

"Ahmed told you about the prison." Khaled closes his eyes.

"Yes, and about the way they tortured you," Taher says, shading his eyes with his hand, "the way they ripped your arms—" He doesn't finish.

"Exhaustion came after," Khaled interrupts. "After I woke up, the next day, and realized I couldn't move my arms. The helplessness was exhausting, not the pain."

"Weren't you glad they didn't kill you?" Taher sits up.

"You make it sound like life is everything, but it's not." Khaled sits up, too.

"What do you mean?"

"Life is not everything; life is not the most important thing. This is what I learned in prison." Khaled stands up and again blocks the sun from Taher's face. "Listen, you need to get up. We need to go now." He starts walking away.

"Wait." Taher is untying his shoelaces.

"No!" Khaled almost screams, then coughs, just like Taher.

"I need to take my shoes off for a second." Taher doesn't stop, even when Khaled grabs his wrist.

"That's a big mistake, big mistake! Listen to me." He towers over Taher, still holding his wrist. "Don't do it, or you won't be able to put them back on."

"I will." Taher takes his right shoe off and then the left.

His socks are soaked. He takes them off, groaning. His feet are covered in blisters, new and old ones, bleeding and filled with pus. The crust of dried blood is mixed with fresh layers. All injuries are from the last seven days of constant walking up and down the mountains. Small drops of blood sink into the soil where he sits.

"And that's why I won't take mine off." Khaled looks at Taher.

"How far to the village?" Taher asks again.

"We have to go. It can't be that far," Khaled says with hope in his voice. "Think, Taher—this is our last task in the training. We're almost done. Let's go."

"I want water," Taher says to himself. "Water, water."

"Get up, let's go!" Khaled repeats.

Taher puts his wet socks back on and, tying the shoelaces together, throws his shoes over his backpack.

"You can't walk like that." Khaled points to Taher's feet.

"Too swollen, I can't put my shoes back on," Taher says quietly.

They walk down a steep and narrow path. Below them, a quiet valley sits in between soft slopes of green hills that grow closer with every step. The chain of mountains on the horizon encircles them, closing their journey in a small womb, silent and spacious, painful and safe.

"How come we were only allowed to take water for four days?" Taher asks.

"They wanted us to find water," Khaled says, turning around to look at Taher.

"I guess we failed." Taher's voice is weak.

"We're still alive." Khaled maintains his composure. "That's an achievement."

"I'm not sure." Taher trips on a rock and almost loses his balance.

"Maybe you should try to put your shoes back on," Khaled suggests, stopping.

"I'm fine. Let's go and get some water." Taher fixes his backpack and continues walking. "I wonder if we passed the test or not," he says after a while.

"If we reach the village today, we're only one day late," Khaled speculates.

"Only?" Taher laughs. "They probably think we're dead."

"No, it has happened before," Khaled continues. "Sometimes people are later than that. It's a huge place."

"You mean sometimes they're dead?" Taher asks.

"Rarely," Khaled answers after a short pause. "The Northern Alliance is still here. They come down as low as this, I've heard." He stops. "Look." He points toward the mountains.

They stand in silence for a moment, observing a bird circling above their heads.

"Is it a vulture?" Taher asks, shading his eyes.

"I told you, put your shoes on." Khaled laughs. "You're leaving a trail of blood. He's after you!"

"Very funny." Taher looks at his feet, now covered in sand and dust, sticking to his socks.

"Do you have your Qur'an with you?" Khaled asks.

"No, Ahmed took it this time—he needed it," Taher answers. "We kind of share it."

"I wanted to tell you about the picture you have there."

"What about it?"

"I saw it on the Internet," Khaled says.

"And?"

"It's not a Palestinian boy." Khaled stops and turns to face Taher.

"Of course, it is." Taher stops. "It's a four-year-old Palestinian boy killed by Israelis."

"I didn't want to tell you back there, with the others," Khaled continues.

"What do you mean?"

"It's a picture of an Israeli boy killed by a bomb on a bus in Tel Aviv," Khaled says, slowly and quietly.

"That's impossible." Taher says, and starts walking again. "Ahmed would know."

"You carry in your Qur'an a picture of an Israeli boy killed by a suicide bomber from Gaza." Khaled insists on repeating his statement.

"That's *impossible*."

"I specifically remember this picture. I saw it on the Internet. I remember we even talked about it. We were wondering if it was a boy or a girl since—"

"Just stop it," Taher says angrily.

"I'll prove it to you as soon as I have access to the Internet."

"Fine, prove it!"

"Maybe we'll never know the truth," Khaled says sadly.

"About what?"

"About the picture. You know, maybe it's a Palestinian boy, maybe it's an Israeli boy. All we can see is our own suffering."

"Just don't start with your poetic crap again." Taher tries to walk faster but can't. His feet are getting worse with each step.

"No, just think about it. If you look at the picture, you see the suffering of your people. I'm positive. If an Israeli would look at this picture, he would see the suffering of his people. And it doesn't really matter who the boy or the girl—"

"For me, it matters, because I want to have a picture of a Palestinian boy in my Qur'an, you idiot!" Taher trips once more and hisses in pain.

"Let's just say you carry a picture of a child as a symbol of all children suffering in the world created by adults."

"You're so full of crap!"

They walk in silence. The sun melts into the sky with golden streaks, falling over the green valley in patches of yellow flowers. The blue and violet backs of the mountains climb up the pink summits. Taher and Khaled reach their destination exhausted, anxious, and happy.

The village invites them in to the ruckus of running children. Several women retreat behind fences, but the men come out to greet them, nodding and waving. Taher and Khaled walk slowly—Taher still in his socks, with the shoes hanging over his backpack.

An old man approaches them with water. Taher nods with gratitude.

"Drink," the old man says, smiling, revealing toothless gums.

"Welcome, in the name of Allah," he adds, handing them two cups.

"Thank you," Taher and Khaled say simultaneously.

They drink thirstily while the old man nods. His eyes fill with sadness or gratitude.

"Thank you, again," Khaled says, and they both hand back the cups.

"More?" The old man squints, and again reveals his pink gums.

"Yes, if we can," Taher answers without hesitation.

A little boy runs toward them, yelling, "There! There!" at the top of his lungs.

They look at him in confusion, and then they look at each other.

"I'll get more," the old man says, leaving.

"There! There!" The little boy's voice grows stronger. As soon as he stands in front of them, he says, "They are already here! They are here! There!" He points toward the direction he came from. They look at him, and then at each other again, both equally confused.

"Who?" Taher asks finally.

The boy looks at them, surprised, his round eyes getting bigger. "They," he says, pointing in the same direction. "They are from the other village. There." Now he is pointing in the opposite direction.

Taher and Khaled look in both directions and stay silent and confused, trying to understand what the boy is talking about.

A red pickup truck comes from around the corner and heads straight at them.

"They," the boy says again, pointing at the truck.

"Here is more water." The old man extends his arms with the cups.

Taher takes the cups while Khaled tries to get answers from the boy. From there, everything happens in a split second. The pickup truck stops in front of them, braking sharply and raising a flurry of dust.

"Hurry up," a man from the bed of the truck yells, gesturing. "Get in!"

"There's no time!" another man, standing next to the first one, yells. "Our men are missing!" He points his gun toward were Taher and Khaled have come from.

Taher tries to hand back the cups to the old man, but instead drops them accidently. Dark patches of water sink quickly into the sand.

"Oh!" The old man kneels. "It's no good to spill water, no good," he laments. "Bad omen," he says.

Taher and Khaled hand their backpacks and guns to the men on the truck and then climb in. They are offered a place to sit down and the truck is on its way, leaving clouds of dust behind.

A group of children follow the truck, running and screaming.

"Do you have some water?" Taher asks after a while.

"Why? Are you sick?" a young man asks back.

"Oh, no, just," he thinks for a moment, searching for the words, "we've been walking for seven days in the mountains."

"We know. That's why they asked us to pick you up here and take you to the village. Because you were late," the same man answers.

"What happened?" Khaled asks.

"We don't know exactly," says the man. "There was a fight with the Northern Alliance, and we've heard someone was killed."

"We missed the fight?" Khaled looks at Taher.

"You did," the man confirms. "You were supposed to go with the rest of them."

"If we only had more water," Taher says. "We were too thirsty and too tired."

"You spilled the water back there." Someone else points toward the village they've just left.

"It was an accident."

"There are no accidents with water." The man's eyes grow wider as he raises his index finger to the sky. "Everything happens for a reason. It was your choice to spill it. It's always a choice. And where are your shoes?" The man points to Taher's feet.

Taher doesn't say anything.

The silence grows in me. Opens and waits. There is no beginning to it. There is no end. Everything is there, in this silence. It comes from outside but belongs to me from eternity. I don't grasp it. I just feel its presence.

The perfect emptiness is filled with everything that has ever been and with everything that will ever be. The point of silence is that in it, everything has its beginning and its end.

This is the place where I spread my wings and fly above my house, above the desert, and above the ocean. This is the place where I reach the cloud and the moss at the bottom of the forest at the same time. Where all is one.

The white and black stones on the paths of my garden. My grandfather's flamingos, my father's words. Bright pools of light on the floor of my room, changed by the movement of the sun, day after day.

The next village welcomes them with stabbing silence. Motionless rows of slender poplars sit on the silver background of the sky—shimmering wings of a dragonfly. A sandy, weaving path climbs a narrow channel toward the soft arches of the green hills. Above it hangs a slim coin of white sun.

The truck slows down when it reaches the clay huts. Their flat roofs divide the lavish greenery behind them with straight lines. Baked in the blazing sun, they emit the warmth of the late afternoon in the barren stillness of the landscape. Small openings in the walls, just under the roofs, don't betray any movement. Only the faint strips of smoke rising here and there signal human presence.

The men on the truck are vigilant. They lower their guns and assess the surroundings. Hut after hut, nothing. Fence after fence, nothing.

Scrawny trails lead to small gates. Behind them, yards are invisible to strangers. Next to the gates, single mulberry trees sit on small patches of grass. Around the corner, a bicycle with a two-wheel cart and milk cans is parked and waiting. Next to it stands a motionless donkey with loads of hay fastened to its sides. A dog basking in the sun lifts its head for a moment to look at the truck, then lowers it again.

On the other side of the village, at the fork in the road, a little girl in a white dress stands motionless—as if part of the landscape. She stands waiting. Her white dress is long, and it shimmers with bright light around her neck, chest, around her wrists, and all the way down to her ankles. The light, reflected off hundreds of tiny mirrors sewn onto her dress, encloses the girl in a crystal aura that seems to be lifting her up above the ground. Her eyes are violet blue, and her wavy black hair covers her shoulders and her back like a cape, falling all the way to her waist.

The pickup truck stops in front of her, but the men on the truck don't move. They look at her, confused and in awe. The slender coin of the white sun. Her white dress. Her strange eyes and the weightless aura.

The girl lifts her arm and points to the west. As she moves, the sun, reflected in the hundreds of mirrors on her dress, illuminates her face, and then spreads further to the sandy roads and the truck with the motionless men. She stands there, pointing, and the light keeps spreading, multiplying, flowing until it joins the soft breeze that lifts her hair. The long wavy strands circle around her back. She says something but doesn't use any words. She sounds like wind or an ocean wave, like an echo reverberating between the walls of a mountain ridge in a long valley. They all watch her and wait as if time could explain what is happening.

Then the men descend slowly from the bed of the truck, leaving their guns behind, one after another, in silence. They lower their feet to the ground, not jumping, but reaching down quietly as if not to disturb the girl, as if to feel their way and make sure to be present.

They approach the girl slowly. She still holds her arm up, still points in the same direction. She looks at them, scanning each face carefully. And then she starts walking—hovering in the crystal light above the ground—to the west. And the men follow her.

She walks slowly. Her white dress moves gently in the breeze, billows from time to time like a flower turning towards the sunlight. The strands of her hair bounce gently—as if defying gravity—following the rhythm of her steps. She leads the men, and they don't mind following her. Taher is right behind her—his feet in socks, still bleeding—and he tries to keep up with her pace. No one tries to pass him. Step after step, they form a procession of followers, but none of them know where the girl is going.

When she stops at a smaller fork in the road and turns around to face the men, she lifts her arm again. She points to an island of dwarf trees and a metal container the size of a small truck with a date written in fresh red paint: 1999. The numbers are dripping—parallel lines run down—to the grass beneath. The grass is red—drowning, dying all the way to its roots.

The metal container hums in the flaring sun, the way hot metal hums. It is a low, buzzing sound like a string pulled and left alone for a moment. The air above the container rises in a wavy pattern—clearly noticeable—and when lifted by the wind, travels in a white, nearly translucent cloud toward the turquoise mountains, toward the horizon of far, far west.

The little girl steps up on a flat rock and lifts three fingers high above her head. The men look at her, surprised and confused again. They look at one another. Taher looks at his feet.

"What is she saying?" someone asks finally.

Taher is mesmerized.

"What is it?" Khaled asks Taher.

Taher steps forward, closer to the rock where she is standing. She looks down and their eyes meet.

"What are you trying to tell us?" Taher asks her.

She moves her hands in a flowing motion, waving her wrists, and then lifts up three fingers again. She shakes them three times and circles the air with the other hand three times—an incantation of movement in place of words. She closes her eyes and turns her face up toward the sky. Two streaks of silver run down her cheeks. Taher keeps his eyes on her. Her tears are mixing with the light on her chest—shimmering, sparkling water. Then she lowers herself from the rock, flowing with the air, and places her palm on Taher's chest. Her touch is soft and warm. It closes the space between them and through her palm, Taher can feel the beating of his own heart. One pause two, one pause two, one pause two.

The crystal light bouncing off the mirrors on her dress swallows me. There is nothing else but the light. My mother and father are dancing, their laughter embracing me further and further. The desert is safe. With the dolphins arching above the waters, I am alive. And Holy Words in the garden. My garden, the place that pulls me, pulls me strongly. This is the place that belongs to me. This is the place I belong to.

The blood of the gazelles comes back to me. And the amber eyes of the lions in high grasses. The refugee girl, Aisha, and her dying brother. He is in me without a name. And Aisha's lips moving, "When will he die?" My own words—"I don't know."

"What did she say?" Khaled puts his hand on Taher's shoulder.

Taher turns around to face the group. No one moves. They all wait for him to answer Khaled's question. Mountains and sky and them.

"Where is she?" Taher looks around.

"Gone. What did she say?" Khaled asks again.

"She says—" Taher closes his eyes for a moment, then opens them and turns to face the metal container. "She says," he raises his arm, just like the girl a moment ago, "that the foggy vapor, the cloud above the container, has been there for three full days."

"What is it? Why clouds?" someone asks.

The bodies of the murdered. My strange words are silent. They were baked in the container, in the blazing sun. And their souls, ripped from their bodies by the heat, left in the form of clouds. I can't speak the words aloud.

"Did she say?" Khaled asks again.

"She said three days." Taher takes Khaled's hand. "Help me" he says quietly.

They both approach the metal container. The humming sound gets louder. The air gets hotter. It is an oven. It smells sweet and sour. The door of the container is padlocked.

Khaled picks up a rock and with a strong swing, breaks the lock. For a long moment, no one moves. The sound of the rock's impact reverberates through their bodies, replacing hope with fear.

Khaled is still holding the rock when he and Taher move back from the door. Taher doesn't want to enter the grave. Khaled doesn't know what to do.

Another man opens the door with a screeching sound of metal and rushes inside. Then comes his scream that joins the vibration of the door. Both sounds became one, howling—"Where is God?" the man inside the container screams. "Where is God?" His words echo inside the metal walls.

"Where is God?" The container grows with the scream—it swells, it towers, it takes the place of the mountains and the sky. It takes the place of the entire world.

All the other men, except for Taher and Khaled, run to see inside. "What is it? What is it?" the ones near the back ask.

Ahmed was late—the way I was late. He is not here. He is alive. I know it. He is alive.

*

The Sacred Room opens again. Taher closes his eyes and turns his face up toward the ceiling—the canopy of brilliant stars. He doesn't have to look. He knows it is there. The high walls around him are covered with engravings, and they are divided into three sections, equally tall and parallel to the floor. The lowest section is filled with ocean life, the middle with life on the land, and the highest with life in the air.

The power is in me and only in me. I can bring it to life. I can make it stop. I can create. I can refuse. I can give. I can take. Black and white rocks. White and black rocks. I am.

Taher raises his arms. "Here!" He conducts the motion of hundreds of swallows in the perfectly blue sky. "Here!" He conducts the bodies of the gray whales and makes them move and spout fountains of water toward the sky. "Here!" He orders the sharks to stop. "Now! I am!" He screams at the top of his lungs. "I am!" He screams again. "Ahmed is alive!"

Ahmed is alive.

*

"You'd better come—" Khaled puts his hand on Taher's shoulder.

Taher opens his eyes. He is kneeling, but he doesn't understand why. *How come?* There is blood on the white and black stones around him. *How come?* His feet are still bleeding.

"Taher, you should come." Khaled kneels next to him and helps him up.

Everyone except Taher is involved. They bring the charred

human bodies from the metal container outside. One by one. They pick up the bodies slowly and gently and step carefully, as if holding newborn babies. They cradle them, press them to their chests and sob. Some cry loudly, their faces covered in tears and mucus.

They place the remains in rows, one next to the other. When they are done, they have three rows of frames, bones in wrinkled shrouds—the final attire, as black as hair, dry and dull. Lips open wide. Nonexistent throats. Hollowed ribcages.

In the distance, the white and silver river holds the memory of life, where women knead dough for flatbreads. In a slow manner, their hands move in the soft light of the late afternoon. Sometimes they look up at the snowcapped mountains in the distance, sometimes their eyes are focused above the flame of the campfire, where their young sons with glad eyes hand them more brushwood. When they get up, they think of the future—straightening their backs, tired with swollen bellies—and wait for their husbands to come back home.

"I can't recognize anyone, my God. Who are they?" An old man beats his head with both hands.

"This is Yunis," someone says, pointing to a corpse. "I recognize his wristwatch."

"And this is Sayed!" another man says, wiping his tears. "He is holding the turban he got from his father last week, the new turban."

"Ismail and Amir, the twin brothers from Pakistan," another man says, pointing to two bodies holding hands. "They both had gold teeth in the front. See?"

"Not Ahmed. Not Ahmed. It isn't Ahmed," Taher says out loud to himself every time he hears a name.

*

The day Ahmed took twelve-year-old Taher to Luxor, and Karnak was dry and hot. The giant statues in the Luxor temple were cold. Taher touched them in awe. "This is you, Taher. This is you," Ahmed said to him, putting his arm around the boy's shoulder. "This stone is in your blood," he explained. "This stone runs in your blood." Taher looked at him with gratitude and love. "This is us," Ahmed said, walking with the boy in the Valley of the Kings, on the west bank of the Nile. "This is us. All of this, you see. Always remember you come from the giants of the world, from the great and majestic necropolis of the millions of years of the Pharaoh, life, strength, health in the west of Thebes, Ta-sekhet-ma'at. This is your heritage. This is what runs in your blood."

*

Khaled is waiting. Just standing at some distance and looking at Taher. Taher doesn't move. They look at each other. The distance between them grows heavier and heavier, with every breath, with every second, with every second.

There is the broken fountain on the first level of the house in Ismailia, the little one, at the back of the house where I go to be alone. I can see the garden out the window. The flower pools and azaleas, where spiders spin their sticky webs to catch blue butterflies, are always the same. The surface of the water at the bottom of the fountain is still and silent until the drops come, one after another—hitting the surface and making waves that follow each other in the never-ending journey to the edge of the pool, just to disappear and come back in a new drop from the broken spout.

Taher approaches Khaled slowly, looking at his eyes. *This is not Ahmed.*

At Khaled's feet lies a corpse, as small as the rest of the corpses. This is Ahmed, Taher's cousin, brother, twin. So small, one could hold it like a loaf of bread. The same hands that held the metal bars in a citadel prison, the one on the hilltop overlooking the streets of Cairo. But this can't be him. This is a child. The same hands that touched Khaled's arms when they were ripped out of the shoulder sockets. *It will hurt for a moment. Scream, Khaled, scream. It helps.* The same hands that killed a giant lizard in the desert. *Taher did it. We are twin brothers forever.* The same hands that helped the sick and the wounded in the refugee camps in Jalozai. The same hands that gave medicine and injections to save lives. The same palms that faced the winter sky on the mountain, next to Little Omar. The palms brought together in front of his heart. *Put your finger in Little Omar's wound and you will believe, and you will remember, and he will become a part of you, your brother forever.*

Taher's feet are still bleeding. He becomes aware of it when he falls to his knees next to the corpse, when Khaled whispers—"Taher, this is Ahmed." He disconnects from everything and becomes a tree struck by lightning. The tree leans forward and Taher presses his forehead to Ahmed's chest. The nauseating smell jerks the tree back. Ahmed's body is cold and hot. Stiff like a piece of wood. Dry. An object. *Why not me?* He doesn't try, it just comes to him and he remembers Naim who said, "Why not me?"

Taher sinks his fingers into his own hair and pulls. Pulls and holds it. The tree struck by lightning rocks back and forth, back and forth. His throat is a ball of fire and snow. *This is death.* Hot and numb, an avalanche that freezes the blood and stops the breath. *This is my death. His death is my death. Death brings death.*

He touches what used to be Ahmed's face, gently. Eyebrows, sunken eye sockets, two dark cavities, places for round pebbles. He rocks back and forth, back and forth. *My Qur'an. Ahmed's Qur'an. Our Qur'an.*

> *Death ends everything that needs to be forgotten.*
> *It erases the longing for love that cannot be found.*
> *It erases the loss that cannot be dismissed.*
> *It erases the joy that can never last.*
> *It erases the smell of the skin that cannot be changed.*
> *"When will he die?" Little Aisha asks.*
> *"Kill me!" The girl with almond eyes begs.*
> *"Man chooses between the black and white rocks on his path," Father says.*
> *Rocks are rocks. They are the same, just the color is different. Like twins.*

A dead man is like a piece of wood or a rock you throw into the water. It's an object—like there was no life before. Nothing stays with the body. Nothing stays with you. Nothing stays after you, except a piece of wood or a rock.

Is there a life or is there only my life?
Is there a truth or is there only my truth?
Is there God? Or is there only my God?
Is there evil or is there only their evil?

Khaled removes the Qur'an from Ahmed's hands, kneels next to Taher and embraces him. They both rock back and forth. The scent of blood and of rock is the same. The forest falls to the ground but doesn't make a sound, just as the night doesn't offer any shape.

Ahmed is a drop of water and a rock.
He hits the surface of the ocean.
I am a drop in that ocean.
For what do we die? For what do we live?

Taher looks around—the burned bodies and the lamenting men. For the first time, he knows he belongs to this place, he belongs to them. Here, in the valley where the sun melts slowly and long shadows withdraw the light of the day, he belongs. The world is slowly falling away, ceasing to exist.

I will drink your blood from the white clouds.

The Qur'an opens while Taher and Khaled are embracing each other and a small piece of paper falls out, landing on Ahmed's body. Someone picks it up.

"Here," the man says, handing it to Khaled, but stops and looks at the picture. "Who is this?"

Khaled takes the picture from the man, and for a moment, looks at it as if he is seeing it for the first time or as if he is trying to remember a long-forgotten answer.

"It's a child," he answers finally. He kisses the picture and places it back between the pages of the book. "This is where it belongs."

*

That night, Taher lies on the floor in the Sacred Room. The room is dark. He can't see the walls. The floor isn't obsidian the way it was before. It is translucent and illuminated with lights, and he lies in the lustrous center.

He doesn't have to look down to see everything. It simply comes to him and fills his hollowed body, seeping through his skin that separates the space from *here* to *there*. The outside of his skin is cold, and the inside of his skin is hot, refining the time, differentiating *now* from *then*.

The city's buildings—made of glass and mirrors—stand on an island surrounded by water and connected with the sky. The clearness and lightness of both makes them seem as one, with no beginning and no end.

The gates of the world encircle the city on the island, opening and closing, inviting and refusing, throughout the centuries.

On the south sphere of the city are the gates of Cairo, with aged Ahmed leaving the prison. He says, "I didn't recognize you. You are someone else, Taher."

> *Am I betraying Ahmed?*
> *Am I betraying myself?*
> *Where do I begin and where do I end?*

On the east sphere of the city is the yellow basalt Gateway of India in Mumbai with British troops—the First Battalion of the Somerset Light Infantry, the last ones to leave India. The date on the banner reads February 28, 1948.

On the west is Madrid's Puerta del Sol with the square and the clock whose bells mark the traditional eating of the twelve grapes—with each new beginning, a new year. In the middle of this square stands the old watchmaker from Afghanistan. He is holding a shield made of a clock dial with no arms, just Roman and Arabic numbers running in a trail from the center of the shield all the way to the edge.

And on the north sphere of the city is the Crane Gate at the Baltic City of Gdańsk with Nazi soldiers marching in perfect order, their boots echoing on the cobblestones of Długa Street. They lead the sea of naked men, women, and children with Stars of David tattooed on their chests, above their hearts. Behind them, another sea of men, women, and children follow under signs in red: "Solidarity!" They all sing, "Ave Maria."

The soldiers going to battle are everywhere, among them girls with blonde hair, blue eyes, and such young, young faces. Their uniforms are encrusted with thousands and thousands of tiny mirrors, reflecting the fires of explosions that light up the night sky. They scream as they storm their targets.

Taher sees mothers breastfeeding their infants in a hospital on a hill in Cairo, and a sea of cars flooding the narrow paths of the metropolis below them. Their husbands stand with armfuls of white roses, waiting for the bells to give a signal for the coffins to be lowered into the dark soil of the children's graves.

And there is one grave with a headstone that reads *Marek Aaron Abdullah Kowalski*, and under the name is the poem Taher remembers from their last meeting in the park.

Lying in the center of the bright pool, Taher recites the poem. His voice is pure. *Taher means pure in Arabic.* It rises from Taher's skin to his throat and becomes an extension of his flesh, like truth—easily defined. The words unwind in a language he understands, though he is hearing it for the first time. *English? Polish? Arabic? German? Russian?* None of them and all of them.

And those who expected signs and archangels' trumps
Do not believe it is happening now.
Only a white-haired old man . . .
Repeats while he binds his tomatoes:
There will be no other end of the world.
There will be no other end of the world.

Wings

Fire and ice, fire and ice—they made the world for you and me.
Their sweet sweet heat, and sweet sweet cool
will end the world for you and me.
They make up all the things we see,
the birds, the trees, and the flowers.
And anything that gets in their way
will be burned or frozen for hours.

—Alex, age eleven

It is early in the morning, almost three hours before sunrise, when
Taher stands in the shower with his forehead turned up, allowing
the hot stream of water to run down his face and chest. When
he turns his face even higher and steps back to look at the wall
in front of him, he sees a small, orange, nearly translucent spider
tirelessly pacing the labyrinth of the narrow dark spaces between
the tiles. After a while, the creature disappears into an invisible
crevice and doesn't come back. *What a strange life,* Taher says out
loud, waiting for the spider to come back, and then reaching for a
bar of soap.

*In the name of God, the most merciful, the most compassionate—In the
name of God, of myself and my family—I pray to you God, to forgive me for
all my sins, to allow me to glorify you in every possible way.*

The parchment paper from the soap falls under his feet and
circles the surface of the water, as if trying to find a way to stop, but
the current just keeps pushing it, turning it around and carrying it
closer and closer to the drain. It touches Taher's foot and then stops,
covering the drain hole. The water rises slowly to Taher's ankles as he
examines the surface of the wall, the tiles, and the darkened grout.
Finally, he picks up the paper and places it on the wall in front of
him, but the paper seems to have a will of its own. It slides down

a couple of inches, then following the fast, wavy ribbons of water, falls at his feet.

Taher moves the razor blade slowly over his skin—not to miss anything—following along his fingers, the back of his hands, his wrists, and up his arms. He turns off the water and stands there in silence, in the shroud of the night, in the beam of the bathroom light, alone, focused.

Remember, the angels forgive the clean ones. He rinses his arms and checks the smoothness of his skin, and then turns the water back on.

When he sits down on the shower floor, he notices the water dripping from the faucet, single drops hitting the surface of the small pool that formed around the drain.

Mesmerized, he watches for a long while—the ripples above the darkness of the hole, the thickness of the fluid, the soapy bubbles, the rhythms of the movement, the drops falling, one after another.

A memory makes its way through the image: the back garden of the house in Ismailia. The edge of the fountain. The broken spout. The quiet garden. And the patch of bright light coming from outside that would spread across the floor.

I am here and there, he says out loud, closing his eyes. A cold shiver runs up his spine. *Remember, the angels forgive the clean ones.*

Then he shaves his legs and groin, rinsing the blade in the pool of water under his feet. He checks every spot twice, running his fingertips lightly over his skin, almost not touching. He follows the blade and watches it tentatively.

Finally, he shaves his torso. Again, the blade moves slowly from the outer edges of his chest toward the sternum, in straight lines from the left to the middle, from the right to the middle, straight down and straight up.

All the rays of smooth flesh, uncovered by the blade, end in the soft niche of warmth above his heart where his hand twitches, sending a red drop sliding down his stomach, a fast-dissolving trace, bringing the memory of Ahmed with it, and resurrecting the agony of the loss that changed his life.

Taher kneels and lowers his forehead to the floor. The water runs down his back while he sobs quietly. He finds himself back in the stillness of that late afternoon, in the quiet valley at the foot of the Hindu Kush, where the smell of slowly burned blood hung above the green plains, where Ahmed's body was reduced to a loaf of bread.

Taher presses his forehead to the bathroom floor as he realizes that all he has lived through, all he has known survives within him, in a strange inner place, just below his skin.

Remember, the angels forgive the clean ones.

He doesn't need to use a mirror. He doesn't need to look. He knows the map of his skin well, every hollow, every rise, every birthmark, and every scar. He feels it, shaved clean, there in the place pierced by the fingers of others, in the middle of Little Omar's chest, in the center of his heart, where the thick white fog, found by the tiny hand of a girl in a long white dress, wandered above the summer plains of the valleys, carrying the scents of the world that passed away.

The instructions are burned in his mind: *The night before the mission is the time for you to focus and pray. Only you can overcome your own fears. Only you can win your own victory. Remember to pray. Remember to ask for guidance. Prayer will give you the strength you need. God is with you at every step, always.*

His blue shirt is stiff with heavy starch from the cleaners. The buttonholes are stuck, and he needs to go closer to the window, where he can catch more light, to push them open. He breathes deeply and closes his eyes.

This is my prayer, he says softly, facing the day that is waking behind the curtains.

I know I don't understand it all. He opens his eyes and peeks through the narrow opening. *Marek said it doesn't matter. Marek said, "It doesn't matter whether one knows what he serves. Who serves best doesn't always understand."*

*

Taher leaves the hotel room when the first flames of the sun spill from the edges of the sky. As soon as he turns the corner, he sees a group of homeless people strewn along the sidewalk. Some of them are still asleep. Others are getting up slowly, turning their gazes toward the first light, their faces bruised with time and darkened with sorrow. They are shrouded in colorless, shapeless attire.

Two of them wander aimlessly among piles of rugged fabrics and plastic shopping bags that guard long-forgotten items with tight double knots. Others sit among their belongings—cardboard boxes, buckets, and shopping carts filled with yesterday's treasures, seeking no one's attention at this early hour.

He quickens his pace and checks the tips of his freshly polished shoes. They are as presentable as they should be. He looks up to check the direction to the taxi stand marked for him by the streetlights. He remembers that he needs to turn right at the lights that are changing from red to green at regular intervals.

As he passes two homeless women focused reverently on the contents of a trashcan, one of them extends her hand. "Can you spare a quarter?" Her voice is clear and pleasant.

"No change," he says tensely, his eyes rising to the woman's face.

Her face is white, almost translucent. He sees her turn around as he walks past her. Her eyes are a watery blue, and her long dark hair falls down in a heavy cape, covering her shoulders and breasts.

Ageless, Taher thinks, turning around with her in an invisible dance. Their eyes meet, and the air around them slows and becomes quiet. She smooths her hair at the sides of her face, and then slowly unbuttons her sweater as if attempting to show him something. Taher stops and looks at her small hands, as white as her face. He follows their movement until he feels a strong tug in his navel when he sees his own image exposed on her chest.

"Ja Rab." My God, his lips move silently. *"Ja Rab,"* he whispers, dropping his bag. The woman smiles serenely. Her entire body becomes illuminated. She seems to hover slightly above the sidewalk in a warm, golden aura.

"I *am* God," she says softly. "And you are here forever. Remember that," she says as she points to her chest. "Remember me. Remember me," she says and smiles again, her watery blue eyes on him.

Taher looks at her in awe. The world around them falls away, and all that is left is the woman and him—locked up in a crystal paperweight globe. Nothing can come in, nothing can get out. They face each other, enshrouded in the silence of the new space. Silvered light slides down the crystal sphere which pulsates with brightness, expanding and contracting, revolving around the center where the two of them stand. The woman smells of lavender and burned ginger—the scent of his childhood home in Ismailia. Her eyes remind him of someone he knows well and deeply, but for some reason, he can't recall at this moment. *Maybe later*, he thinks. Her skin reminds him of children, but her gaze is wise. *Ageless*, he thinks again. Looking at her is confusing and reassuring at the same time, and Taher tries to decide which feeling is stronger. He longs for clarity. He needs clarity before he leaves.

"It's a mirror!" he finally yells, pointing at her chest. "It's a mirror. Nothing else!"

"It is, of course," she agrees.

"We knew you would see it because you know the truth." Now the second homeless woman answers in unison with the first. "Everyone really knows the truth. We all carry mirrors, Taher."

Only now does he notice that the two women are practically identical, with the second one's hair a bit shorter and graying slightly at the sides.

"How do you know my name?" Taher demands, feeling a cold shiver run down his spine. "Are you twins?" He listens to the echo of his own words, as if they are spoken by someone else.

"We all are. It's the only way we can truly see and understand each other and ourselves," the two women continue in a chorus. "We all carry mirrors in our hearts, and so do you." They both point to his freshly pressed blue shirt.

"There's nothing here!" Taher cries, looking down at himself.

"Oh, yes there is, but the only way you can see it is to look at someone else. I can see myself in your heart the way you can see yourself in mine," the first woman explains.

"Yes, the same is true for me," the second woman confirms.

"No!" Taher screams, terror filling his voice.

"Don't forget: the truth is there when you choose between the black and white rocks. It's all up to you," the women say. "Remember me. Remember me," they say in one voice.

Taher grabs for his bag and turns around, his heart pounding. He looks at the horizon, suddenly remembering where he is going, suddenly hurrying to get there. In his haste, he trips over an uneven section of the sidewalk and falls to his knees. *The angels forgive—the angels forgive the clean ones,* he whispers and gets up. He turns around to see the two women once more, but he can't see them. He stops and scans the street, trying to find them, but they are not there anymore. He turns again and looks at the streetlight. The light is red. The sky stretches evenly in a luminescent azure all the way to the horizon, where it meets the sapphire waters of the calm ocean.

*

Men in red headbands emerge from the aisles, ordering everyone to stay in their seats. Taher follows their movement, still holding the flight attendant. An elderly man asks for permission to go to the lavatory, but hearing, "Just piss in your pants!" he slumps in his seat.

Suddenly the passengers in the front of the plane are jolted by a loud sound. Someone slams the cockpit door, sending a metallic thump reverberating through the cabin.

"Open the door! Open the door!" comes the repeated command.

There is no response on the other side. When the hijackers start speaking Arabic, tense anticipation fills the faces of the passengers.

"Jesus, I've studied Arabic for five years, and I can't understand a thing!" a young woman with big, terrified eyes whispers to an older man sitting next to her.

"*Nothing?*" the man whispers back.

"Well, I can say they're angry . . . they don't have enough time. They're saying there is no time . . . " She picks at her fingers, lowering her gaze.

"That's okay." The man exhales, looking at her with disappointment.

When the hijackers raise their voices, arguing among themselves, both the young woman and the older man move to the edges of their seats and focus on what is unfolding.

"Please, just listen. Maybe you'll understand something," the older man pleads.

"I will," the young woman says.

The loud argument between the hijackers stops, and nothing changes. For a moment the air seems still, as if all movement has ceased. Only wide-open eyes exchange forceful gazes. Passengers and hijackers wait, not knowing for what, until someone again pounds on the cockpit door, this time screaming in Arabic.

"Oh, my God," the young woman whispers, covering her mouth. "Oh, my God," she whispers again, moving back in her seat, pressing her back against it.

"What?" the older man whispers back, running his stiff fingers over his forehead.

"They want to kill her." She looks absently out the window, bringing her feet up onto the seat, embracing her knees tightly. "*Kill* her," she whispers, tightening her grip.

"Who?"

"Her." She points discreetly towards Taher and the flight attendant, still looking out the window.

"What are they saying?"

"They're ordering him to kill her, but he's asking questions . . . "

"What questions?" The man looks at the flight attendant.

"I'm not sure. I think he doesn't want to do it." The woman starts rocking back and forth and looks out the window again.

"Why?" The man stops and listens to the echo of his own words. "I mean, what's going on?"

An avalanche of commotion and screaming fills the scene, but it takes a while for many to understand what exactly is unfolding. Some ask for an explanation; others don't want to know. "Hush, hush," they whisper softly. All flinch at Taher's command, "Stay in your seats!" A little boy runs down the aisle to the back of the plane. "Stop! Stop!" Taher screams toward the boy, squeezing the flight attendant harder, as if she is the one who is running.

The boy, maybe six years old, has suddenly decided to join his mother, sitting about twenty rows behind him. He is running now, screaming, "Mommy, Mommy!" His long blond hair bounces with the rhythm of his steps. There is Taher's voice and another man's accented voice, screaming, "Sit down! Sit down!" There is the boy's cry, "No!" until he trips and falls on his belly, sliding straight under someone's feet. He quickly picks himself up, only to end up in the arms of the other hijacker. The man looks at Taher. Taher nods.

"Mommy! Mommy!"

The mother stands shaking, crying along with the boy. "Don't do it . . . " she screams, lifting her hand, but no one understands if she is trying to stop her son or the hijacker.

"Stay!" The hijacker, holding her son, points his finger at her. "Sit!" he barks.

"Better to listen. Better to listen for now." A man next to the mother helps her to her seat. "Let's stay calm." Another passenger taps on her shoulder.

The mother sits back down, looking at her son. "Hush, baby, hush," she says through her tears. All her muscles are reaching forward, trying to bridge the gap between herself and her son. "He doesn't understand," she says to no one in particular. "We know, we know," the helping man says, again unsure if she means the little boy or the hijacker. He doesn't care to find out.

A skinny girl with round blue eyes and headphones too big for her head sits on the opposite side of the aisle. She stares at the woman for a long time, motionless, with her chin slightly up. Strong. And then she says, quietly but forcefully, "Mom, look at me." The woman looks at her, surprised, as if seeing her for the first time. "He will be okay. I promise you that," the girl says, and smiles. The woman looks at her with adoration. "I love you, baby."

"I love you too, Mommy." The girl's smile widens, revealing a big gap between her front teeth.

*

The flight attendant cries as loudly as the boy now. She lifts her arms and flaps in the air helplessly, like a bird caught in a net. Once, twice. The passengers look at her and Taher with the horror of questions they can't ask. They wiggle in their seats, obeying the orders to stay, but many look like they want to jump forward. A woman in the first row sees the flight attendant's extended hand, and says to her husband, "Jesus, she's engaged, just like Betty."

"Let go of me," the flight attendant whispers, but Taher can't hear her. His mind is somewhere else. It floats above the city of Ismailia, his childhood home, the flower pools in the garden, and the black and white pebbles on the paths shaded with pink blooms, where Aisha was turning around to look at him in awe, like the rest of the crowd.

"I want my mommy!" the little boy cries out.

"Shut up!" The hijacker twists the boy's arm and lifts his elbow.

An old lady sitting next to the crying boy extends her shaking hand with a Hershey bar. "Want some chocolate?" she asks, waving it in the air in front of him.

"No! I want my mommy!" the boy cries even louder.

The old lady pulls back and sinks into her seat under the reprimanding gazes of those around her.

"For the last time, open the fuckin' door!" The command jolts the young woman, who is still hugging her knees and looking out the window.

One of the hijackers turns toward Taher and gestures, barking his orders. Then he turns to the hijacker holding the boy and yells something at him. The boy is released. He runs down the aisle and jumps into his mother's lap. "Thank God!" She hugs and kisses him. He embraces her with all his strength, leaning against her chest, soaking her blouse and skirt with his wet pants.

After a moment, the mother glances at her daughter. "Told you!" the girl says in a high-pitched whisper, smiling and hugging herself, rocking from side to side, knowing to stay in her seat.

"Let's hope they let all of us go," someone says to the mother.

"Let's hope so." She nods, rocking her sobbing boy. "It's okay. You are okay," she whispers in his ear.

It is understood that the hijacker giving orders to Taher and to the other one is in charge. He is the tallest of them, with dark skin and sad eyes. He paces the floor between the cockpit and Taher several times, before he says something that makes the young woman, hugging her knees and looking out the window, jump.

"I studied Arabic," she repeats, rocking in her seat. "For five years . . . "

"Don't worry," the man sitting next to her embraces her. "Come here," he says, stroking her hair. "Everything will be all right. Trust me," he pleads with her.

"How do you know?" she asks.

"I'm a psychologist. All they want is money."

"Money?" she asks, looking him in the eyes with openness, accepting all the answers he gives.

"Oh, yes, I'm sure of it."

"Why do they want him to kill her then?"

"I don't know for sure," he says, losing his composure, but not giving up.

"The tall one says that he can do it himself, if the other one doesn't have the guts."

"Oh, that's easy then," the man is happy to explain now. "It's between them. Power struggle. He wants to prove who's stronger. Beasts. They're just using this poor girl to resolve something between them. It probably has nothing to do with the hijacking."

"No, it does. It has something to do with the cockpit door." The woman rocks in the man's arms.

"Bithib ana aamalha lak?" Do you want me to do it for you? the tall hijacker asks Taher. *"Bithib ana aamalha lak?"* he repeats, leaning forward, grabbing Taher's elbow and pushing it hard before Taher can resist.

Her skin doesn't provide any resistance under the short blade intended to cut boxes, strings, and duct tape. One stroke, unintentional really, is enough. Just one simple move to the right, slightly up.

The flight attendant follows the movement of the knife, turns to the right, and with her arm drawing a wide arc in the air, catches Taher's neck and looks at him. He embraces her tiny body, not letting her fall. She is surprised as much as he is, though for a different reason. She can't believe the sudden silence and the pleasant warmth entering the rhythm of her heart, slowing it down. He can't believe how much *his* heart is slowing down and how, looking at her face, he thinks of the pink blooms in the garden of his childhood.

He cradles her head with one hand and her waist with the other. The plastic handle of the knife hits the floor with a muted sound. He can hear it bounce twice. And then there is the strange stickiness of the substance washing over his hand and the embrace of the woman's body, soft and fragrant, beautiful and free.

Time stops. Space disappears. All is here and everywhere. All is now and forever. Her hair, freed from the silver pin, reaches the floor in slow waves. Falling and falling many times. Shining with the coolness of a rock. Her white blouse is soaked with all the sunsets he has ever witnessed; drowning in crimson, carmine. Her round breasts are rising and falling in short bursts. Her eyelids close for a moment, as if she is trying to rest, then open again when she whispers to him in Arabic, "*Ana aihtadara,*" I am dying, looking straight into his eyes. He says, "No, no!" looking back.

*

Taher closes his eyes and immediately feels a strange sensation— the woman's blood rises up in tiny droplets and encircles the two of them like a cloud suspended in the air. The scent of the woman, her warmth, the lightness of her body is resting in his arms. Her almond eyes are quiet in the dark frame of long eyelashes, and for the first time he notices her lips—full and soft, outlined with a pink pencil. He shakes her gently and waits.

Finally, he sees the woman move. First, she spreads her wings wide and takes off—majestic movement and the swishing of feathers, a dancing heron. Then she breaks through the cloud of droplets, pulling a trace behind her, and glides away into the distant horizon. As soon as she is gone, the first droplet from the cloud hits the floor and reminds him of the broken spout in Ismailia. Back then, he wanted the drops of water to be reborn in the fountain. He wanted them to come back. He waited for them to reach the edge of the pool and come back to the spout. Now he wants the drops of blood to be reborn and rejoined, but all he can see is the carpet soaking up the dark moisture. Nothing is coming back. "*Ana aihtadara*," I am dying, he says.

The passengers are ordered to move to the back of the plane and sit on the floor. Everyone obeys. Everyone wants it to end, and all believe that following orders is the best solution for now.

"This is your captain speaking," a voice with a heavy accent reverberates in the speakers.

"That's him!" the young woman who used to study Arabic says, grabbing the sleeve of the man who used to sit next to her.

"Who?" the man asks, taking her hand gently.

"The tall hijacker," she says, focusing on the voice, clenching the man's hand.

"We will reach our destination soon," the voice continues. "Everybody will be safe if you listen."

The passengers look at one another, waiting for more. Nothing else comes. This is the end of the message. Some ask questions, others are eager to give answers. Hopeful speculations fill the conversations among families and strangers. They try to recount previous hijackings and outcomes to learn how to behave.

"All they want is money," the psychologist says again.

"Let's stay calm. The government will take appropriate action soon," someone else adds.

"Our president is the one to handle it. He knows what to do." An older lady closes her eyes and starts praying.

"I'm sure negotiations are already in progress," someone else adds.

The little boy and his sister sit on the floor with their mother, embracing her from both sides.

"Are you okay, Markie?" the mother asks.

"I'm okay," the boy answers, closing his eyes and burying his face in her cardigan.

"And you, Julie?" The mother looks to her right.

"Mom, where are they taking us?" the girl asks, her eyes focused on the air in front of her face, thinking, waiting.

"I don't know, but I'm sure it's not too far away," the mother says, kissing her daughter's forehead.

"They can't take us too far, like . . . over the ocean, that's for sure," the psychologist offers to the girl.

Julie turns toward him.

"How do you know?"

"That's simple." The man smiles, happy to help. "They don't have enough fuel for that."

"That's smart." Julie smiles back.

"I'm telling you all," the man says, "they want money, and we can give them all the money in the world." He looks around, finding more and more eyes turned in his direction.

A sense of hope marks the faces of many.

"Did he kill her?" A woman sitting next to the mother asks.

There is a long silence with gazes turned toward the floor.

"The one in the front . . . " the same woman asks, looking at the mother.

"I don't know," the mother says, pressing her children to herself a bit harder. "All I could see was the top of his head. He kind of looked down. Even when the tall one yelled at him. I don't know what happened. But I have a feeling she was released."

"He killed her," says the young woman, covering her mouth, still holding the psychologist's hand.

"Please, don't," the mother moves her lips silently, pointing to her children with her eyes.

"Sorry," the young woman says quietly. "Well, I didn't really see anything," she adds louder for the children to hear.

*

There is tension in the cockpit. Taher wants to ask questions about the flight attendant, but understands he needs to wait. Satam, the tall hijacker, is leading the mission. He is also the only one who knows the entire plan from takeover to landing.

"How long did you practice flying?" Satam asks calmly, as if nothing happened back in the cabin.

"Seven months," Taher answers just as matter-of-factly.

"I'll fly the plane myself." He looks at Taher. "But in case I need to go to the back of the plane to check . . . "

His hesitation alarms Taher. *He doesn't trust me. He doesn't know how much I know. Killing her was useless. Useless. Yes, he needed to ask me several times. Because it was useless.*

"So, if I need to go to the back . . . I was told you know how to fly."

"Yes, I do." Taher keeps his eyes on what's in front of him. "No problem."

"Good."

"I just need precise directions." Taher faces Satam, but noticing the surprise in his face, adds quickly, "I know the landing place . . . "

Satam masks a too-long silence with random movements and unnecessary tasks, moving his hands between switches as if looking for the right one.

"Oh, you know more than I thought." The statement comes too late, leaving Taher in distress. "You know our knowledge of the mission can't overlap. You have your part, I have mine."

"Sure," Taher says, looking ahead, deciding not to disclose what was included in his instructions.

"So, going back to landing—" There is the silence again, filled with random movements. Looking for controls, touching switches. Here and there. Clicking his tongue and waiting.

"Yes?"

"So, landing," Satam repeats, busying himself with controls.

"What about landing?"

"I will land the plane myself, but in case I need to go to the back, can you take over?"

"As I said, of course I can." Taher says. "You already cut off the connection with the tower, right?" Taher straightens his spine and nods.

"It was about time!" Satam's nervous laugh tears the air. "One more thing . . . "

"Yes?"

"I need you to lead the prayer."

"Which one?" Taher asks after a moment of reflection.

"In case of death." Satam waves his hand as if saying something obvious. "You know anything can happen," he adds.

"Sure. Of course," Taher answers reassuringly, against all the questions that are rising within his unsettled mind.

*

The sky over the city is sapphire blue all the way to the horizon, where it joins the water fading into the silver strokes of the morning sun. The air is unusually clear, devoid of dust specks or pollen, like a flawless diamond—shimmering with brightness.

People are busy with their morning routines, rushing to meet their obligations. Women are changing into high heels in elevators, doing last-minute touch-ups to their hair in front of freshly polished mirrors. They put on thin layers of reds, puckering their lips like exotic fish in an aquarium. "Mary said they're having a huge sale," one says to another, tucking the lipstick away into a narrow compartment of her purse.

"I don't really need anything," says the other woman.

"Neither do I, but I'm checking it out anyway. You never know." The first one smiles, lifting up her shoulders.

"I'll go with you." The other smiles back.

"Great. See you at noon." The first leaves the elevator, waving.

"See you! Mwah!" The second blows her a kiss.

Men, as usual, are checking the stock market with the steady conviction of people planning their lives sensibly. They exchange greetings and polite comments, shaking hands and nodding respectfully. "In two days, we'll be in Florida," one says on the phone. "No, just for three days, but still, it's nice to get away. It's our anniversary. Yes, sixteen years. Time flies. Thanks. You too."

The latecomers hail taxis, waving on street corners. Some jump up, signaling with folded newspapers. "Downtown. Quick, please. I'm already late." "What a beautiful day!" a red-haired woman says to her taxi driver. "Yep, you can say that again."

"My dogs, I have two golden retrievers, didn't want to go inside this morning." She continues, looking out the window, "They were running in the backyard like crazy." She smiles at her early morning memories. "Made you late?" the driver asks.

"That's okay. I enjoyed watching them."

"I know. I have a goldfish."

*

The hijacked plane makes a sharp turn to the left, changing its course to the southeast. No one is concerned. The passengers wait for the flight to end—hoping no one else gets hurt. "How many did you see?" someone asks.

"I think five. Yes, five of them."

"I thought there were seven of them." They exchange whispered speculations. "What do they want? Money?"

"Of course, what else?"

"What if it's about Israel?"

"What about it?"

"Nonsense!"

"What happened to the pilots?"

"What about them?"

There is confusion. Many questions open too many avenues of unsettling predictions. It isn't welcome. No one needs to think about horrors, especially those trying to get to the other side of things, back to normal.

"What about oil?"

"What do you mean, Palestinians?"

"What prisoners?"

"Nonsense, we have nothing to do with it!"

The passengers, brought together by unexpected circumstances, find themselves joined in a union of mutual support. Family members and friends embrace each other, talking about the little details of their daily lives. "Cocoa Puffs cereal and Nutella, that's his breakfast." They find simple humor in brief moments of forgetfulness and remembering. "Ten more pounds and I'll be at my ideal weight, then I can wear my favorite jeans!" Even strangers touch one another, placing their hands on each other's backs, forearms, elbows, and hands—finding comfort in closeness, in the warmth of each other. They look into each other's eyes a little bit longer than before, holding the moments close.

"What if they ask for too much, for some astronomical sum of money?"

"If they want to get it, they'll ask for a reasonable amount. And they know how much that is. Besides, no amount is too big for our lives." The conversations bring consolation to all. No one is able to imagine demands that would be impossible for the government to meet. It brings hope and confirms the previous assumptions that only deliberate prudence can save them all.

*

"I changed my mind," Satam says firmly.

"About what?" Taher asks.

"I want to make sure everything is fine in the back of the plane," Satam says, looking straight ahead.

"Yes?"

"I'll stay here, and you go to check." Satam keeps his eyes forward.

"Whatever you want," Taher answers obediently, but with a note of tension. He looks out the window, taking in the spaciousness of the blue firmament. The sky and water are joined seamlessly, and he focuses on the distant horizon, trying but failing to find the thin line of their connection. All is one. The entire length and breadth of both elements is filled with subtle sparkling light. It is both still and moving—expanding and contracting, full of steady energy, alive. He stares for a long while, his eyes burning, until he hears the voice again.

"Go!" Satam says.

"What?"

"Go to the back of the plane!" Satam repeats harshly. "The silence back there makes me nervous."

"Okay," Taher says slowly, still caught up in the contrast between the serene image of the sky blended with ocean and Satam's sharp tone reverberating in his ears.

As soon as he reaches the back of the plane, to where the passengers have been moved, he stumbles upon Khaled. Two others are standing on the opposite side of the aisle.

"He wanted me to check on things."

"Fine. We're ready," Khaled says.

"For what?" Taher asks, but immediately regrets the question.

"For everything," Khaled replies, looking at him sharply.

Taher is ready to go back when, out of the corner of his eye, he sees a woman slowly approaching him, her eyes both questioning and bold. He stops, and as soon as he faces her, she stops, too. Then she stretches out her arms—slowly—in a strange, mesmerizing motion, revealing her body in an invitation he can't refuse. Her chest is suffused with flame but it doesn't burn. When she rises slightly above the floor and stretches her wings—white with the tips of the feathers dipped in gold—he recognizes her. She is as beautiful as Marek described in the park on the day Taher visited.

Ja Rab, my God, it's you, he whispers.

"Oh, my God, my God, it's you," the angel woman whispers.

Pulled by a power stronger than he could ever imagine, Taher steps towards her. In an instant, he and the woman come together into a place they both know well. They need no words to describe it.

The place opens and unfolds fast, resurrecting their friendship—all that was theirs, marking all that can never be changed.

They both reach forward into the longing. She touches the pendant she is wearing, and he remembers—an anchor, a cross, and a heart. He touches his left forearm, where the warmth and softness of little Julie's skin melted into his.

The books together, he thinks.

The cookies together, she thinks.

Julie's runny nose, he thinks.

The story of the Virgin Mary and Hans, she thinks.

The story of the Virgin Mary and Hans, he thinks.

"Oh, my God, Taher, it *is* you!" the woman cries out.

Oh, my God, Irene, it is *you,* he thinks, sickened.

"Where are these people taking us?" Irene asks, her lips quivering, "Taher, please, tell me."

I don't know. Where are we taking you? Taher wants to answer but can't. He doesn't know the answer. He suddenly feels split between two worlds, the past and the now. He stands above the rapture and is being pulled in two opposite directions.

"Talk to me," she demands softly.

Talk to me, he hears the echo one more time but stays silent. He simply can't speak. Something in him wants to scream "No!" but he doesn't understand why.

Slowly, the twins, Markie and Julie, come closer and stand beside their mother, holding her hands. Markie presses himself tightly to his mother's side and buries his face behind her arm. Julie—her curiosity overpowering her fear—steps forward to see, and as she looks up, she recoils in shock. She knows this man! She remembers his face from the faraway past, frozen in pictures displayed in her living room. She knows him from her father's stories of the faraway country hidden behind the snowcapped mountains, where everything stays the same, even when everything changes.

Julie reaches for her pink sack, hanging across her chest, and presses it to her side.

No one moves for a long moment, as if searching for something lost, hoping it will appear if they stay. They are asking without words and patiently waiting for the indescribable future that is opening in their presence.

Finally, Julie steps forward. She looks at Taher—seeking his attention—her eyes wide open, her blonde, wavy hair forming a soft light around her face. "Excuse me," she says quietly, her body shaking. "Excuse me," she repeats a bit louder, taking her enormous headphones off slowly and placing them under her chin.

Taher looks at her, surprised, still trying to understand what is happening.

"Why are you doing this?" she whispers, when their eyes finally meet.

Taher doesn't answer, torn between wanting to leave and wanting to stay. He wants to stop everything, and he wants everything to end without him there.

"Why?" Julie asks again.

Irene tries to pull her back, but Julie doesn't move. Markie peeks at his sister and immediately draws back, one hand clutching his mother's cardigan, and starts to sob.

"Baby," Irene says to Markie and, letting go of Julie's hand, picks him up. He embraces her tightly, leaning on her shoulder, and hides his face.

Julie steps closer to the man towering over her and demands again, her voice breaking, "Why are you doing this?"

Taher remains silent, but feels himself being pulled into the past that he has forgotten for a long time, almost forever. The little girl is resurrecting his memories without hesitation, unknowingly, making him reclaim all that has been lost. She doesn't do it with words. She does it simply by being. He recognizes her power. There is greatness in the small frame of her body and strength in her childish weakness.

She is different than before, yet the same, he thinks. The memories of their first meeting rush in. *She is as forceful as ever,* he notices, but feels as if someone else is saying those words for him.

"Why?" Julie repeats, but he can't hear her. Instead, he is trying desperately to recall his purpose. He tries to answer Irene's question for himself—*What am I doing here?*—to make sure he remembers the vision he shared with his comrades and the faceless ones who orchestrated the mission.

Suddenly, he wants to know the person who left the instructions for him. *Angels forgive the clean ones*, he whispers, the words etched into his mind—but he realizes he no longer understands their meaning. Now, he wants to meet the person whose face is made of the numbers changing from month to month in his bank account. Transferred: $9,500.00—that is all he knows.

He closes his eyes.

"A man makes decisions by himself." His father's voice is as calm and clear as before. "And why is that?" his father asks. "Because he is a man!" Taher whispers, turning his face up, breathing heavily.

He feels the floor slipping away from under his feet, the same way it did on his seventh birthday, on the journey to the desert, when the sun infiltrated his lungs and heart. It was the day of recognition, when God spoke to him directly, revealing all that was to be learned.

Taher opens his eyes and looks at the child standing in front of him. *Little Julie*, he thinks, but doesn't say anything. He wants to scream "No!" again, but he still doesn't understand why.

Irene, with Markie on her arm, places her hand on Julie's shoulder and tries to pull her back for the second time, but the girl resists, busying herself with looking for something in her bag.

The four of them—Taher, Irene, Julie, and Markie—are standing at the back of the plane; but in another time, another realm, they are standing in the center of that old place of fusion, where all remember and all in the present exist as one. They form the primordial circle of meetings, facing each other and belonging to one another, together and separate, different and the same. They reach the point of stillness that enfolds them, absorbing all else.

"Will you tell me?" Irene asks, looking at Taher, tears now running down her cheeks.

"I don't know," he finally says, feeling his two separate worlds collide in him with increasing violence.

"What?"

"I don't know everything. I only know my part, which is to fly the plane.," he says, lost in his struggle.

Julie steps closer, but Taher—still looking at Irene, her face begging for more—doesn't see her.

"Excuse me," Julie says, and trying to get his attention, touches the sleeve of his shirt gently.

He jumps, pulling his arm back, and cries out, "No!" but it is too late. He feels a sudden burning in his chest and understands that he has been awakened by the child standing in front of him. He realizes that they are closely related. They are twins, as they have always been, from the beginning of time.

"Ja Rab." My God, he whispers, letting it happen.

Time stops, and the space expands. Taher realizes that there is nowhere to go and nothing to change. All he wants is to stay in the presence of this child, and he recognizes that it is the same longing he has carried in his heart all his life. At this very moment—connecting with Julie the same way he did on the day of their first meeting— he becomes one with truth, and he doesn't need reassurance from anyone anymore. He simply knows who he is—and he is complete.

Julie extends her trembling arm toward Taher, trying to hand him something she has retrieved from her bag, her palms cupped as if shielding a small bird. She waits, and their eyes meet again as Taher slowly kneels in front of her. Now, they face each other directly. Taher breathes heavily. Julie sniffles, her face covered in tears.

At this very moment, Taher's attention is suddenly drawn by a noise he can't immediately recognize. He holds his breath and focuses, and then he realizes it is the soft sound coming from Julie's earphones, and as he leans closer, he hears—*I'll hold out my hand, and my heart will be in it.*

A second wave of heat overpowers his entire body. He looks up at Irene and lets it happen again. The images of Marek's apartment rush in. Their family. Their happiness. Their life.

Little Julie is still standing there—facing Taher—suspended between the past and the present, as if holding both in her extended arm.

Taher reaches toward her almost automatically and takes the object she is handing him. The object is pink and round. He gets up fast, ready to leave.

"Remember," little Julie says as Taher is turning away.

"What?" he asks, looking at her for the last time.

"Remember me. Remember me," she says softly.

Irene and the children stand there, watching Taher walk away. Even after he disappears down the aisle, Irene is rooted to the spot, unable to turn around to go back. She doesn't understand what is happening and who Taher has become.

"Mommy, let's go back," Julie says, pulling Irene's arm.

"It's too late." Irene says, looking at the floor, answering something she can't grasp. "Too late to go back."

"Hold my hand," Julie says, slowly pulling her mother, turning to go back.

My God, she knows him! Irene hears whispers following her.

"Are you *with* them?" one passenger, a big man asks, approaching her hesitantly.

"What?"

"Do you have anything to do with this?" the man asks her, his eyes wide with panic. "Where are they taking us?"

"I don't know!" Irene cries, suddenly afraid.

"What do you mean, you don't know? You just talked to one of them." The man steps closer and towers over her.

Irene looks at him and two silent tears run down her cheeks.

"Sir"—Julie steps in between her mother and the man—"my mom doesn't really know him. Please, leave her alone."

"So how does she know him if she doesn't really know him?" the man says.

"She knows him just a little," Julie answers.

"Did you hear that?" The man turns to the others. "Just a little? Anyone else know a terrorist *just a little?*"

*

Taher stops at the cockpit door, realizing he is holding something in his hand. It is the round object Julie gave him. Flat. Pink. He can't put a name to it. He turns it in his palm several times before noticing a tiny latch, and when he presses it, the lid opens. The object looks like round wings connected by a tiny hinge. Strange.

What is it? He decides to go over to a window and examine the object more closely. It is a mirror. Actually, it is only partly a mirror. One wing of the object holds a mirror—he sits down and holds it closer to the light—and the other wing holds a picture.

"*Ja Rab,*" he whispers. It is a picture of him with Marek and Ahmed in Afghanistan. There is Marek in the middle, smiling, with a Kalashnikov across his chest, embracing Taher and Ahmed. Above their heads there is one word written by a child's hand—*forever.*

The letters arch in a colorful rainbow on the blue sky's background. The F is red. The O is orange. The R is yellow. The E is green. The V is blue. The second E is purple. And the R is white. Many colors, the way little girls like it.

"*Ja Rab,*" he whispers again, lowering himself into the seat. His body becomes heavier and heavier with every second, turning to lead. A metal girdle on his chest tightens its grip, and Taher stops breathing. He falls. His fall is long and slow. The air turns to fire, and the ground disappears. There is nothing left except to move downward through the burning heat. There is nothing to stop and nothing to change.

*

It is eight-twenty-two in the morning when Marek sits across the table from Katie, the second office manager.

"So, what do you suggest?" Katie asks, finishing a chocolate-covered donut.

"I think you should replace the damn thing," Marek answers.

"It costs money." Katie wipes her mouth with a napkin. "Mmm. Mmm. This is delicious," she says, closing her eyes, soaking in the taste delightedly and shrugging her shoulders.

"If you keep it, it will cost you money too, you know." Marek reaches for a powdered donut. "When the printers jam and spill ink like this, it's time for a replacement."

"You don't like the chocolate ones?" she asks. She points to the donut box on the table.

"No, I prefer the powdered ones." He takes a bite. White powder spills on his fingers.

"That's why I don't like the powdered ones. So much mess," she says, handing him a napkin.

"I have my reasons." He laughs, wiping his mouth.

"Oh, really? What reasons?" she says, reaching for a cup of coffee.

"You don't have the time for all my reasons." He laughs again and takes another bite.

"We have about fifteen minutes before Robert comes. You know he needs to make the final decision about the printer, so go ahead. Make my day." She laughs too, shaking her long dark hair.

"Okay," he says. "Where do I start?"

"You know I like your Polish stories. Is this one of them?" She reaches for another chocolate-covered donut.

"No, you don't. My story is just an excuse for you to have that second donut you'll regret later." Marek points at Katie's face.

"The next time I see Irene, I'll tell her you're a nut case," Katie says, laughing.

"She knows. She knows." Marek takes a sip of his coffee.

"I like the powdered ones because they remind me of snow," he says.

"You shouldn't be fixing fax machines, Marek. I'm telling you, you should be a stand-up comedian."

"I am! For my family and friends!" he says, and they both laugh.

"Okay. I'm ready for the story." She leans back.

"You know, it's funny how everything always somehow comes back to childhood," Marek says, taking a deep breath.

"Like what?"

"Like the powdered donuts," he says.

"Hmm," she says, waiting for him to continue.

"When I see this white powdered sugar on donuts, I see myself better." He wipes his mouth and continues his story while folding a napkin, slowly and intently. The movement of his fingers supports his thoughts.

Katie crosses her arms as if hugging herself, knowing what's to come.

"Why snow?" she asks.

"My mom used to make *pączki.*"

"What's that?"

"Similar to donuts, but without the hole and—and just different, really—completely different, denser, not as sweet, a bit flaky, and with a teaspoon of thick strawberry jam inside." Marek closes his eyes and tilts his head back.

"First, my mom would mix the yeast with a bit of hot water. It was live yeast. Grayish, chalky, and cold. We would buy it in the store just a block away from our apartment. The lady in the store would cut it with a long knife and weigh it on a scale with a vertical arrow swinging from side to side. I remember we used fifteen decagrams for this recipe.

"I remember my mom checking everything twice—the weight of the yeast and the price. I loved eating it. My mom always objected, saying that I would get sick from it. But I just loved the texture melting on my tongue.

"I remember she would cover the yeast mixture with a linen cloth and put it on the radiator in the hallway for the yeast to rise. She would always tell me not to peek under the cloth because lifting the cloth could make the yeast cool off and drop to the bottom. I always thought if I did it slowly enough and just for a little while, the yeast wouldn't notice. I was sure the yeast could somehow notice things, since it was alive."

Marek smiles at his memories.

"Making the dough was always fun. We would laugh and knead the dough for eternity. We had so much fun. Then she would ask me to form these dough balls with my hands. She said my hands were the perfect size for it. I was five or six. Then she would make holes in the balls with her finger and put the jam inside. Then she would close it and flatten the balls to make them look more like flying saucers. Finally, she would gently put them, one by one, in deep frying oil, telling me to stay away from the pan. She didn't want the hot oil to splash on me accidentally."

"You talk a lot about your mom," Katie whispers.

"Only when I see something that reminds me of her—which is—kind of—always." Marek opens his eyes.

"What about the snow?" Katie says.

"I still remember her hands whitened with the powdered sugar we would sprinkle on our *pączki*. It looked like snow to me. We used a small aluminum container that had tiny holes in the bottom. She always allowed me to do it, to use the container. And of course, I would make it *snow* all over the table. 'Mom, it's snowing, it's snowing!' I would yell.

"'Just like outside. Look! Look!' she would say in such an excited voice. We would look out the kitchen window to see snow coming slowly in the pools of streetlights at night. I would make it snow on her hands, on her wedding ring, on her other ring with the little pale pink stone." Marek stops for a while.

"Her eyes meant the world to me. I feel her so close sometimes," he whispers. "Especially when I see Julie. My little Julie looks so much like my mom. Sometimes I imagine how wonderful it would be to see them together."

*

It is eight twenty-two in the morning when Taher returns from the back of the plane and enters the cockpit.

"What took you so long?" Satam asks him nervously.

"I—" Taher looks around, confused, searching for words. "I just met some people I know," he says.

"You know someone on the plane?"

"Marek's wife and the twins," Taher says, lowering himself into the co-pilot's seat.

"*Whose* wife?" Satam asks, now turning his head, but the tone of his voice is somewhere else. He doesn't care about the answer. *He is too busy, too focused on something else, too gone,* Taher thinks—looking at the boundless sky—and he realizes that he has reached the end and nothing can be changed.

*

His blood turns into a frozen fire. His body becomes a solid block that is melting. His eyes see the unseen, and his skin shrinks into a single fingertip that can feel the emptiness of the air. Madness—how everything stops and everything rushes at the same time—locked in a place where every single pain of every single person is stored and revisited forever, day after day, hour after hour, second after second—in an eternal cycle.

"I don't want to kill them," he says, putting his hands under his armpits, embracing himself.

*

Grandmother Rumaisa's voice pierces the silence of the house. "Aisha, take the kittens out!" Aisha can't hear her. She is busy playing on the edge of the flower pool, lowering her hand to touch the surface of the water. Yellow flowers sway softly. She taps the water twice to make them move faster.

In the same place of forever, Irene lifts little Julie. "Be a good girl now. Your brother is sick. We must be quiet." She embraces the one-year-old softly and kisses her forehead, caresses her cheek. "I love you," she says, looking at her baby's sparkling eyes.

"Ov you. Ov you." Little Julie bounces on her mother's arm.

"My precious girl," Irene says, giving her a bottle. "Now, here you go," she says, putting her back in the playpen.

Next to them is the dead baby in the arms of his mother in the refugee camp. Both of them are shaded from the cold with a single tarp. The sand is still filling the baby's nose and eyes. There is no will left, no life. The mother is as motionless as the baby in her arms. She looks into the empty space above the tents, far away, where the mountains meet the sky. She doesn't cry anymore.

And the little girl in the long white dress with tiny mirrors stands in the middle of the refugee camp with her arms spread above the heads of the women and children. "One life," she says sadly. The mirrors on her dress sparkle with thousands of lights and spread outward in a sphere all the way to the farthest corners of the world.

Taher is still sitting on the last step of the broken fountain. As he leans forward to look out the door where he can see the garden, he reaches down and places his palm on the surface of the water. He taps it twice to make waves. When he looks up, he sees a drop of water hanging in midair in front of his face. *How beautiful,* he whispers and touches it with the tip of his finger. The drop moves within its own boundaries but doesn't fall. He pokes it gently again. It is there—reflecting the colors of its surroundings, all the shades of the house, all the shades of the garden, all the shades of all the places Taher remembers—all the colors. "I want to be the drop of water," he says out loud.

"You already are." The answer is firm, but he can't tell who is speaking.

*

Marek and Katie leave the conference room and go back to the office with the broken fax machine. It is eight-thirty.

"If you weren't here, I would have had another donut," Katie reveals.

"You would have another reason to dwell on your lack of willpower," Marek points out jovially.

"I'm telling you, you should be a stand-up comedian," she says. "Look." She points to the window.

"What?" Marek pushes the fax machine closer to the wall.

"That plane is too low," she says, stepping closer to the window.

"Weird," Marek says and comes closer to her.

*

The last night falls upon the world when Taher enters the Sacred Room.

"I want to see them again," he pleads. "All of them, alive." He steps into the darkness of the room. "The elephants and whales."

He wishes for his words to become flesh. He reaches with both arms in front of him, but nothing happens. "I know you are here!" he screams. "Let me see you!" he yells again, raising his arms, but nothing happens. "I *am* the force! I am!" His voice echoes several times before it fades. "I want to see the mountains! I want to see the birds flying high! I want to see the lions! And the fish!" The words of his last prayer come in fast. "I want to make the world real again!"

He stands there waiting, but nothing happens. Then suddenly, he remembers about the matches he has in his pocket. "Yes! A man makes decisions by himself. No one can do it for him." His father's words come back to him. "I am the man of the desert!" He is excited, almost happy. His hands are shaking. "Yes!" he whispers as he strikes the match. "Yes!" he whispers, as he sees the glowing flame in his hands. "Yes!" he whispers, extending his arm.

Finally, he sees the room. The floor and the ceiling are pitch dark, but the walls are covered in mirrors glowing with tens of thousands of flames—all of them born as a reflection of the tiny flame in his hand. He turns around and brings his arm higher, trying to find the images he remembers—dolphins, colorful macaws, horses. Nothing. He steps forward, closer to the wall. "Here it is!" he shouts as he sees something moving. It is the image of his own face. "No!" he says, moving back. He drops the match and the room becomes brightly lit. "I want to see the blue macaws!" He closes his eyes and takes a deep breath. "I want to see the blue macaws!" he yells.

He slowly opens his eyes—hopeful—but all he can see is his own image, multiplied. Countless repetitions of his face—thousands and thousands of them—stare back at him, and he recognizes himself for the first time. Now, he knows who he is. He steps closer to the wall and looks himself in the eyes. He says, "Don't remember me. Don't remember me."

Acknowledgements

In the many years of research for this novel, I was supported by my family, friends, and numerous strangers who became my friends in the course of my studies. Their generosity and guidance made the journey rewarding and made this book possible.

Rabbi Martin Siegel: I am deeply indebted for your guidance in my studies of the Torah. This two-year endeavor would not have been possible without your wisdom and deep knowledge of the world's history, cultures, and religions.

Dr. Harris Chaiklin and Sharon Chaiklin; Mark and Ina Oxman from Israel and the USA: Thank you for opening your homes to me and helping me to understand your personal stories as well as key aspects of the culture and traditions of the Israeli people. Your insightful narratives helped me to appreciate the complexities of Israel's history.

Najad Tuffaha from Palestine: I am immensely grateful for the numerous times we met to discuss the history of Palestine, its people, and your own life, a story that helped me imagine the struggle and the beauty of your homeland. I am still thinking of the olive trees.

Khaled Tantawi from Egypt: Thank you for your translations into Arabic, and for sharing your beautiful city of Ismailia with me. You made me fall in love with its history, architecture, and people. I hold in my memory the image of embracing your mother and our conversation through tears and laughter, with gratitude and affection.

Azar Nazeri from Iran: Thank you for sharing the story of your life and your country with me. The way you talked about politics and the women of Iran made me think of women in the Solidarity movement in Poland, the similarities in their attitudes were at first surprising and then empowering. To me, you are the embodiment of grace, wisdom, and strength.

Shahlo Karimi from Afghanistan: You will always remain the generous student who brought your world to me to learn from and to admire. Thank you for sharing with me your story, your country, and your dreams. I am waiting for the day when Afghanistan becomes the country you envision.

Tahir Yunus, M.D., from Pakistan: Thank you for reading the first drafts of the novel and identifying the places in the story that were inconsistent with Middle Eastern cultures and traditions. I am grateful for your family's suggestions, and especially appreciative of your medical knowledge and expertise.

I am especially indebted to my teachers who, throughout the years, fostered my curiosity and understanding of the world's history, traditions, cultures, politics, and religions—Maria Janion, Ewa Nawrocka, Stanisław Rosiek, Marek Adamiec, Stefan Chwin. And to those who encouraged my desire to exist as a writer in my second language—Sven Birkerts, Amy Hempel, Jill McCorkle, Askold Melnyczuk, Davis Gates, Lynne Sharon Schwartz.

Special thank you to Alan Roth, my agent and screenplay writer, ever optimistic, ever kind, ever supportive, who holds an impressive vision for the novel.

Very special thank you to everyone at Plamen Press: the ever-patient Roman Kostovski for his vision and expertise; Rachel Miranda, my editor, whose love of language and its nuances turns editing into an adventure; Nicole Suozzi, my copy editor and thoughtful reader; and Walter Carlton, the greatest cover designer. I cannot imagine a more supportive and talented team.

The following sources were essential to my understanding of the history, religion, and politics of the Middle East:

The Lion's Grave: Dispatches from Afghanistan by Jon Lee Anderson

Through Our Enemies' Eyes: Osama Bin Laden, Radical Islam, and the Future of America by Anonymous

West of Kabul, East of New York: An Afghan American Story by Tamim Ansary

No god but God: The Origins, Evolution, and Future of Islam by Reza Aslan

Palestine: Peace not Apartheid by Jimmy Carter

Power and Terror: Post-9/11 Talks and Interviews by Noam Chomsky

Against All Enemies: Inside America's War on Terror by Richard A. Clarke

My Jihad: One American's Journey Through the World of Usama Bin Laden —As a Covert Operative for the American Government by Aukai Collins

Price of Honor: Muslim Women Lift the Veil of Silence on the Islamic World by Jan Goodwin

The Last True Story I'll Ever Tell: An Accidental Soldier's Account of the War in Iraq by John Crawford

The Sacred and the Profane: The Nature of Religion by Mircea Eliade

Journey of the Jihadist: Inside Muslim Militancy by Fawaz A. Gerges

Inside Al Qaeda: Global Network of Terror by Rohan Gunaratna

Chain of Command: The Road from 9/11 to Abu Ghraib by Seymour M. Hersh

Soldiers of God: With the Mujahidin in Afghanistan by Robert D. Kaplan

Why Courage Matters: The Way to a Braver Life by John McCain with Mark Salter

My Forbidden Face: Growing Up Under the Taliban—A Young Woman's Story by Latifa, written with the collaboration of Shékéba Hachemi, translated by Linda Coverdale

Perfect Soldiers—The 9/11 Hijackers: Who They Were, Why They Did It by Terry McDermott

Sixty Years, Sixty Voices: Israeli and Palestinian Women by Patricia Smith Melton

The Interrogators: Inside the Secret War Against al Qaeda by Chris Mackey and Greg Miller

Inside Islam: The Faith, the People, and the Conflicts of the World's Fastest-Growing Religion, edited by John Miller and Aaron Kenedi, introduction by Akbar S. Ahmed

Guantánamo: What the World Should Know by Michael Ratner and Ellen Ray

Israel/Palestine: How to End the War of 1948 by Tanya Reinhart

The Greatest Story Ever Sold: The Decline and Fall of Truth by Frank Rich

Bin Laden: Behind the Mask of the Terrorist by Adam Robinson

Why Do People Hate America? by Ziauddin Sardar and Merryl Wyn Davies

The Two Faces of Islam: The House of Sa'ud from Tradition to Terror by Stephen Schwartz

Genghis Khan and the Making of the Modern World by Jack Weatherford

Al Qaeda: Brotherhood of Terror by Paul L. Williams

Inside 9-11: What Really Happened by the Reporters, Writers, and Editors of Der Spiegel Magazine

The 9/11 Commission Report, Final Report of the National Commission on Terrorist Attacks Upon the United States, Authorized Edition